VOLUME 1
DOLL OF THE DEAD

A NOVEL BY
MIKE WOLFER

Special thanks to Christopher Paul Carey, Natalie Jane, Todd Luck, Phoenix Grimm, Holly Golightly, Michael Mundy, and all those who supported the production of this novel on Kickstarter.

Mass market edition, December 2022

Published by Mike Wolfer Entertainment,
Wyoming, Delaware

CONTENTS

A Dire Warning ....…..….....1

Shrouds ....…..…..17

A Walk in the Woods .....…...….............29

The Edge of Mania ....…...37

Lifeblood ....….......45

The Eternal Bond ....…..57

Life! ....…..69

Magdaline ....…...................79

Beyond the Door ....…....91

The Consultation ....…....109

Oraculum Obscura ....…....117

The Soul Awakened ....…..133

A Ghostly Visitation ....…..143

Dark Communion ....…......151

A Midnight Stroll ....…......159

Reflection of the Dead ....…..181

Revelations ....…........197

Descent into Darkness ....…....207

Point of No Return ....…......217

Denouement ....…...............…....237

CHAPTER ONE
A DIRE WARNING

Their whispers danced like gossamer strands of spider silk upon the night breeze and were barely audible above the cobblestone streets of Kleinburg. The young man's protests lacked sincerity, as he quite enjoyed the slow strokes of her hand up and down the length of the stiffened cock seeking freedom beneath his trousers.

"Odette, really, what if someone sees?"

"Is it such a crime for a woman to touch her fiancée?" She giggled as she tightly squeezed his shaft, leaning in to playfully suck on his lower lip. "But have it your way, Conrad. I'll stop. In fact, since it's so dreadfully sinful for me to have natural, human desires, I'll not fuck you again until our wedding night. When is that? Three months from now?"

Conrad straightened his pants and vest as he rocked away from the alley wall against which she had pinned him. "Three months?" he simpered. "There's no need to go to extremes, is there?" He glanced down the narrow passage between the village's two main thoroughfares, both avenues lined with cottages of alpine design, their windows securely shuttered for the night. There was no one to be seen at that late hour, and no one to see them, and his throbbing was quite insistent. But as he turned his head to Odette, he found that she was already swaying away from him down the unlit pathway, playfully waving goodbye over her shoulder.

"See you in June, my love," she teased, as he jogged to catch up to her. With their arms intertwined, the young lovers giggled as they strolled from the alley onto the moonlit street, the rich scent of the encroaching pines flavoring the night air.

A fanciful but weathered sign hung over the ornately-painted doorway, but despite the colorful attempts to entice customers into the small shop, there was rarely a visitor to the dark abode of Madame Sabina, Cartomancer. It was well past midnight when respectable men and women were home in their beds, and the few villagers still on the streets summoned all of their strength to navigate from the town pub to their destinations without passing out in the gutters. One such man lingered before the window of the fortuneteller's shop. After cautiously scanning the lantern-lit avenue, his hand found the door handle behind him. It was unlocked, but he quickly turned and shuffled away as the young voices grew nearer.

As they strolled down the walk across the street, Conrad discerned Odette's interest in the small shop. "Have you ever been in there?" he asked his radiant companion.

"Once, with my Tante Hilda, when I was a little girl. She believed in all those kinds of things," Odette replied, slowing her gait. "Ghosts, goblins, demons. Witches, even," she whispered, almost reverently, turning her head so that her eyes could remain on the shop as they walked past.

He took her hands into his. "Let's see if she's open!" he impishly suggested. "There's a lamp lit in there, so...Let's give it a go?"

"You read my mind," she giggled, taking Conrad's hand as she pulled him across the cobblestone way.

Madame Sabina's cartomancy shop was a fixture in Kleinburg for as long as anyone could remember. It had been there at least since George II assumed the title Duke of Brunswick-Lüneburg fifty years prior in 1727, and maybe even longer than that. The village elders of Kleinburg insisted that Madame Sabina was already an old woman even decades ago, a notion that could not possibly have been true. The unintentional distortion of fact is common among the aged, and surely that was the case with the local lore told of the fortuneteller. The truth could have been easily ascertained by simply asking Madame Sabina her age, but small talk and pleasantries were rarely exchanged between the villagers and the old woman. Most of the townspeople ignored her, even despising her for her Romani heritage. The less tolerant among them had carefully watched her shop for decades, suspecting that at any time others from her homeland would assume residency with her. There was a traveling troupe of carnival performers that pitched their brilliantly colored tents outside the village each fall, and the townspeople watched them suspiciously until they pulled up their stakes and rolled out of town, but never did the Romanis venture into Kleinburg. Madame Sabina had always lived alone, save for a few black cats that occasionally basked in the sun in her front window. As far as the town was concerned, the old Romani was just a confidence artist who preyed upon the foolish.

Ironically, deep-rooted superstition which none would admit kept the villagers from driving out Madame Sabina from Kleinburg entirely. Not even the Bürgermeister had the nerve to determine if the mysterious recluse truly possessed supernatural powers. The prevailing sentiment among Kleinburg's residents was to pretend Madame Sabina did not exist, except when it was time to collect from her the village taxes.

The youthful couple entered the tiny establishment. The shop was wedged tightly between a chandlery and a tobacconist, the two businesses hedging the cartomancer's shop fairly choked it as if they intended to engulf the unwelcomed boutique and devour it. Dimly lit by a single oil lamp whose wick was set at its lowest adjustment, the shop's front room was sparsely furnished and as quiet as a tomb. Odette gripped Conrad's hand just a bit tighter when the voice croaked a welcome from somewhere in the dark.

"I can provide more accurate services between the hours of ten a.m. and six p.m.," said the voice, "but if you are in dire need, I will do what is necessary to accommodate you."

They still could not see who had spoken, so Odette replied to the darkness. "Oh, it's nothing dire. Actually," she hesitated, "We're visiting on a whim. I apologize for disturbing you, Madame. We'll leave."

Two emaciated and frail hands parted the beaded curtain behind the front counter. From the blackness beyond the veil emerged a stooped figure, draped in a hooded cloak dyed the deepest shade of juniper. "I am Madame Sabina, and I do believe I remember you, young lady," she stated with certainty. "If memory serves me, at the time we met you were less interested in the words of a wise, old woman than you were in trying to catch a frog to impress a little boy named Conrad, am I correct?"

"I was that little boy, Madame," Conrad offered with pride, "and that frog wasn't the only one to be snared by this lovely lady." Odette turned her head in mock demureness, but her eyes and wide smile belied her gesture.

The old woman quipped, "Frogs and boys, always leaping from one thing to the next with not a single thought of caution, until they're too fat to leap at all."

"Oh, I'll be sure that this one gets enough exercise to stay nice and slim," Odette responded cheekily.

The corners of Madame Sabina's mouth turned upward, drawing the ancient wrinkles of her face to the edges of her smile. "Good girl," she imparted. "But it's very late. What is it that you seek from wise, old Madame Sabina?"

After the visitors confessed to entering the shop more out of drunken curiosity than anything else, the old woman courteously ushered them behind the counter and through the beaded curtain.

The eyes of Odette and Conrad grew wide, for they had both expected Madame Sabina's inner sanctum to be as devoid of vitality as the shop's antechamber. Instead, they found a small room that practically breathed color and light. Dozens of candles illuminated the parlor, over whose walls were draped luxurious tapestries splashed with the vibrant tinctures of faraway India. Intricate wood totems, gaily painted pottery, and glass bottles filled with herbs adorned every shelf. Along the periphery of the room were bookshelves packed with crumbling tomes whose decorative spines exuded prestige, and in the center of the glowing chamber sat a simple, wooden table with two opposing chairs. A large glass orb was situated at the table's center, a "crystal ball" so often associated with the artistry of fortunetelling.

"You're soon to be wed," Madame Sabina stated.

Odette smiled. "We are. How did you...?"

The dark eyes of the old woman burned into those of Odette. "The forces from the other side whisper all of your secrets to me, girl." The words caused a shiver to run the length of Odette's spine. "I'm joking, my love," Madame Sabina laughed, warmly taking both of Odette's hands into hers. "The engagement ring on your finger has given you away, and your brother speaks much too loudly when he walks past my shop on his way home from the tavern each night." Odette's shoulders relaxed with relief, as did the expression on her lovely face. "Divination is not necessary when one can learn all they need by simple observation. Now. Sit and I'll conduct a reading. An early wedding gift." Odette happily complied.

"How do you foresee the future, exactly?" Conrad asked, standing closely behind Odette's chair. "Do you just look into that ball and..."

Madame Sabina's laugh was gravelly. "This? This is for tourists," she said, her long nails tapping the glass orb as she patted it with her palm. She removed the globe from the table and replaced it with a dark wooden box adorned with ancient brass hinges. "But this...this is what will give us the truth."

The slightly inebriated couple watched with rapt attention as the old woman opened the lid of the box and removed a deck of large, worn cards with ornately decorated backs. In a precise, fluid motion, Madame Sabina placed the deck very carefully on the table before her with a delicacy that seemed unusually ceremonial. "These are oracle cards," she whispered.

"Tarot cards?" Conrad assumed.

"Oracle cards," Sabina responded, bluntly. "What is the difference between the two, you wonder?"

Conrad raised an eyebrow. "I was just going to ask."

"I know you were. Now hush, boy, and listen. And learn." The cartomancer rested both of her bony hands upon the oracle deck and continued. "Others in my profession use a variety of scrying methods. The crystal ball. The tarot deck. Astrology. 'Sit down, have some tea, let me gaze at the remnants left in your cup and I'll tell you that a wealthy, handsome man is about to enter your life.' I can do all of that for you if you prefer that I lie." She gently tapped the oracle deck. "Or," she smiled knowingly, "together we can reach through the veil of eternity and pluck divine guidance from the tree of truth."

Conrad kissed his betrothed on the side of her head. "Odette quite enjoys a good plucking," the dark-haired man bawdily quipped. As a reprimand for his lewd remark, Odette tapped her heel into his shin.

Madame Sabina smirked. "There's more to life than 'plucking,' young man. You'll learn that when you're fully grown," she replied with a twinkle in her eye. "Now. Let us take a tour of the oracle deck."

With that, the ancient Romani woman spread the cards before her in a perfect arc. "Some in my profession will tell you that they have supernatural abilities, that they can commune with forces from beyond. They will tell you that they wield magic. But what they will not tell you is that all of us—you, Odette, you, Conrad— all of us have natural magic within us."

"When I was a boy, I was sure that the local apple peddler was a clairvoyant," Conrad recollected. "She always seemed to know when I was thinking about stealing an apple from her cart."

"That was not magic, my boy, that was an observation. Your intent was probably written all over your nervous little face." Conrad's laugh affirmed that Madame Sabina's assessment was most likely correct. "That is not what I am talking about," she continued. "I am talking about anticipating our futures, heeding our instincts, and blazing a divine path of our own creation, using the 'magic' that is within us all."

Odette watched the old woman carefully, intrigued by her words. "Are you saying that one can change their destiny? How is that possible?" the blonde beauty enthusiastically asked.

"That's the unusual thing about destiny," Madame Sabina replied. "Destiny is not written in the stars. It is not written anywhere. It is not an absolute, and it is the exact opposite of what it purports to be. The concept of destiny is fraudulent. It is a lie," the old woman said authoritatively. "Let me show you what I mean, through the oracle cards. But it is not I who will perform this 'magic'...it will be you, Odette."

With a dexterity that belied her age, Madame Sabina scooped up the cards and began to shuffle the deck, rotating the worn cards randomly as she thoroughly disorganized their previous orientation to one another. She returned the deck to the table and leveled her gaze at the attentive young woman sitting across from her.

"Now, in your mind, ask a question to which you seek an answer," Madame Sabina explained.

"Oh, I don't know. What do I want to know? What kind of question should it be?" Odette asked.

Madame Sabina's eyes—or what could be seen of them beneath the hood of her cloak—narrowed a bit to emphasize her point. "Understand, this is not a game, Odette. If you are not pure of soul and clear of mind, the message from the oracle cards will mean nothing. If your question relates to worldly goods, the acquisition of wealth, the shallow vices and pleasures enjoyed by the hollow of heart, you will be wasting your time."

The statement was cautionary, but Madame Sabina knew Odette possessed unique qualities that the pious of the village sanctimoniously labeled as sinful. In life, Odette pursued happiness but never at the expense of others. Always did she extend a hand to those in need without the expectation of recompense or the desire for reciprocation. Most importantly, she never denied herself personal pleasure, for abstinence breeds only bitterness and frustration. Odette was pure, at least by Madame

Sabina's standards, and the old woman was prepared to open a whole new world to her.

"I know," Odette whispered with conviction. "I have a question."

The old woman nodded her head in approval. "Good. With that question in mind, choose one card from anywhere in the deck, then place it face down in the center of the table." After the young woman completed the task, Sabina continued, "Place your palm upon the card. Now, ask your question aloud."

"What can I expect in the months leading up to our wedding?" Odette spoke into the sage-tinted air, her eyes closed.

Madame Sabina was pleased. "Now. Turn over the card to reveal its face."

Odette complied. Adorning the card were two full circles at each end and two semicircles on both of the longer sides. The card had four words written on it, one word near each of the circles, and in the card's center was an intricate illustration. "Now," the old woman said, "draw the card from the top of the deck, expose its face, and lay it across the first card in the form of a cross. That will reveal the message of guidance." When Odette did as Sabina told her, the semicircle of the top card joined with the full circle of the bottom card, the individual words from each aligning to create a two-word message. "And what do the oracles reveal to you, young lady?"

"'Unexpected arrival,'" Odette read, a hint of trepidation in her voice.

The couple sat quietly in the soft glow of the candlelight, absorbing the strange cards' message and applying it to their pending nuptials.

Conrad gently broke the silence in the chamber. "Unexpected arrival. That could mean anything."

"Exactly," Madame Sabina smiled. "That is exactly the point, Conrad. What is life, if not an unending string of events both minuscule and grave, whose sum comprises the entirety of our life experience, an ever-shifting totality that makes us who we are, differing from one day to the next?"

The young woman repeated Madame Sabina's prior conjecture. "Our destiny is not set in stone. A change of heart today could alter the course of one's life. It could change everything." She let the concept sink ever deeper into her mind.

The soothsayer added, "Consider, too, that a misguided decision or a simple mistake can do the same and have repercussions for years to come, even altering the lives of those around us."

"Unexpected arrival," Conrad repeated to himself. "Is it a warning, Madame Sabina?"

"Maybe it is, and maybe it is not," she responded with uncertainty. "That is up to you to decide. The message you have been given is merely a suggestion and nothing more. It is intended to make you think. To consider alternate possibilities. To contemplate actions before they are made. To joyfully leap like a happy frog while exercising caution," Sabina added and winked at Conrad. "How might an unexpected arrival affect your upcoming wedding, Odette?"

"The first thing that comes to mind is my uncle Edgar," Odette replied. "My family does not plan to invite him to the wedding. He's a drunken sot who starts fights everywhere he goes. He ruins every family gathering." Even as she spoke the words, an idea was taking root within her mind.

Conrad snapped his fingers as the same idea began to blossom in his mind. "Yes...But think about it a minute, Odette. Won't your Uncle Edgar be upset that he was not invited, and might that not spur him to attend anyhow, drunker and angrier than usual because of his purposeful exclusion?"

Odette looked at Sabina, nodding her head slightly as her imagination began to consider scenarios that she had not previously entertained. "I was just thinking the same thing, Conrad. If Uncle Edgar is sent an invitation to the wedding, at least we know what to expect, and we can prepare for his usual antics. And after all, he is my father's brother. He should be invited."

Sabina relaxed, melting against the back of her chair. "There you have it," she said pleasantly. "Then again, that might not be what the oracles were referring to at all, but...they have done their job. They have stirred the natural magic within you, the magic of your conscience, your awareness, and your compassion."

The oracle cards were returned to their case and the enlightened couple was ushered to the doorway of the cartomancer's shop. Odette turned and gave Madame Sabina a warm hug and thanked her for not only allowing them into her shop at such a late hour but also for the oracle reading.

"Are you sure we can't pay you, Madame?" Odette offered. Sabina smiled and demurred, but the young woman reached into her coin purse and placed two pieces of silver in the parched hand of her elder. "For the advice you tried to give me when I was a girl," she explained. Arm in arm, a happy Odette and Conrad walked into the night.

"It's three months until our wedding," Conrad stated after only a few steps.

"It is. I can't wait," Odette replied cheerfully.

"But an 'unexpected arrival'...You know, that could be something else entirely, other than your uncle. What if it means..."

Odette stopped in her tracks, the weight of Conrad's conjecture hitting her bluntly. "Oh, my God, Conrad. Oh, my God."

Conrad's eyes widened. "Odette, you're not...you know," he said, not wanting to speak the last word of his sentence for fear of jinxing them both.

"No, I'm absolutely not!" she replied defensively, but confidently. "And we're not going to risk that possibility, either, you hear me? If it happens, it will be after we're married, right? We only have to wait three more months."

He hugged her in relief and reassurance. "I can wait. But on our wedding night, all bets are off in our bed." The couple kissed deeply and disappeared into the night.

In the front window of her shop, Madame Sabina smiled and whispered to herself, "Yes, the oracles have done their job."

Only a few minutes passed after Odette and Conrad's departure before the furtive, drunken man returned to the door of the cartomancer's shop. He again tried the door handle and again found it unlocked. He slipped into the darkness of the parlor and quietly shut the door.

Verner Keller stood in the blackness, breathing deeply to calm the nerves that were not already numbed by tavern ale. Very little was visible to him, but the swaying of the beaded curtain that concealed the entryway to the backroom told the shabbily dressed drunkard that Madame Sabina had just passed that way. His visit to the ancient crone's shop after the witching hour had nothing to do with securing her services, and if a confrontation occurred, he could deal with her easily enough. He was there for money, not blood, but Verner was a man who had no qualms about extracting both from the old woman, if necessary.

The visitor of ill intent stiffened suddenly and his eyes widened as he took a quick step backward. Something in the darkness of the shop had brushed past his lower leg. Again, he started, as the fluid, ebon shape leaped to the counter and sprang toward the beaded curtain. In the blink of an eye, the black feline disappeared into the back room of the fortuneteller's shop. Verner spat on the floor. "God damn cat," he hissed to himself.

"We're closed," a voice said, final and sultry. She stood in the parlor doorway, holding wide the beaded curtain, the tilt of her hips accentuating her feminine curves rounding beneath her hooded cloak. Her dark eyes fell upon Verner with an intensity he had never experienced, and her striking beauty made it difficult for him to formulate a coherent sentence. "Wait...I sense something," the cloaked woman added.

Verner stood stock still, his calloused hand finding the handle of the blade in his patched coat pocket. In all of the times he had passed the old woman's shop, never had he seen this dark beauty. He was expecting the old lady to be the only person there, not this elegant creature, whose wavy, black locks poured from beneath her cloak hood and spilled across her chest in ringlets.

"I'm looking for money," he proclaimed. "I'll hurt you if I have to, gypsy." He thought for a moment. "And I might hurt you even if I don't have to."

The woman held out a hand and beckoned for him to follow her into the dark back room. The situation was not what Verner had expected. He imagined walking in, grabbing the cash box, and leaving, not—what was it—seduction? The lack of fear displayed by the woman angered him, as did her turning of the tables. "Oh, no, I'm not following you back there. I'm not fucking stupid, gypsy. Give me all your fucking money, you hear?"

She spoke in an even tone, a hint of melodic playfulness in her delivery. "I think you would be quite unsatisfied with the two silver coins that I have. But I have something that will be of much more value to you."

"What's that? Pussy?" the lout slurred.

She was unfazed by his lewdness. "No. I can see things most people cannot. I sense that your destiny is tied to a treasure greater than you could possibly imagine. Come with me, and I will reveal all to you."

Surely, it was a trap. More of her kind probably lay in wait in that back room, eager to pounce upon him the second he penetrated the beaded curtain. But the knife in his pocket—and the ale that filled his belly—assured him that he would be leaving with exactly what he came for, and perhaps even more.

"Come," she repeated, one olive-toned hand still extended toward him in the dark.

He cautiously entered the room. To his relief, there was no one else in the inner parlor other than the shapely beauty, but Verner was in no mood to entertain foolishness.

"What have you got to show me, huh?" he blurted. "Show me, and make it fast."

She beckoned for him to sit in the chair and placed the dark wooden box with brass hinges on the table. Verner swayed anxiously in his seat as the woman replicated the same routine with the oracle cards that the old woman had performed for the young couple. In this instance, however, the hooded woman chose and placed the cards herself, but she did not read aloud what they said. Whatever message the cards held mattered not, as she had no intention of performing for him an actual oracle card reading. No, she had in mind something else entirely.

"It is as I suspected. You are surrounded by a charm, a very strong charm. I can see it in your aura. A stream of gold that flows to you from..." She stopped, pressing her hands against the crossed cards and tilting her head backward. Her lips parted and formed an ecstatic oval. "Yes...I see it all...a great treasure," she breathily exhaled.

"Where?" Verner shouted, pressing forward against the table. "What kind of treasure?"

"Gold. Chests of gold. Hidden away."

"Where?" he demanded.

"A castle. On a high peak. Abandoned. Forgotten. Riches beyond belief, hidden under the stones of the wine cellar." As if possessed by an urgent impulse, she rose suddenly and frantically rifled through the items on the small table next to her, then hastily wrote something on a scrap of parchment as if the information she had just received from beyond would vanish into mist at any second. "Here," she said, handing Verner the crudely drawn map. "Here is where your destiny lies."

"I know that place. That's Văduva Castle. There's nothing there, hasn't been for two hundred years. Rotting timbers and crumbling stone, that's it," he muttered. "I hunt in those hills, I should know."

"Yet," she interjected, "have you ever gone down to the castle's wine cellar and loosened the flagstones to see what lies beneath?" She stared directly into his eyes, condescension highlighting her smirk.

The rough drunkard stood abruptly, pulled the knife from his pocket, and pointed it directly at the face of the beauteous seer. "If you're lying, I'll be back for you. Believe me, I'll be back for you."

She smiled and tilted her head to one side, unintimidated by Verner's threat. "Closing time," she said nonchalantly, as she blew out one candle, then the other. "Oh, by the way, when you receive your just reward, don't forget who sent you there."

Verner stumbled down the street, the folded parchment in his tightly clenched fist. Minutes before, as they sat in the parlor, the fortuneteller had seen the image on the top oracle card, but Verner had not. If he had, he would have beheld an ornate illustration of a nightmarish beast from Hell itself, blood dripping from two gleaming fangs.

Verner Keller would not discover gold at the castle on the peak. Instead, he would come face-to-face with a much different destiny.

As the door was locked, laughter at once youthful and gravelly briefly wafted from the cartomancer shop of Madame Sabina, then all was silent. The hooded figure sat in the darkness, the oracle deck before her, and she hesitated briefly and concentrated before turning the top card in the reading she had just dealt for herself. The circles aligned as she positioned the card, and her stomach sank when the message was revealed. Her question had been, "Of what on the horizon should I beware?" The message relayed by the oracle cards was as mysterious as it was chilling. It read, "Unholy creation."

But even more concerning was the black area within the central frame of the card, for it was not adorned with an illustration.

Every card within the deck was black by design, the image on each conjured by the Oracle at the moment it is gazed upon by its reader. Yet, the card that lay exposed before the dark-haired mystic remained ebon, as if it possessed a secret as yet unveiled, the image of a being who, at that time, did not exist.

At least, not yet.

GUIDANCE

SUPERNATURAL

UNCANNY

WISDOM

CHAPTER TWO
SHROUDS

The straggling remnants of the night's revelers shakily climbed the wooden stairs of Kleinburg's rathskeller, some still warbling the strains of some unintelligible drinking song. Four of the men were handsomely dressed, but their expensive garb did not conceal their vulgar dispositions. Among the group, Erwin Engel seemed detached from the inebriated antics of his friends. He tapped the bowl of his cherry wood pipe against his palm as he watched the attractively dressed blonde woman step up from the stairs onto the cobblestone. She lingered under the rathskeller's above-ground lantern, her azure gown glowing in the golden light, the dim illumination accentuating the shadowy crevasse that melted between her ample breasts.

Two of the men paused in silence to drink in the woman's beauty. Erwin gave his drunken friend a knowing smirk, but he did not have to voice what was on his mind. Instead, he casually greeted the woman, who immediately locked arms with him, and the two left the rest of the men behind to stew in their envy of Engel's brashness.

Ivonette gripped his ass tightly, pulling him toward her to increase the depth of his rhythmic thrusts. It was completely out of character for her to engage in any form of immoral activity. Even more shocking to her was that she now found herself in his arms after only first meeting Erwin earlier that evening. When he had walked into the rathskeller, something about him immediately snared her attention. Perhaps it was his dark locks that attracted her, or maybe it was the way that he moved with such assurance and fluidity that he would shame the most highly-trained ballet dancer. Or perhaps it was the polish of his black shoes, which stood in stark contrast to the scuffed work boots worn by most of the village men. Whatever it was, he had caught her full attention.

She had arrived in Kleinburg just over one year ago. Ivonette was still attempting to navigate through the new social circles in which she found herself, with varying degrees of success. Before her arrival, she had been struggling to make a living in her home hamlet of Braumstadt, over two hundred kilometers away, but a chance meeting with a traveler through her village changed the course of her life. During small talk exchanged with a stranger she was serving at the tavern where she worked, Ivonette learned that he was a doctor who was passing through Braumstadt on his way to Kleinburg. There, he would assume residency in a stately castle he had inherited.

The doctor seemed greatly impressed with her and when he paid for his meal he presented her with not only a generous gratuity but a most attractive offer of employment. If she agreed to his terms, she would act as his purchaser of supplies, to be delivered weekly to the castle where he would be immersed in important medical studies and experimentation. His estate, he told her, was a family holding that had not been occupied for decades, and although she would not live in the castle with him and his staff, her generous wages would be more than enough to lease a small apartment at Kleinburg's boarding house. Taking up the doctor's intriguing offer would be her way out of a dreary existence that was both mundane and stagnant, and without trepidation she heartily accepted. Within two days, she had packed a small case, bid farewell to her family, and traveled the long, forested road to a new life in another hamlet.

Ivonette and the handsome, well-dressed man said very little to one another on their short walk through the dark from the rathskeller to the village boarding house. The two quietly climbed the wooden staircase on the exterior of the house and after locking the door to her flat, Ivonette succumbed to her irresistible urge to kiss him. Erwin eagerly reciprocated, his hands pulling her into him so closely that he could feel her breasts against his chest. What followed was a flurry of unbuttoning and unlacing, thoughts of foreplay completely disregarded. She wanted him inside of her, immediately.

Ivonette pushed Erwin roughly to the bed, and he did not object in the least when she climbed onto him and straddled his hips. His manhood bobbed against her silken lips, parted them, then slid inside of her. It was not an easy feat to accomplish as the fit was exceptionally tight, but with a concerted thrust, he was deep within her. Ivonette let out a sharp cry and her fingernails dug into his muscled chest as he buried himself within her fully, but after a few strokes, she relaxed her grip and fell into euphoria. She rode him slowly, and after only a few short minutes, Ivonette tensed again, her hot breath in his ear, as orgasm overtook her senses.

Erwin wrapped his arms around Ivonette and rolled so that he could look down upon her, sweat tracking down the sides of his chiseled jawline. He still excitedly throbbed within her, so very close to orgasm himself. With one hand he massaged her breast and lightly pinched her pert nipple as he withdrew his cock from the warmth of her and began vigorously stroking his shaft. So enraptured was he by passion that he failed to notice the streaks of blood on his penis, which quickly disappeared by the motion of his hand. Erwin smiled as he gazed deeply into her pale, blue eyes. Moving from her breast to the back of her head, his hand made a fist in her hair and pulled her face toward his glistening rod. She knew what he wanted. Submissively, she opened her mouth and extended her tongue just inches from the darkening head, and as he groaned in release, he came in several squirts upon her tongue, into her mouth, and upon her flushed cheek.

His muscled back hit the sheet beneath him, and he panted furiously. For Erwin, it was simply another sexual conquest. For Ivonette, however, it was the beginning of thoughts she had previously been far too busy to entertain since arriving in the secluded, mountain village of Kleinburg. But more so, the stirrings of romantic thoughts within her were compounded by the fact that for the first time in her life, she had given herself to a man.

The notions that flowed through both of their minds could not have been in more direct opposition.

"That was incredible," she whispered, wiping the warm fluid from her face. She giggled in slight embarrassment. "You know, I don't even know your name," she admitted.

"Erwin," he responded, retrieving his pants from the wooden plank floor.

"Just Erwin?"

"Erwin *Engel*," he said, arrogance dripping from his tone as if she should have known who he was.

"Don't you want to know *my* name?" she teased.

Silence.

The handsome man's lack of response was crushing. Time itself seemed to stop and her heart felt leaden within her chest. She reminded herself to take a breath. Because she was not prepared to hear an uncomfortable truth, she nervously spoke the first thing that came to mind. It was not what her pride urged her to say.

"I've only lived in Kleinburg for a short time. I'm still learning who's who." Suddenly self-conscious of her nakedness, she pulled the sheet above her breasts as she sat upright and watched him search for a missing shoe.

As he finished dressing, he grabbed his suitcoat from the back of a chair. Neither of them noticed as something fell from the coat pocket, bounced on the throw rug at the foot of her bed, and disappeared just beyond the footboard.

"It's been my pleasure spending the evening with you. I'm sure it was your pleasure, too, hmm?" he said, feigning a friendly demeanor. It appeared that he was trying not to look anxious to leave, but Ivonette knew in her heart that he had no further use for her. He had gotten what he wanted and would probably never speak to her again. She should have realized what kind of man he was when she first noticed the highly polished black shoes that he wore.

Her voice was devoid of cordiality as she imparted a closing comment. "My name is Ivonette." It was an affirmation of her integrity but possessed a chord of warning. He kissed her lightly on the cheek then closed the door behind him, leaving Ivonette alone in the candlelight, the sheet on which she sat damp with her blood.

With the darkened boarding house behind him, Erwin retrieved the wedding ring from his pants pocket and returned it to its rightful place on his finger. He mentally congratulated himself for being such an experienced lover, a sentiment shared with him by dozens of women, many of whom he had fucked after his marriage. He considered himself a trophy that should be shared, rather than locked away in a display case, and he cared not whether his wife agreed with such an amoral attitude. Regardless, although Kleinburg was a relatively small village, Engel's surreptitious dalliances were never reported to his spouse. Wealth has a way of silencing rumors before they begin. He walked the cobblestone street, toward the rathskeller and his carriage.

Behind the gates of the Engel estate, Josephine Engel again glanced at the clock on her nightstand, as she had every fifteen minutes for the past few hours. Again dejected and again suspicious—as she so often was—she sank into the bed pillows, wondering what Erwin's excuse would be this time for returning home so late if he could be bothered to return home at all.

Castle Zorn loomed like a mute sentinel over the village of Kleinburg, a gray reminder of past glories whose significance grew increasingly dusty over time. Once an opulent symbol of wealth and power, the castle had become nothing more than a crumbling refuge for vermin, whose shrieks echoed through the dark catacombs beneath its foundation. At present, however, the ghosts of Castle Zorn retreated into the shadows, as the blood of the living once again pulsed through its stone veins, the glow of candlelight illuminating the cobwebbed chambers for the first time in years. Castle Zorn lived again, host to its new master, Dr. Aldo Zorn.

It was Aldo's father, Wilhelm Zorn, who had assumed ownership of the intimidating edifice in the hills above Kleinburg twenty-two years hence. Wilhelm Zorn was a powerful man and one who was not averse to flaunting his wealth before others, for he was immensely proud of the success that was a creation of his own two hands. Although he began his professional career as a soldier, he was abetted by an inheritance that allowed him to also pursue land acquisitions in his spare time. Those financial endeavors led to his elevated station upon his retirement from the service to his country, and he enjoyed his lucrative civilian occupation for several decades, during which he married and was blessed with three children.

But it was the elder Zorn's profitable business dealings that created within the family a detachment among its members. He was usually absent from the home, pursuing lucrative deals of one sort or another, and when he was in the company of his family, he showed little or no interest in the lives and well-being of his children. He was a virtual stranger to his progeny, to their dismay. Catherine Zorn fared no better than her children in vying for Wilhelm's attention, and her frustration and abandonment manifested as overbearing scrutiny of their young son Aldo and his sisters. The trio of children was scolded constantly for the most menial of transgressions, for Catherine demanded absolute perfection from them. It was an overwhelming burden to thrust upon the sensitive psyches of children. It was not only the children's behavior that was criticized, but also, oddly, their physical appearances. All of the youngsters' natural and minute imperfections were subject to Catherine's obsessive critique. Aldo was continually jabbed because his mother considered him too thin. The hair on the arms of his sister Freeda was considered masculine by her mother. Little Agatha's upturned nose made her look like a swine, or so Catherine always reminded her youngest child. It was painful and abusive, and it was an inevitability that their mother's behavior ingrained deep insecurities in the minds and personalities of all three of the Zorn children.

The castle that loomed over Kleinburg was one of many estates owned by Wilhelm Zorn and was to be utilized as a family vacation home, a plan that never came to pass. The Zorn family's formal residence was in Hannover, where the elder Zorn conducted his lucrative business of buying and selling land, a profession that not only made him one of the richest men in the region but also afforded him privileged information not available to others. That insider knowledge alerted Wilhelm to the existence of the castle, whose owner and single inhabitant was a wealthy widow with no living heirs.

In the spring of 1755, Wilhelm paid a visit to the hilltop estate and immediately fell in love with its aesthetic and domineering stance above Kleinburg. He met with the widow who resided in the ancient edifice and made a most attractive offer to purchase the huge estate, a holding that was much too large for her to manage at her advanced age, he assured her. To his inner displeasure, she had no intention of selling. Zorn changed his bargaining tactic, assuring her that should she claim him as her heir, he would ensure that the castle's glory never dimmed, for he would oversee the upkeep of the estate, with her name forever attached to it. For hours they conversed, through lunch and well past sundown. Throughout the meeting, the widow had no legal representation nor anyone with whom she could consult, but Zorn's credentials reassured her that he was a man of great repute.

The only other person in attendance was Wilhelm's son Aldo, who had no interest in his elder's business, but the boy was still at his father's side, as was demanded of him. Wilhelm's powers of persuasion were indeed formidable, and at length, a deal was finally struck. The widow affixed her signature and waxen seal to a document that Wilhelm hurriedly prepared, and after tea, he and his son departed for Hannover. It was only two nights later that the old widow passed away in her sleep after a sudden illness, and within days, her former home became known as Castle Zorn.

Aldo was always a peculiar child, extremely self-absorbed, and often seeking to ingratiate himself in the eyes of others through spurious means. If a concocted lie would elevate his worth in the eyes of other children or even adults, he would pursue it with relish, a distasteful trait that was a result of the inattention of his father. It was at a very young age that Aldo learned the art of manipulation, and the fact that he was naturally inclined to overachieve and was indeed quite bright was exploited by the young Aldo at every given opportunity.

Of the three Zorn children, it was upon Aldo that the greatest degree of his mother's parental authoritarianism was heaped, and she decided when he was but a child that he would one day become a doctor. Every effort was made to ensure that eventuality, including the beginning of biological and anatomy studies when he was just seven years old.

As Aldo matured and reached his teen years, the pressure imposed upon him by his mother increased. He had grown into quite a handsome young man, and Catherine feared that the eyes of some country girl might lead him astray from the destiny she had chosen for him. She would not have it. Any time a female showed interest in her son, Catherine would cruelly disparage the girl's looks and fill Aldo's head with unfounded accusations that were nothing more than vicious attacks upon the character of the young woman. In her eyes, no one met her unreasonable standards; no one was good enough for her son. Not a day passed that she did not remind Aldo of his princely status. He believed every word of it.

In his later years, Aldo's father Wilhelm was not content to live out his remaining days as an elderly aristocrat, as greater glories called to him. It was because of his innate arrogance and entitlement that he returned to military service as an officer in the Army of Observation during the French invasion of *Kurfürstentum Hannover* in 1757, just two years after he acquired Castle Zorn from the elderly widow. He purchased his title of Field Marshall and was entirely convinced that his wealth and stature—and the bodies of common soldiers—would shield him from harm. Unfortunately, it was during the Battle of Hastenbeck that Wilhelm Zorn's fanciful delusions of being hailed as a decorated military hero were terminated when he was decapitated by a cannonball.

No one in Kleinburg knew the full details, but it was rumored that upon the death of Wilhelm, Castle Zorn was willed to his three offspring, each of whom would enjoy one-third of its occupation and value, should they mutually agree to sell the estate when they were of legal age. But after the death of the vacation estate's master, neither Catherine nor her children ever visited the castle, which seemed to close in upon itself as ivy overtook its stone exterior and encased it in cold solitude.

The truth was that neither Aldo nor his sisters were interested in the least in occupying the castle; conversely, neither were they interested in selling the property. It was an impulsive purchase of their father and nothing more, and it held no sentimentality by his grown children. Castle Zorn became forgotten, as all three heirs led separate lives, apart from one another and apart from their heritage. In their early adulthood, both Freeda and Agatha Zorn had married prominent doctors and began families of their own, while Aldo had followed his mother's persuasion and devoted his life to scientific research at university in Prague. But for reasons unknown, Aldo had emerged from the seclusion of his mysterious medical studies one year ago to take ownership of the neglected edifice known as Castle Zorn.

The two ebon steeds snorted as their shooed hooves clattered upon the steep, stone road that wove up the hillside, to terminate at the cobblestone driveway and *porte-cochère* before the mouth of the dark manse. Through a candlelit window on the second floor, a young woman watched with curiosity as the horse-drawn wagon slowly approached, then veered to one side of the driveway and disappeared into the shadows on the east side of the castle. It was another delivery, conducted in the dead of night, as always. She let the curtain drop and blew out the candle, and after gathering her nerve, she quietly crept away from the window and toward the darkened staircase.

Leuthar stepped down from the driver's box and stood silently in the night. He was unnaturally enveloped in shadow; his black suit, top hat, and straight, shoulder-length, ebon hair seemed to make him practically merge with the darkness at the gate of the castle's cellar entrance. Hugo, much shorter and less fashionably dressed than Leuthar, bounded gracelessly from the wagon and proceeded to attend to the canvas tarp that enshrouded the freight they had hauled up the winding forested road. It would be no stretch of the imagination to envision the pair as a mortician and a gravedigger, for in truth, that is exactly what they were in the not-too-distant past. With a clank, the reinforced wooden door was unlocked and the rusted iron hinges screeched in protest as it slowly swung inward.

Aldo Zorn held higher his oil lamp to illuminate the face of Leuthar. The tall man's soulless black eyes and black mustache and mutton chops only accentuated his deathly pallor. "What have you brought me?" the scientist intoned flatly.

"Come and see. I think you'll be pleased," the dark man replied with a devious smirk.

Hugo drew back the tarp to reveal the cargo. It was the body of a woman, her clothing thoroughly soaked, a mingling of seawater and blood pooling beneath her prone form. "Why is she soaking wet?" Zorn inquired.

"Fished her out of the sea near Wolfsburg," Leuthar replied proudly.

"She must have drowned," assumed Zorn.

The tall man grinned. "Hardly. She had a three-meter-long boathook shoved clean through her belly." It was as if the dark man relished the thought that the woman was murdered, but Leuthar's disturbing demeanor did not chill Zorn in the least.

"Any idea who she is?"

"When has that mattered, sir?" the undertaker quipped. He was only being truthful.

Over the past several months, Leuthar and Hugo had been supplying Aldo Zorn with bodies for his medical experiments, and they were paid handsomely for both their assistance and their silence. A public revelation of the unseemly deeds of the trio would surely lead to nooses around their necks but Zorn spent little time preoccupied with that possibility. He was a doctor, a scientist, and a researcher into the mysteries of life, and should the activities that fueled his experiments be revealed, he trusted that he would escape conviction because of the altruism of his endeavors. Still, the unusual specifics of the work he entrusted to Leuthar and Hugo were suspicious. The unsavory duo was tasked with covertly delivering bodies to Zorn's castle, but not just any bodies. They must be young and they must be female. Exactly how those corpses were obtained was unimportant to Zorn. The scientist's directions to his suppliers never tread into the territory of their methodology, for he did not care if they were simply grave robbers or, in fact, murderers. Never did Leuthar and Hugo admit to such crimes, but Zorn had suspicions, which he kept to himself. Pondering the morality of his scientific endeavor would result in a distraction that he could not afford, particularly not now. Time was of the essence, but what it was that he was rushing to complete remained a mystery to his two accomplices.

"Roll her over," Zorn instructed.

With a mien of professional detached, Zorn lifted the dress and underclothes of the corpse. He held his lantern high as he focused his attention on her pale buttocks, sliding one hand over it and gently testing its firmness with a reverent—and almost loving— touch. Leuthar turned his eyes to Hugo, intent on silently communicating his disgust, but the surly gravedigger was lasciviously gazing upon the dead woman's derriere.

"Perfect. Simply perfect," Zorn whispered. "You've done well." With that, the scientist instructed the two men to rewrap the corpse and carry it down the mossy stone steps that descended into the dark bowels of the castle. As with every delivery, the men placed the corpse upon a wooden trolley before a deeply-pitted iron door whose portal they had never crossed, nor had Leuthar and Hugo ever caught a fleeting glimpse of what lie beyond it. Zorn paid the men for their night's work and the ancient gate leading to the cellar steps was locked behind him.

"What do you think he's doing with all of those bodies?" the dark mortician asked his companion. Hugo did not respond, nor could he. The fall he experienced in his youth while working in Wolfburg's shipyard had not only left a deep crease on the side of his forehead but also robbed him of the power of speech. In truth, Leuthar did not expect an answer to his question; he was merely expressing the curiosity that burned within both of the unsavory men.

Aldo Zorn wheeled the trolley bearing its grisly cargo into his inner sanctum and bolted the door behind him, muffling the low mechanical hum that emanated from within the chamber.

She waited in the shadows of the hallway, and once certain that the scientist would not be leaving his laboratory, the young woman who watched the approach of the midnight visitors silently ascended the stone stairwell to the main floor of Castle Zorn. She still had no idea of the substance of her employer's scientific experiments, but Falcona now knew one thing: The primal matter employed in his studies was ghastly.

CHAPTER THREE
A WALK IN THE WOODS

It wasn't until well after breakfast that Josephine Engel finally spoke to her husband. As she adjusted the plume on her hat, he descended the stairs from the second floor to stand directly behind her as she stood before the gilded mirror beside the front door.

"Have you seen my pipe?" Erwin asked flatly.

"Oh. So you're aware that you don't live here alone," she intoned with palpable disinterest.

He paused, drew in a breath, and exhaled loudly to make Josephine aware that he was prepared to give her the usual reminder of who was the man of the house if she wished to persist with her attitude. Words weren't necessary, as they had played this scene numerous times over the past few years, the frequency of those confrontations coming more and more often.

After her husband finally made his way home the previous night, Josephine feigned sleep when he entered the bedroom and undressed. She listened to Erwin's every move and every breath as if anticipating some telltale indication that what she suspected about her husband was true. It was when he walked past her side of the bed to hang his shirt in the closet that she detected not an unidentifiable perfume or the scent of another woman, but the strong odor of his sweat. For a man who spent nearly every waking hour balancing ledgers behind a desk, physically exerting himself—enough to make his body reek—was highly unusual. And highly suspect.

Josephine awoke at dawn after several hours of fitful sleep. She considered asking Erwin why he had felt the need to bathe upon returning from the rathskeller, but she instead decided to file away her suspicion for another day, a card that she would play when the time was ripe and he was least likely to have an entirely-concocted explanation prepared.

"Where are you off to?" Erwin asked.

"I'm going into town," she replied.

"To spend money, I assume?"

It was typical of Erwin to change the subject and point the finger at some imagined wrongdoing of Josephine when questions about his unexplained comings and goings arose. His was a juvenile and transparent technique, but Josephine would not allow her husband to deflect the morning's tone from the underlying conversation that remained unspoken. "Yes, perhaps I will spend money," she responded, "but primarily, it will give me the time I need to be alone, to think." Josephine shot a withering glance at him in the mirror and without even a goodbye, she turned, the loud slam of the heavy oaken door punctuating her departure.

Erwin watched through the window as Josephine declined their houseman's offer to drive her into town, and she steered the carriage onto the lane and into the forest. He laughed to himself and prepared to return to bed. It had been a long night of drinking and fornicating, after all.

Before he could climb the stairs back to the bedroom he shared with his wife, there came a knock upon the door. Erwin answered it, but it was not his wife returning to ask his forgiveness for her rudeness. Instead, before him stood Ivonette, more radiant in the sun's late-morning rays than she had been in the soft, orange glow of the rathskeller lantern light the night before.

Erwin Engel's adulterous dalliances were numerous but never had one of the objects of his sexual conquests visited his estate. It was so highly unusual and so unexpected that he was at a loss for words. He felt an uncomfortable warmth gather in his temples.

"Well, hello, Erwin Engel," Ivonette gaily chirped, accentuating his surname just as he had done the previous night.

He nervously glanced over her shoulder, but there was no sign of Josephine's carriage, and the houseman had gone around to the back of the estate to attend to the stable after the departure of the lady of the house. All that was out of place was the modest, horse-drawn buckboard sitting in the drive.

"Hello," Erwin finally responded. The air of composure in his voice was belied by his furtive glances around the mansion's grounds, which did not go unnoticed by the beauteous visitor. "It's so nice to see you. I was just on my way out, to take a walk," he offered. "I would be honored if you would join me." Josephine took immediate note that he did not use her proper name, not once. She assumed that he could not remember it.

Birdsongs filled the pines along the narrow path that meandered through the woods. Ivonette walked behind Erwin, who moved at a very casual pace. In light of their sexual encounter the previous night, the conversation between them was understandably awkward, considering that neither of them knew anything at all about the other. To compound Ivonette's frustration, she could not get a straight answer from Erwin when she asked questions of a personal nature, such as what he did for a living, how long he had resided in the area, or if he had any romantic interest in anyone. Every instinct within her urged her to ask Erwin if he had a wife, but he couldn't possibly be married, could he? He was so handsome, so charming, and despite his avoidance of her questions, that didn't necessarily make him a liar or a scoundrel, did it? If only she wasn't so attracted to him, she could assess him from a different perspective, but in this case, her heart adamantly overruled her head.

With his estate no longer in view through the thick, spring foliage, Erwin stopped and pressed his back against an oak, his hands folded behind him. Deftly, he slid his wedding ring from his finger, as just moments before he had realized that the gold band was in full view of Ivonette, but she had not yet remarked on it. He was safe, he assured himself. She had not seen it. To test his assumption, he smiled at Ivonette in a way that he knew would warm her heart. What he could not know was that it also created a slight tingle in the core of her womanhood, but her rational mind pushed aside her sexual urges and demanded to be heard.

"You're not afraid for me to be seen at your home, are you?" she asked bluntly.

He laughed dismissively. "Of course not. What would make you say that?"

She locked him in a dead stare. "Because as soon as I arrived, you whisked me away from the house without even asking me in. It's almost as if I'm... unwanted here." It was not the words she wanted to use, but they would suffice.

Erwin responded not with words, but by extending his hand. Pushing back all her misgivings, Ivonette allowed herself to be pulled into his embrace and a deep and primal kiss.

Almost immediately, Erwin's hand found its way under her dress, rubbing her aroused clitoris through her silk undergarments, his other hand in her hair at the back of her head. She kissed him deeply, their tongues intertwining passionately, as both of her hands worked to unbutton the front of his breeches. She could feel his pink shaft pulsing in anticipation, and once she freed it, Ivonette stroked him slowly, causing his penis to become increasingly rigid. The world around her melted, the trills of the forest birds dulled, and all of her misgivings about Erwin evaporated at that moment as she was swept into the throes of sexual abandon.

Without breaking their kiss, Erwin spun her so that Ivonette's back was now against the bole of the tree. With a solid surface behind her, he pressed upward with two fingers to more deeply penetrate her and the slippery wetness within her eased his manipulations. Still, she gasped sharply as his fingers rubbed across the area that had been torn and was still raw from Irwin's oblivious taking of her virginity the night before. Ivonette's passion far overwhelmed her pain, however, as his fingers found the location inside of her that would lead her to orgasm. She gripped him firmly at the base of his cock, her other hand working the head, using the clear fluid that came from within the shaft to lubricate both his rock-hardness and her supple hand.

"Turn around and lift your dress," he panted.

She did so without hesitation, exposing her round behind. He pressed his shaft between her cheeks, gliding his cock up and down between them as he squeezed her ample breasts through her dress. For both of them, the rush of passion was dizzying. His cock teased at her tight, puckered opening before sliding down between her velvety lips, glistening with her own, sweet honey. He thrust hard, burying himself within her to the hilt, his girth eliciting a high-pitched moan of surprise and satisfaction from Ivonette. She rocked against the tree as he thrust again and again, faster and faster, both of them exhaling in unison with each smack of his hips against her ass. It was only a few minutes before he withdrew his cock and pressed it against her rear, his pelvis continuing to thrust as if he was still deep within her warm, tight pussy. Ivonette instinctively lifted the back of her dress higher to her waist, revealing herself fully to him, and with that, he ejaculated in several short bursts onto her buttocks.

The sexual episode that had just occurred was not the reason Ivonette had come to the Engel estate. It was not why she had cautiously inquired about the location of his home from the town baker when she purchased two scones that morning. Fucking him again was the farthest thing from her mind. During the carriage ride to his estate, the scene she intended to enact played through her head like a shadowy theatrical production, with all of her lines pre-written and rehearsed to perfection. But upon seeing his face—and his devious smile—she succumbed willingly to her suppressed, lusty urges. As she let her dress fall once again to her feet, she cursed herself for sabotaging her plan to tell him of her unexpected feelings for him without ties to a sexual union.

They stood silently, smiling politely at one another, but neither of them spoke. In truth, they knew not what to say. In a voice tinged with embarrassment, Ivonette told Erwin that she had a chore to perform at the behest of her employer, Dr. Aldo Zorn. Hopefully, she would again see Erwin in town on some other occasion. In point of fact, she had no task to perform for Zorn that day, but it was a convenient excuse to depart, to create distance between her and the object of her curious infatuation. She needed time to put her feelings in order.

To her frustration, those feelings were about to be twisted once again.

"I'm a very busy man," was Erwin's curt and dismissive reply, in response to Ivonette's suggestion that they might next meet in public. Again, he was aloof, again he played games with her. But if that was his way, perhaps she could grow to understand why he strove to maintain a distance between them, or at the least, she could learn to tolerate his odd behavior. Somehow, she would find a way to break through the gruff exterior of the man to whom she had surrendered her virginity the night before.

Ivonette found her way back to her carriage, but other eyes followed her through the woods. Seeing all there was to see—including the unsettling truth of Erwin's secret life at last revealed—Josephine Engel crept through the rust-colored pine needles that blanketed the forest floor. Her knuckles were white and her mind was aswirl with a cascade of emotions as she ascended the embankment to her carriage. Only minutes after leaving her home, she had turned around and parked after another carriage bearing a pretty young woman passed her on the road, the road leading toward Josephine's home, and her husband. Now she knew the truth. She had seen it with her own two eyes. Now she knew the truth.

But the anger that rushed through her soul was not without direction, nor was it unbridled. There was more evidence to uncover before her inevitable confrontation with her philandering husband.

Ivonette, too, was lost in thought and her mind was a tempest of unanswered questions, self-doubt, and disappointment in her actions. As her carriage rolled down the dirt road toward Kleinburg, she barely took notice of another carriage, parked and unattended, on the side of the well-worn road. No driver or passenger was within the polished black conveyance that sported a monogrammed "E" on the rear of its bonnet, but as quickly as she noted those facts they were immediately dismissed. She had other more important things on her mind.

Had Ivonette considered the innocuous carriage a few moments longer, she would have noticed that it pulled back onto the road after she passed and followed her carriage into town.

After returning her borrowed conveyance to the stable hand at the Kleinburg boarding house, Ivonette climbed the wooden stairs to her apartment. From the alleyway adjacent to the two-story cottage, Josephine watched the door close behind her new rival, then shook the reins and clicked her tongue to urge her horse to draw the carriage with the monogrammed "E" on its bonnet onto the main thoroughfare of the hamlet and back to the countryside.

CHAPTER FOUR
THE EDGE OF MANIA

In the darkest corner of the rathskeller, Erwin Engel sat alone. After Josephine had returned home from the village, and for the remainder of the daylight hours, she was nothing more than a ghost, a silent, morose specter who strolled aimlessly through the halls, neither speaking nor acknowledging Erwin's presence. He did nothing to draw his wife from her introversion, for it would surely lead to an argument and accusations that he was in no mood to deflect. Instead, he searched the home for his pipe, which, for the life of him, he could not find.

Erwin took another sip of wine, the fourth glass he had consumed since his arrival at the underground pub shortly after sundown, but the pouch of tobacco in his coat pocket was calling to him. What could he have done with his pipe? Throughout the day, he searched the bedroom, the study, the carriage, the kitchen, everywhere, several times over, but there was no trace of it. He asked the landlord of the rathskeller if he had found it—which is what brought Erwin there that evening—but neither the old man, his wife, the barman nor the two barmaids had seen it. Again and again, Erwin retraced his steps of the previous day, the craving for the sweet, comforting smoke gnawing at him. Where else had he gone? He remembered last smoking the engraved, dark cherry wood pipe when he stood outside the drinking establishment the night before, but he could not recall if he had used it again after that. If it had fallen from his pocket he would surely have noticed and that probably couldn't have happened, unless he had taken off his coat and…

And then it struck him, just where it was that he had taken off his coat. It was in the apartment of the girl he had fucked twice in the past day. Ivonette was her name, wasn't it? He could not be sure.

The porcelain bathtub had seen better days. It was slightly discolored and spider-web cracks adorned its exterior, but cosmetic imperfections mattered not to Ivonette, who was immersed in the water's warmth. With so many conflicting thoughts in her mind, and unsure how to reconcile both her attraction to and distrust of Erwin, she hoped that a hot bath would soothe her and hold at bay the moral phantoms that vexed her.

It did not work.

As she gazed at her own body beneath the water, she could not help but recall how she had surrendered herself to him. She closed her eyes, recollecting all that she had memorized about his face. His dark hair, the prominent and strong curve of his nose, his full lips, those penetrating eyes. The silence in the small, lantern-lit room created a vacuum that filled with her sensual thoughts and she drifted willingly into the realm of fantasy. Ivonette's fingers stroked against her belly under the water. She drew them upward to her breasts, cupping them, squeezing them. She tilted her head back, resting it against the rim of the tub and her lips parted as she lightly pinched her pale, pink nipples, sending velvety tingles through her breasts. Her nipples were now fully erect, hard, and round, begging to be taken into his mouth and sucked. In her mind's eye, she imagined Erwin doing just that and more. As if moving of its own volition, her right hand found its way between her legs, her middle and ring finger finding their way inside of her...

Ivonette opened her eyes with a start as the knock on the door rudely pulled her from her fantasy. "Yes?" she called. "Who is it?"

On the other side of the door, the man with polished black shoes nervously scanned the deserted street below. "It's Erwin Engel. May I speak with you?" At times when he drank too much, Erwin did not care what he did and who had seen it. Whether or not it was a premonition, something told him that tonight he should exercise more caution than usual and it would be best if no one knew of his visit to Kleinburg's boarding house.

Now discreetly robed, Ivonette ushered Erwin into the small room. She assumed that he was there for one thing, but she would not, she would *not* give in to him. She had to be strong. She had to resist the primal urges that even now contracted between her thighs. If the relationship between her and Erwin Engel was to progress, mature elements of responsible, intellectual behavior needed to be nurtured. Even though she was barely clothed, and only moments before she had been fingering herself while she recalled how gloriously he had fucked her from behind that very afternoon, she would not give in. They would talk, and that was all that would transpire, although she was warmed by the thought that Erwin would pay her a social visit so soon after that morning.

He had an air of distraction about him that she could not quite identify. "You look... concerned," Ivonette offered, cautiously.

"It's not concern," he smugly assured her. "It's frustration." She felt that she knew where the conversation would then lead until he continued. "I've lost my pipe, and can't find it anywhere. I thought that maybe I left it here. Have you seen it?"

She was a bit relieved. This wasn't a social visit with the expectation of a sexual encounter. Although perhaps the story of a lost pipe was just an excuse for him to be welcomed into her apartment. *It shouldn't be like this*, she thought to herself. *I shouldn't be questioning everything this man says*, her instincts screamed out to her.

"I haven't seen it, no," Ivonette conceded. "You didn't smoke it here."

"I know that. I was drunk, but I wasn't that drunk," he slurred. "I've looked everywhere with no luck. This is the only other place I went yesterday where I might have dropped it."

Even though she enjoyed being in his company, something was off about the situation. The conversation was strained and his focus on the misplaced pipe seemed strange to her. She stood before him in nothing but a silken robe, her legs and breasts barely concealed by the diaphanous material, and he had not even told her that she looked lovely? It was odd. And telling. It was assuredly true that he was concerned about recovering his lost belonging, but another realization sunk in: Erwin Engel was nervous about leaving behind a physical clue that would prove that he had visited Ivonette's apartment before. He wanted to erase any possible link to their sexual dalliance, or so she concluded. It stung, but it was now all so apparent.

She wanted him to leave immediately but did not want to be overtly rude. "I haven't seen your pipe, but I don't know, maybe it fell out of your coat when we…You know," she said, referring to their passionate disrobing of one another the night before.

He muttered a grunt of agreement. Steadying himself with his left hand upon the footboard, he bent to look under the bed. Ivonette glanced downward, and a bolt shot up her spine and into the base of her skull. There it was, in full view for the first time: A gold band upon his ring finger.

She grabbed his hand and pulled it upward, distracting him from his search, and although Ivonette trembled, she did not say a word as she held Erwin's hand in front of his face. His initial expression of dismay melted into one of indignation, and a short, exhaled chuckle escaped his lips.

What could he say? Nothing. There was nothing to say. He roughly snatched his hand from her grip to assert his dominance, but Ivonette's steely gaze voiced her indifference to his action. She was broken, disappointed, and shocked, but mostly she was embarrassed for being so foolishly trusting of an absolute stranger.

"When were you going to tell me, or were you not going to tell me at all?" She tried to speak in an even tone, but it was next to impossible to suppress the bitterness that welled within her.

"It would be best if I leave," he offered, drawing himself upright, his thumbs tucked behind his lapels.

Ivonette would have none of it. "I'm sure you only ever consider what would be best for you. That is not what is best for me. What would be best for me is for you to explain to me just what you thought you were doing seducing me since apparently you're a married man."

Erwin scoffed at her accusation. It was entirely on target, but he scoffed nonetheless. "I seduced you? That's not how I recall it. What I recall is that you willingly took my arm last night and led me to this hovel you live in. And was it not you who tracked me down to my home today, like a dog in heat?"

The crack when her open palm met Erwin's face resounded through the little room, but it echoed within his head like a thunderous explosion. All expression drained from his face, save for his eyes; they blazed with a demonic fury as Ivonette had never before seen.

"How dare you strike me," he hissed through clenched teeth, before adding, "Ignorant whore."

Ivonette clutched her robe closed at her chest and pointed to the door. "Get out, now, you bastard! Get out!" she demanded. But he did not move. He simply stood there, his hands dropping to his sides in fists as rage boiled within him.

"Get out!" Ivonette screamed again, forcefully striking his chest with the balls of her palms, momentarily disrupting his drunken balance.

"I want my pipe!" he yelled back at her, leaning into her face so close that she could smell the sickly sweet odor of wine on his breath.

"Fuck your pipe!" she shot back, again striking his chest with both palms. A veil of blood-redness fell across Erwin's vision. He would suffer no more of her violent anger.

Before she could move away from him, Erwin was upon her, both of his hands shooting outward and wrapping around Ivonette's throat. Utilizing his weight, he backed her against the door. He squeezed tighter, with such force that she could neither speak nor breathe. Tighter still, fire in his eyes, pressing her head against the door. She could do nothing. He was bigger than her, stronger. She tried kicking him, to no avail. Ivonette's face began to grow pale as flashes of light danced before her eyes, and fleeting glimpses of her past cascaded through her memory.

When he finally loosened his grip, her body fell to the floor, reddish-purple bruises in the shape of fingers embedded in the soft flesh of her neck. Ivonette breathed no more.

As Erwin looked upon the prone corpse at his feet, a wave of panic swept over him, manifesting itself as a chilling sweat that crept up his spine, circled under his arms, and washed over his temples and forehead. He had many sins to account for in his life, but murder had never been one of them. Until now.

Every few minutes, the call of a nearby owl mocked Erwin Engel, as if to remind him that his criminal act was not going unnoticed. With his bare hands, he had cleared the pine needles and branches from the ground at least one hundred meters from the road, deep within the blackness of the forest. In his drunken stupor, he was confident that no one had seen him carry the sheet-wrapped burden down from the second-floor flat, load it into his carriage, and transport it out of Kleinburg. That large bundle now lay next to him as he furiously dug deeper into the moist earth. *She was new in town. She had no friends. No one will miss her*, he assured himself.

Again, the owl cried hauntingly, and as he wiped the stinging sweat from his eyes, he nervously scanned the surrounding area, to be sure that only the owl was observing his nocturnal mission.

But he was not alone. Standing in the shadows among the trees that encircled the small clearing, two men watched silently. One was taller than the other. He was dressed entirely in black and wore a tall top hat and a knowing smirk. Erwin considered that he was hallucinating. Surely he was imagining that a phantom undertaker had arrived with a gravedigger in tow to perform the interment of the body of Ivonette, lying cold and still and wrapped tightly within the white sheet. Erwin's dark eyes widened in panic as the tall stranger in black raised his lantern to illuminate the grisly scene.

"Nice night for a bit of skullduggery, isn't it?" Leuthar chuckled.

There was nothing that Erwin Engel could do but sit on his knees in the dirt, his hands encrusted with earth, the evidence of his crime lying stiffly at his side. He had been found out. He would lose everything; Josephine would assume his fortune and he would soon find himself dangling at the end of a hangman's rope. It was over.

The voice of the tall man broke the silence among the trees. "Don't misunderstand, sir. Skullduggery is our stock in trade, isn't it?" he asked of the silent man beside him. "Before you continue with what you have to do tonight, I'd like to suggest a business proposition that could benefit all of us. But that will depend on what's wrapped in that sheet, there."

Knowing that he was at their mercy and unsure if the two mysterious men were armed with pistols or other weapons, Erwin stood impotent as the tall man undraped the corpse and examined it, as a jeweler examines precious gems.

"I'm definitely interested," the tall man whispered.

Erwin's fear of blackmail quickly dissolved as he listened to the undertaker's pitch, which was quite succinct: If Erwin paid the men a small emolument, they would forget what they had seen and never speak of it again. They would also see to the disposal of the woman's corpse in a way that could never be traced to the man who killed her. All Erwin had to do was pay them, walk back to his carriage, and return home. He could put the entire affair out of his mind as if it was only a delirious fever dream.

He had no choice. Erwin did exactly as the man asked then departed without a backward glance, driving toward his estate through the darkness that encroached upon the wooded lane. Behind him, the tall man counted the money once again and let out a sandpaper cackle. "Nothing like getting paid twice for the same slab of flesh, is there?" he asked his speechless partner. Together, the two men carried the sheet-shrouded corpse of Ivonette to their carriage and ultimately delivered the horrific prize to the cellar door of Castle Zorn.

CHAPTER FIVE
LIFEBLOOD

A silken tapestry of cobwebs hung limply in the rafters above the head of Aldo Zorn as he stood before the vat, an erect, copper coffin whose murky interior was aswirl with yellow-green liquid and bubbles that issued forth from the oxygenation propeller at the tank's bottom. Beneath the vat, an orange glow emanated through the faceplate of a flat, wrought iron furnace. The heat generated by the furnace warmed the contents of the case and draped the entire laboratory in a sickly shroud of amber. The vat, with a round, glass porthole on the face of its top end, was the centerpiece to not only the cold, stone-walled room but also to the mysterious endeavor to which Zorn had devoted his life.

Some, actually all of his contemporaries in Prague would have called for the suspension of Aldo Zorn's license to practice medicine if they knew to what dark depths his experiments had plunged. Zorn viewed his contemporaries as short-sighted fools who were more fearful of God than they were of rotting in their graves without ever having accomplished anything in their lives other than attending to sickly old people, children, and unfaithful husbands with venereal diseases. It was on more than one occasion that he had hurled accusations against a fellow man of science; to him, they were nothing more than public servants who attended more to their self-interests than to the concerns of their patients.

Zorn's calling, he knew, was to illuminate a path that had never been blazed, an avenue that led to the golden, intellectual vault containing the secrets of life itself. It was an endeavor that he alone would pursue, for the superstitious fools of the world still shivered in fear at the mention of witchcraft, an ungodly practice of which he would surely be accused if the nature of his studies was uncovered. For true science to thrive, Zorn believed, one must disengage from the constrictive oversight of what modern science and the patriarchs of the church defined as morality.

At a table near the bronze-hued, rivetted vat, Zorn moved his hands over the round dials and switches of an odd, metallic box, making adjustments and writing notes to record the location of the needles on the multiple gauges that extended upward from its body.

The entire chamber hummed with an unnatural drone that pulsed forth from another larger apparatus that towered in the darkest corner of the laboratory. It also glowed from within, fed by coal stored in a large bin at its side. Reminiscent of some hideous, metallic spider, it reached across the floor with several thick, cylindrical canvas tubes that attached to the base of the copper vat just above its small furnace. Steam generated by the larger furnace traveled through the tubes fastened to the lower portion of the upright metal casket, providing the propulsion for the propeller that vigorously rotated the liquid within the strange chamber. But there was something else within the vat that could be barely glimpsed through the opened shutter of the glass porthole. It was something intangible yet familiar, floating like a dark apparition cocooned within the bubbling fluid. Something almost…

Zorn angrily slapped down his notebook on the table when he heard the faint banging from above and outside. Someone was at the gate that led to the cellar, and they were trying very hard to rouse him from his studies. Estevan or Falcona—Zorn's meager house staff—knew better than to interrupt when the din of the steam-driven equipment churned forth from his workroom. Even if it was the housekeepers who knocked, they would have done so on the chamber door in the dark hallway beneath Castle Zorn, not on the exterior iron gate that led to the basement lab. There was only one explanation and only one person who possessed a key to the padlock at the gate that barred entry to the steep drive leading up the hill to the castle.

"You were just here only last night," Zorn reminded Leuthar, speaking to him through the iron gate. The undertaker and his companion were uncertain how to interpret the scientist's statement. Had Zorn not instructed them to use their discretion and bring to him any female corpse that fit his peculiar and fastidious specifications? Did he not tell his dubious assistants that they could call on him at any time, as long as the corpses were fresh and that no crime committed by the two could be traced to him?

Hugo glanced at his much taller associate with an aura of suspicious confusion written on his face. If the doctor was now relenting in his bizarre convictions, it could spell trouble for his conspirators. However, it was a moment that both of the shadowy men had anticipated and for which they were prepared.

"Are you saying that you're not interested in what we've fortuitously stumbled upon?" Leuthar whispered sarcastically through the rusted gate. "Because if you're not, that would be an absolute shame, considering her... freshness," he trailed off.

The scientist glared through the bars at the grim undertaker and aired his concern. "The raw material my experiments require is indeed unique, but it seems," he hesitated, "it seems a bit convenient that you've found yet another corpse so soon after last night. Are deceased young women now falling like leaves from the trees of Kleinburg?"

Leuthar smirked, "This one did." He paused and gathered his thoughts, well aware of the veiled accusation that the doctor implied. It was time, Leuthar concluded, to proceed with a topic of conversation that he knew would one day come. "Hugo and I have been talking, Dr. Zorn. Well, I talked and Hugo listened. But we're in agreement. We would like to know just what it is you're doing with the bodies."

Zorn stood silent, weighing his options.

"Now," Leuthar continued, "when we met, as you skulked about the cemetery that night doing God knows what, you offered to employ us to keep us silent about what you were up to. We're not stupid. You intentionally made us accomplices so that if you hang, we hang. But since you trust us so much, we should know what it is that we're helping you to accomplish up here. That is fair treatment among business partners, wouldn't you agree?"

The remark sickened him, but the scientist remained silent as the man in black continued, delivering the ultimatum that Zorn knew was inevitable. "The way we see it, if we don't get what we want—which is full knowledge of what your experiments entail—we can covertly alert the authorities. Here is why that is bad for you, and not for Hugo and me. We are nobodies, not prominent area aristocrats. We can disappear into the night and never be seen again. You cannot. We are two wanderers who will never be missed should we disappear, and never be found if we don't want to be found, while you are rooted to this estate by your very name. You can never escape that, or the hangman's noose. So," Leuthar concluded, "satisfy our curiosity. Tell us what you're up to, Dr. Zorn."

Silence.

With barely concealed aggravation, Zorn unlocked the iron gate and nodded his head toward the visitors' wagon. "Hurry it up, then," he bitterly acquiesced.

Leuthar and Hugo each carried one end of the sheet-shrouded body down the dark stairwell and to the reinforced portal to Zorn's laboratory, where the scientist stopped them before they entered. "What you will see behind this door is to remain in your strictest confidence," Zorn ordered, even though he had been coerced into revealing his secret and was in no position to make demands. The two men agreed and carried the body into the amber-lit chamber. Zorn locked the door behind them.

"Place the body there," the castle's master directed, motioning toward a steel table like those found in surgical operating theaters. The men complied, and Leuthar rubbed his hands together as if wiping away his involvement in the unholy delivery. Zorn could see the astonishment on the faces of his cohorts as they gazed around the dark laboratory. They were duly impressed by the unidentifiable array of equipment that surrounded them.

"There. You've seen it. It's a laboratory."

"The bodies, Doctor," the taller man said flatly. "What do you do with the bodies?"

But Zorn was not listening. He had unveiled the face of the woman on the operating table, and all color drained from his face.

"You fools!" Zorn screamed. "What have you done!"

"We did nothing, just brought you a body, like always. What's wrong with her?" Leuthar demanded.

With rage in his eyes, Zorn looked upon the two men in disgust and anger. "She was in my employ! I brought this woman with me to Kleinburg to live in the village and act as a purchaser of supplies!" He paused, the tone of his voice dark and sallow. "What did you do to her?" He spoke each word as if it was a sentence unto itself.

The tall man emotionlessly explained the events that led to the acquisition of the dead body of Ivonette, albeit a revisionary interpretation that excluded their blackmail of her killer, Erwin Engel. Honor among thieves is something that truly exists, at least for Leuthar. His story detailed how he and Hugo had encountered a man dragging the corpse into the woods, but as they approached, the killer fled the scene so quickly that they were unable to identify him. The road on which they found the woman was dark, deserted, and rarely traveled, so they simply took advantage of the situation, as they had in several other instances over the past few months. Zorn expressed skepticism, but the undertaker assured him that the tale was the absolute truth.

"In my thirty-eight years on this Earth, I've not once stumbled upon a dead body," Zorn said cynically, "but you two seem to fall over corpses left and right. I find that extremely curious. But, your unfortunate luck—and the untimely demise of so many young women—promotes the advancement of science, for which all of humanity might one day benefit."

"But how?" asked Leuthar, his voice not unlike the hiss of a serpent.

"Blood," the scientist intoned solemnly. "The blood. Blood is life, and through the study of it, I hope to discover something never before dreamed of."

"What?" questioned Leuthar.

Zorn looked him squarely in the eyes. "Immortality," he responded.

The undertaker stiffened. "You're a god damned vampire, is that it, Zorn? You're a fucking vampire?"

Aldo Zorn laughed. "I am shocked that a man who appears to have had a reasonable education and who is of greater-than-average intelligence believes in fairy tales." The comment was condescending but still laced with compliments meant to massage the ego of the man in black. It appeared to work, based on the way Leuthar straightened his posture upon hearing the back-handed commendation.

"I do have one other question about all of this, Doctor," Leuthar stated respectfully.

Zorn smiled. "We're business partners. Go ahead."

"I don't quite understand," Leuthar began, carefully choosing his words. "If it's blood you're interested in, why do you examine the bodies? Seems like each time we make a delivery, you look at some specific part of them. An arm. A leg. An ear. A breast."

"Are you a doctor yourself, Leuthar?" Zorn snidely replied. The undertaker shook his head. "No, you're not. You therefore could not identify the early physical manifestations of diseases like diabetes mellitus. What about variola great or small? Consumption?" Again, Leuthar shook his head. "No, you could not. To answer your question, I need bodies—and blood—in perfect physiological states. Is there anything else you would like to know?" Zorn asked as he casually pulled the sheet over the dead stare of Ivonette.

Leuthar tipped his hat to the doctor. "Just asking, is all," he said sheepishly. "We'll be going now." With that, the undertaker slapped his speechless partner to get his attention and the two were escorted to the door. The tall man draped in black hesitated before departing, pausing in the doorway to look back into the laboratory.

"What's that contraption, by the way?" he asked, tilting his chin at the tall, copper-plated vat. There was an air of suspicion in his voice, a subtle indication that he knew the machine held some great importance to Zorn's work that the scientist had not disclosed and did not want to reveal.

"You wouldn't understand the function of that device, let alone the scientific principle behind its construction," Zorn admonished.

"You're probably right," Leuthar conceded. Their footsteps echoed hollowly through the dark hallway, and the scientist locked the iron gate behind them as the two shadowy individuals returned to their horse-drawn cart.

The wagon rattled as it descended the steep drive, through the pines, and back to the main road at the base of the hill. Leuthar looked up at the few lighted windows of the castle that loomed over the valley. "There's always more to every story than what's visible," the undertaker said to Hugo. "It's what's left out that reveals the true tale." Hugo nodded his head in agreement, and the two proceeded down the lane toward Kleinburg, leaving the carelessly unlocked gate behind them.

Aldo Zorn looked upon the pale features of Ivonette, her eyes now gazing beyond eternity. The marks upon her crushed neck were still visible, but they were growing paler as the blood within her prostrate form began to pool in her back. *Such a shame*, he thought to himself. Now Estevan or Falcona would have to ride into Kleinburg for supplies when they had other more important duties to perform in the castle. The death of the woman in his former employ was nothing more than an inconvenience to him. However, Ivonette would still serve one last purpose.

Zorn rolled the corpse onto her stomach and turned the crank wheel beneath the metal table to elevate one end. He pulled her forward so that her chin extended past the edge, then retrieved a large, glass basin, which he placed on a short stool beneath her neck. With deft precision and professional detachment, Zorn slid a scalpel across Ivonette's neck and sliced through skin and muscle, opening both of her carotid arteries. As the blood began to drain from the corpse into the glass receptacle, the doctor raised the far end of the table higher to accelerate the evacuation of the crimson fluid from her body.

Within the hour, the container was filled with thick, dark liquid, which the doctor carried to one of the wooden worktables that lined the ancient, stone walls of the laboratory. Zorn slid the large bowl between two wooden clamps that held it fast, then pulled forward a fork-like mechanical arm from which dangled two flat sheets of pure silver. To the top edges of the gleaming rectangles were connected two thin copper wires that fed into a strange iron engine, no larger than a shoebox. The contraption had exterior gears which provided the propulsion for several metal wheels enwrapped with a rubber belt, and into the device was fed steam from one of the tentacles of the great, glowing furnace. Zorn adjusted the mechanical arm so that the silver plates submerged into the dark blood in the glass receptacle.

With the flick of a switch, the odd little machine came to life, the gears turning and the wheels and belts rotating in place. A high-pitched hum emanated from the glass bowl, barely detectable above the rhythmic drone of the steam motor, as an extremely low and regulated electric current coursed through Ivonette's blood. Zorn watched diligently, but detecting no irregularities, he removed his thick, rubber gloves and straightened his posture. A smile played at one corner of his mouth as he mentally patted himself on the back. It was another genius invention, another piece to the puzzle that he was constructing in the ebon bowels of the castle.

He was now so very close to completion that he could almost taste it. To his side, the tall, copper tank loomed like a funerary monolith.

Zorn stood before the vat like a nobleman before his queen. He inhaled slowly, held his breath for a few seconds, then exhaled with precision, to calm the turbulent thoughts that coursed through his great mind, and with that, he opened the round portal on the face of the vat. His pupils constricted as the light from within illuminated his face. His expression was not unlike that of a religious pilgrim who had just encountered the visage of the Holy Mary.

He marveled at his achievement. Floating within the yellow-green liquid that filled the tank was suspended the body of a woman. She was a most exquisite beauty, perfect in tone and structure and physical composure, save for the hundreds of incisions in her flesh, held tight by thousands of silken sutures. Like lines on a map tracing the course of a river and its tributaries, the deep red lacerations wrapped around the entirety of her body. If not for the jigsaw puzzle appearance of her skin, and the fact that no hair or flesh covered the top of her skull, she would have been considered a goddess by classical painters.

So very close to completion, Zorn thought to himself as his hand found its way into his breeches and gripped his engorged penis.

One hour earlier in the darkness of the upstairs hallway, Estevan had quietly rapped on the door of his younger sister's bedchamber. He intended to wish Falcona a good night, but upon entering, he found the room shrouded in complete darkness. Falcona stood in front of the window, gazing out into the night. She did not turn to greet her brother.

"Is something wrong?" he asked in Spanish. When they were hired, Estevan and Falcona had been strictly instructed not to speak Spanish in Zorn's presence, but when alone they conversed in their native tongue. The doctor explained that his demand was necessary to exercise control over his household, but it was obvious to the siblings that their employer imposed the rule out of distrust; they might conspire against him right in front of him and he would be none the wiser. It was paranoia, pure and simple.

"Those two men in the wagon. They were here," the raven-haired woman whispered with suspicion. "Again." As she had earlier been preoccupied with drying and putting away the copper pots used to prepare that night's dinner, she did not see or hear the approach of the wagon, but minutes ago, from her bedroom window, she caught a glimpse of it leaving. She blew out all of the room's candles to conceal herself in the darkness and spied on the two shady men in the wagon until the conveyance disappeared down the twisting, wooded lane.

The handsome young man sighed, lighting the oil lamp on the bedside table. On multiple occasions, Estevan and his older sister had at length discussed her misgivings but his reassurances that they should trust their benefactor did little to soothe Falcona's unease.

She turned to face him, her arms wrapped tightly around herself. "Don't you want to know…" she trailed off. The sentence did not need completion. He had heard it over and over the past year, since their engagement as the household staff of Castle Zorn.

"Falcona, we've discussed this. I do want to know, but I also don't want to know. It's none of our business. We were hired for one thing: to keep his estate in order. Period. What he does down there is none of our concern," Estavan reminded her.

"I told you what I saw last night," Falcona shot back with steel in her voice. "What those men wheeled into his lab on that table. It was a body, Estevan. I saw a hand. It was a dead body," she reminded him forcefully.

"He's a doctor," Estevan said.

Falcona's heart was full of fire, as it so often was when her brother spoke condescendingly to her. "Doctors work with the sick, Estevan, not the dead."

Estevan exhaled loudly as he took a seat in the upholstered reading chair near the bookcase and adjusted his straight back against the burgundy padding as if preparing himself for a debate. "I've told you before, I agree. The secrecy is suspicious. But that doesn't mean there's anything nefarious going on. He's not just a doctor, Falcona, he's a scientist. He's conducting research, trying to find cures for things."

"Cures for what?" she shot back. "Death? There is no cure for death."

Falcona's brother sighed in defeat and melted into the chair. She was right, and he agreed with her that Zorn's behavior regarding his laboratory was concerning and just a bit frightening. He had admitted as much to his sister in the past. But he reminded her, as he had several times over the last few months, that should the doctor become aware of their suspicions, they would most certainly be dismissed from his service, and then where would that leave them? Stranded in northern Europe, without homes, without jobs, and uncomfortably distant from their homeland of Spain. No, for their own best interests, they needed to remain silent, go about their duties, and collect their wages. In truth, they had no other choice in the matter.

"When we left Valencia, we made a pact, remember?" Falcona said, her demeanor softening. "It was you and me, together, striking out on our own to make something of ourselves. There was a big and exciting world out there for us, so much greater than what we would ever have experienced on the farm. We promised to help one another as a team, and so far, we haven't done too badly, have we? We've traveled, and seen things we never would have if we had stayed stuck in the fields with Aunt and Uncle. But it wasn't as rosy as we had imagined. Some of the jobs we've accepted have been terrible. Then we met Dr. Zorn, and because the money was so good—*so good*—I was willing to overlook what kind of man we were serving." She paused, sitting down on the bed, her head down and her hands clasped between her knees. "But I just can't anymore, Estevan. I can't. There's something about him that feels…"

"I know, I know," her brother interrupted gently. "Evil. And it's not that I don't think that, too, but what do we do, confront him with our suspicions and get dismissed? We just can't do that. We're trapped, Falcona," he pleaded, crestfallen.

She looked at him and smiled, but he detected an undercurrent of defiance in that smile. "For now," she said, her eyes reflecting the flame that danced at the tip of the oil lamp's wick.

WEAKNESS

FORMIDABLE

PRECISE

STRENGTH

CHAPTER SIX
THE ETERNAL BOND

The golden rays of the early morning sun had just begun to peek over the pitched roofs of Kleinburg as Josephine Engel climbed the worn, wooden stairs that led to the second-floor apartment of the run-down boarding house. On the cobblestone street below, a horse-drawn wagon laden with cut grain clattered past the old building, but neither the driver nor any of the villagers on their early morning rounds paid any mind to Josephine. The exceptionally well-dressed woman with the violet parasol knocked repeatedly on the door of the apartment. There was no answer from within but Josephine would not leave until there was.

She waited several minutes, all the while imagining that she was being watched by those on the street. But what did it matter if anyone thought it unusual for the wife of Erwin Engel to pay a visit to the town boarding house, and at such an early hour? Why she was there was no one's business but her own. Should anyone inquire, perhaps Josephine would tell them that she had caught her husband fucking the woman who lived there and she had come to the boarding house for a confrontation about that affair. What difference did it make now? Everyone in Kleinburg probably already knew the sordid details.

Josephine waited and knocked for several more minutes, but not a sound nor a stirring came from behind the door. Unconsciously, she placed her hand on the door handle. Her touch was enough to cause the unlatched wooden portal to swing open, just a few centimeters.

"Hello?" she whispered into the darkness within. There was no response. Josephine cautiously glanced over her shoulder and confident that no one was watching, she slipped inside the apartment and closed the door.

She wasn't sure what to expect but the living space was not as she had imagined. Everything was quite neat and orderly as if the

57

woman who lived there did her best to make the apartment presentable, despite its cracked plaster walls. *Maybe she kept it orderly to impress Erwin*, Josephine thought. She could only assume that her husband had spent time there on one or more of his late nights out on the town, but she had no proof to validate that accusation.

"I am Josephine Engel. I'm here to talk to you," she announced, but no sounds came from the wardrobe closet or the small kitchen. It was a small apartment, the living area only large enough to accommodate a bed, a bathing tub, and a reading chair and table. The apartment's resident was not at home, but curiously, an oil lamp that was very low on fuel burned on the table next to the bed. She gazed around the room and noticed that the bed was slightly askew. It was such a minor irregularity but one that she couldn't help but correct out of habit. As she pushed the footboard of the bed so that the headboard was flush with the wall, she laughed to herself. *Now why in the world am I helping the bitch straighten her apartment?*

Near her foot, something reflected the single ray of sunlight that found its way through the drawn curtains, something that was now revealed after the bed was moved. It was a dark cherry wood pipe, with a silver mouthpiece and bowl. She picked it up and examined the familiar object, and as she anticipated, she found the initials "E.E." engraved upon it.

It was Erwin's pipe. He had been there. But the location of the apartment's female occupant remained unknown, the woman whose name was Ivonette, a bit of information that Josephine had obtained from the boarding house landlord after placing a few coins in his palm. The only other things she knew about Ivonette were that she had only lived in Kleinburg for a year and that she worked for the doctor who had taken up residence in Castle Zorn. She shut the door behind her and returned to her carriage, urging the horse to carry her onto the forested road that led to the secluded mountaintop estate.

Estevan smiled politely at the unexpected visitor as he tried to conceal his dismay at her presence at Castle Zorn. "Good morning, madame. How may I assist you?" he asked the smartly dressed Josephine Engel, whose parasol blocked the rays of the rising sun behind her as she stood at the front doors of the Zorn estate. It was unusual for anyone to come to the castle uninvited and even more unusual that she had gotten past the gate at the main road, a gate that was always locked to prevent entry to the grounds. Dr. Zorn's visitors the previous night must have been remiss in the duties he had entrusted to them, and they would surely be reprimanded severely for their carelessness. If there was anything that Zorn valued, it was his privacy, and he guarded it fervently.

Looking down at her feet, Josephine nervously scuffed the toe of her boot against the marble flooring within the entryway. Now that she had arrived at the castle, the impetuousness of her visit caught up to her. She was completely unsure of what she should say, or how she should explain her presence at the estate without causing some manner of uncomfortable admission. She gathered her thoughts and responded to the handsome young servant.

"My name is Josephine Engel," she said smoothly, "and I thought that I might pay a visit to your master, to extend a belated welcome to Kleinburg, on behalf of my husband and myself."

If Estevan was truthful, he would admit that the visitor's beauty tempted him to allow her anything that she requested, but he maintained his resolve. "Master Zorn is quite a busy man. He doesn't entertain visitors. Ever. However," he offered, her smile melting his stern demeanor, "I would be happy to relay your message to the doctor."

"Oh, that's disappointing," she said solemnly. "I had hoped to speak to him myself. Is there a better time when I might call on him?" she asked.

"He's very busy. I don't..." Josephine fluttered her eyelashes flirtatiously, catching Estevan off guard. "Maybe I can see if he is available."

"Estevan!" Zorn's voice growled behind his house servant. "Who's out there?" he demanded, attempting to keep his voice low to not be heard by the visitor.

"A woman from the village, sir," Estavan replied, closing the door slightly to block Josephine's view of the master of the house. "Somehow, she got through the gate. She says that she's just making a neighborly visit to welcome you to Kleinburg."

"Those careless idiots," Zorn growled to himself, correctly surmising that Leuthar and Hugo had left the gate to the estate unlocked the night before. "Get rid of whoever she is and lock the gate behind her," he barked.

"Dr. Zorn," Josephine said loudly enough for the doctor to hear, while gently pushing inward on the door in an attempt to open it wider. "If I may, sir, I am Mrs. Josephine Engel. I realize I'm a total stranger but I wondered if you would indulge me and.."

Zorn could now see the visitor beyond the periphery of the oak door. She was handsomely dressed, a halo of early morning light illuminating her form, but when his eyes fell upon Josephine, all her other physical attributes dissolved from his cognizance, save one single feature that dominated his attention: She had the most luxuriously wavy, scarlet red hair he had ever seen.

"Please, come in, Mrs. Engel," he graciously bade her. "Welcome to Castle Zorn," he gushed, much to the dismay of the younger man in his employ.

Josephine gazed in admiration at the ornately carved arches that supported the vaulted ceiling of the castle's vestibule. On each side of the chamber rose wide, curved staircases of gray marble, which converged at the balcony that overlooked the room into which Aldo Zorn ushered his beauteous visitor. Although her family had traveled in circles that could be considered high society, Josephine had never before visited a home of such antiquity. Though the stone masonry all about her bore the stain of centuries of wear, the elegance of the castle's design was most wonderful, in her eyes. She reminded herself that she had not come for a sightseeing tour and her visit had nothing to do with Zorn himself, but she could not help but make note of the doctor's youthfulness. She had expected to encounter a stooped, elderly, balding man with spectacles, so she was taken aback by the handsome blonde doctor who had graciously invited her into his home.

Zorn stopped and turned, holding his arms wide. "I'm Dr. Aldo Zorn. I'm afraid it's still a bit dusty in here, but..." he paused, clasping his hands together at his chest, "I'm delighted that you've come to call. How long have you lived in Kleinburg, Mrs. Engel?"

"My entire life," Josephine responded, "like nearly everyone else in the village. We tend to stay close to home around here."

"There's nothing wrong with that. And your husband, what is his occupation?" Judging from Josephine's fine dress, Zorn assumed that Mr. Engel was no mere farmer or blacksmith.

Josephine blanched at the mention of her husband, but it was Erwin who was responsible for spurring her visit to the castle. She'd have to talk about him at some point, so it might as well begin now. "Mr. Engel does legal work for the Bürgermeister," she explained. "He audits and balances the town financial ledgers. On rare occasions, he provides legal representation for the villagers. But as I said, that's rare. Disputes in Kleinburg don't happen often and when they do, they tend to be handled privately. In such a small village, everyone knows everyone else's business. When you're born here, live here your whole life, and die here, it's quite disruptive to escalate disagreements with one's neighbors. Because of his knowledge of legal matters, my husband serves as an arbiter of petty squabbles, before they get out of hand."

Zorn could tell by her expression and a certain drift in her eyes as she spoke of her husband that there was something on her mind.

"To be honest with you," she continued hesitantly, "my husband is the reason I've come here today."

"I see. You may go, Estevan," he said, dismissing his servant. "Let's walk, and you can tell me what's on your mind." he graciously suggested.

The doctor ushered Josephine through two large oak doors into a long hallway, whose walls were adorned with finely painted works of art. She stopped before one of the framed oils. It was a pastoral scene of an impossibly pale, nude woman wading into a stream, trees filled with ripe red apples behind her. "Beautiful," Josephine whispered

"I suppose so," Zorn replied as if uninterested because, in truth, he was not. "I've never been an art critic, nor a connoisseur. My entire life, I've focused all of my attention on my research."

"You can miss a lot of the beauty in life by doing that," she countered with a gentle smile.

Zorn reciprocated the friendly gesture. "Make no mistake, Mrs. Engel. I know beauty when I see it." Josephine was not sure if the comment held any flirtatious intent but it was a distinct possibility, as something about the way the doctor looked at her, particularly her hair, made her uncomfortable. She needed to steer the conversation to the subject that weighed so heavily upon her mind and heart.

What magnificent red hair.

Josephine turned to face both Dr. Zorn and the golden sunlight that streamed through the windows opposite the wall of art. "The true reason for my visit…As I said, it concerns my husband, but it is not pleasant."

Josephine's admission caused Zorn's stomach to drop. Could it be that this woman knew of his work, and in particular, the unsavory tactics by which he obtained the raw materials for his research? Or worse, could it be that Erwin Engel—who worked for the Bürgermeister—had uncovered something about Zorn's activities? What if Leuthar had followed through with his threat to the doctor the night before and had contacted the authorities? No. If that was the case, the visitor Zorn now entertained would be the Bürgermeister himself, not Josephine Engel. The scientist could do nothing but let her speak, and later decide how to respond to what she had to say.

"I understand that you employ a village girl named Ivonette," she said. A chill ran up Zorn's spine.

"Yes. I do. Continue," he responded.

Josephine then told him of the events of the past two days, of her suspicions of her husband, and of what she witnessed between Erwin and Ivonette on the grounds of their estate. Within him, his panic was barely contained, but the doctor listened attentively to the story with an air of compassion. But another voice within his subconscious clawed at its restraints with an urgency not to be denied.

Silken. How playfully it curls. Such a rich, deep shade of crimson.

"It's a terrible situation, Mrs. Engel. You have my sympathy." He paused. "I assume your husband has no idea you've come here today?" Zorn inquired.

"He does not and I do not want him to know. At least not yet, if you understand what I'm saying."

"I do," the doctor assured her. "Are you entirely certain that this affair you allege…"

"I'm not alleging anything. I saw them," she said firmly. "I am not here to cause a scene. I simply want to speak with the girl, Ivonette. I intend to learn the truth, to hear both sides of the story, before deciding how to proceed with my life and my marriage."

It's perfect. So red. So luxurious.

"I've only just met you, Mrs. Engel, but I sense that you are a woman of great composure and grace," Zorn said flatteringly. "If you say that you simply want to talk, I believe you. Yes. Ivonette is here, assisting me in my laboratory. I will take you to her."

Simply perfect.

Zorn led Josephine down the hall, where they descended the stairs into the basement of the castle. At the termination of the dark catacomb, he unlocked the great, reinforced door and ushered her inside, then closed it gently behind her.

Josephine gazed about the laboratory in awe, marveling at the vast array of bizarre scientific devices. As impressed as she was, whatever medical triumph Zorn wished to attain mattered not to Josephine; she was only interested in speaking to Ivonette. The thought had crossed her mind that it would have been polite for her to at least seem interested in the doctor's work, but in light of what she had already disclosed, small talk would have been easily discerned as ingenuous. There was no need for pretense. Not now.

She turned, directing her attention to the large, spider-like furnace that lurked in the darkest corner of the chamber. She had never seen anything like it, and it emitted such an odd sound. But no, the sound wasn't coming from the blackened, iron octopus that reached out across the floor in various directions. Something else was creating a low hum, a rhythmic churning of sorts. She listened, turning her head, and then realized that the drone emanated from the tall, copper tank with a round portal bolted into its face.

Josephine broke from her scrutiny of the odd trappings of the lab and turned her attention to the subject at hand. "So," she stated with the utmost composure, "Where is Ivonette?"

As Josephine turned to face him, she found Zorn only one step behind her. He placed one hand upon her shoulder, then thrust the long surgical scissors upward into the soft region of the underside of Josephine's jaw, through the roof of her mouth, and into the lower portion of her brain. The light left her eyes instantly and she fell limply into the arms of the scientist. He held her close, nestling his nose and chin into the glorious crimson mass of her hair.

Perfection.

As he held her in silence, his mind was deluged by the sheer magnitude of his brutal act. Josephine's blood stained the front of his shirt and vest, but he held her closer still, trying to come to grips with the impulsive action that could now possibly threaten the eventual triumph he had worked so diligently to achieve. But as he felt the weight of her lifeless body in his embrace, a realization came over him like the dawning of a new day: this corpse, this shell, was now nothing more than flesh, and in that rationalization, he found reassurance that he could effectively conceal his crime.

As he drained her body of blood, just as he had done to Ivonette the night before, Zorn considered that the tangled emotional web that strung together Ivonette, Josephine, and Erwin Engel could work to his advantage. It was all coming together in his mind: Erwin held no love for Josephine and her erasure would free him to pursue whatever carnal adventures piqued his fancy. If an investigation into his wife's disappearance was conducted by the local authorities, Engel's questionable actions and idiosyncrasies would come under scrutiny and perhaps his affair with Ivonette would be revealed, which he would most likely wish to avoid. As he weighed possibilities, the doctor continued his gruesome work, surgically dismembering the corpse, just as he had done with the body of Ivonette.

Ivonette. Therein lay the key to ensuring Erwin Engel's silence. The story from the unscrupulous Leuthar was that Ivonette was killed by an unknown assailant. Zorn had previously given no thought to who or why someone would murder his assistant, but now…Now a prime suspect was manifested in the form of Erwin Engel. Although Zorn would do everything within his power to erase Josephine Engel's visit to the castle, he was quite certain that her husband would most likely not create waves to uncover her whereabouts. Doing so might lead to the revelation of his affair with Ivonette, which in turn might lead to an investigation into her disappearance, and thus lead to his unmasking as her murderer. Erwin Engel, he determined, would never become a thorn in his side. He couldn't. In this matter, Engel's silence was preordained.

Zorn casually fed Josephine's bloody clothing and dismembered remains into the spider-like furnace. The fire greedily devoured her, just as it had done to Ivonette. Just as it had done to so many others over the past few months. After disposing of her physical remains, Zorn moved to his workstation and carefully poured Josephine's blood into the glass receptacle containing Ivonette's vital fluids, the blood of the two rivals mingling together in an unholy fusion. Both, at one time or another, had sought the love of Erwin Engel, a man who was probably not worthy of the affections of either of the women, Zorn considered. All that remained of both of them now resided in a single, glass bowl. Such irony. Yet, together, Ivonette and Josephine would serve a much higher purpose in life than being the playthings of some arrogant bureaucrat whom Zorn had never met and hopefully never would.

The doctor's work for the day was only beginning. He explained to Estevan and Falcona that he wished not to be disturbed, as Josephine Engel had a very delicate medical condition that needed treatment. He also informed them that Ivonette, unfortunately, had to rush back to her home in Braumstadt to attend to a sick relative, so Estvan and Falcona would now need to immediately ride into Kleinburg to retrieve some medicines he required from the village chemist. The siblings were supplied with a list and sent on their way, leaving Zorn alone in the cold, dark castle.

The doctor next drove Josephine Engel's carriage up the overgrown path behind the castle, a forgotten service road that led to the derelict mill that had fallen into disuse decades ago. He untethered the horse and with a smack on its hindquarters, it bolted into the forest and down the far slope of the mountain. As for the carriage, he cautiously pried the monogrammed "E" from its bonnet, then pushed the vehicle into the great, dark pit that had formed when an underground cavern yawned wide and devoured the old well at the mill several decades ago.

He flung the silver "E" far into the overgrown forest where it would never be found and walked back to the castle. He had work to do and he would not rest until it was completed.

The medical operation that he performed behind the locked door of his laboratory continued until sundown, long after the return of his servants. Falcona apologized for their delayed return to the castle, but Zorn was unconcerned. He explained that his treatment of the patient with what he had on hand went better than expected and Mrs. Engel had returned to her home. He shooed away the siblings and continued his work.

Several hours later, Zorn stood before the tall, copper vat, drinking in the momentousness of the occasion. *It was perfect*, he thought. *Perfect.*

Before closing the faceplate of the portal on the facade of the metal tank, Zorn took one last look at his accomplishment. Floating like a weightless angel in the murky yellow-green fluid within the vat, the patchwork body enjoyed the oblivious sleep of non-existence. But now, her head was endowed with a most luxurious mass of wavy, crimson hair, which seemed to dance with a life of its own in the liquid that embraced her naked form.

CHAPTER SEVEN
LIFE!

So engrossed was he in his work that Dr. Zorn failed to notice the chime of the small silver bell that hung in the lab. Dinner was now ready to be served, but since the doctor did not respond to her summons from the kitchen, Falcona walked to the basement and attempted to rouse him by knocking on the door.

"Go away!" Zorn barked. "Do not disturb me again tonight, do you hear?"

With each passing day, Falcona's suspicion of her employer had been increasingly piqued since their settlement within the walls of Castle Zorn but the harshness of his response gave those misgivings even more weight in her mind. He was always less than polite but tonight there was something in the shrill tone of his voice that spoke of fanaticism, even desperation. In compliance with his demand, Falcona briskly moved through the darkness and ascended the stairwell, more than happy to distance herself from Zorn and whatever it was that he was doing behind the locked door of his laboratory.

After stitching Josephine Engel's scalp and hair onto the cranium of the patchwork corpse one hour before, Zorn embarked on a most ghastly task. After being removed from the copper tank, the body now lay face-up on the lab table. The doctor inserted two thick, hollow needles into the soles of its feet, and with great precision, they were fed upward into the tibial veins of each leg. Rubber tubes fed both hypodermic needles, and through them, Zorn pumped the electrically vitalized blood from the glass bowl, the blood of Ivonette and Josephine. The process was an arduous one, requiring the very precise manipulation of a bellows and plunger system of his design, but at last, the glass bowl was drained and the circulatory system of the corpse was filled with the sanguine fluid. A harness was strapped across the torso of the body, after which the scientist cranked the metal wheel on a winch system that lifted the body from the table until it dangled like a marionette in the center of the laboratory.

Zorn continued to work feverishly, rushing about the lab, redirecting steam hoses, and pushing his various work tables away from the suspended body and against the walls. He then proceeded to use a crowbar to pry loose sections of the ancient stone floor and removed the dusty tiles to expose the metal grates beneath. Once revealed, the grates formed a rough circle of dark holes that surrounded the dangling cadaver. He next rushed to a hidden chamber directly beneath the floor of the lab, which housed a great vat of boiling water, fed by a fire that he began stoking after the killing of Josephine.

He knew that today would be the day, as the final piece of his grand puzzle had at last fallen into his hands: Josephine's gloriously curly crimson mane. Zorn threw several more logs into the brazier beneath the gigantic cauldron and nodded in approval as clouds of steam drifted upward and belched into the lab through the circular configuration of metal grates embedded in the ceiling overhead.

He bounded up the wooden stairs back to the lab. Now shrouded in steam, the room's sickly yellow glow was greatly magnified by the damp mist that billowed up from the floor and enshrouded the body in its undulating grip. The ambient temperature of the chamber had risen precipitously, as calculated. Within minutes, every surface was covered by a fine layer of moisture droplets. Zorn removed his vest, rolled up his sleeves, and fully unbuttoned his shirt to minimalize the effect of the cloying heat that now permeated the dank confines of the laboratory. The increased ambient temperature was an absolute necessity and he would happily endure it as it was a means to an end.

In the kitchen on the main floor, Falcona breezed past Estevan, who was placing the silver entrée dishes upon a wheeled cart. She spoke not a word to him.

"Is he coming to dinner?"

"No," she growled, then snatched a glass from the cabinet and half-filled it with bourbon from a bottle on the bar cart in the adjacent dining room. She downed the contents of the glass in one gulp.

"Since when do you drink so early in the night?" Estevan chided.

"You were right," Falcona conceded. "He was angry that I disturbed him. He shouted at me. But not in the usual way. He sounded, I don't know, frantic."

"Frantic? What do you mean?" her brother asked.

"I don't know exactly," she admitted. "I'm telling you, Estevan, there's something really strange going on down there and I think it's more than just medical experiments."

"But what?" he queried. He crossed his arms and leaned against the door frame, thinking deeply. "We know there's something odd about those two men making deliveries in the dead of night. Now we know what they're bringing. You saw it. They're delivering bodies. But there's nothing overtly wrong with that. Medical researchers dissect cadavers all the time."

"Exactly," Falcona added. "So why does he keep their visits a secret? Why has he never mentioned them to us? It's because he has something to hide. But what could it be?"

"I don't know," Estevan admitted.

"Also, remember what his sister told me," Falcona reminded her brother.

Estevan recalled the event. He and Falcona had been working in a traveling carnival caravan, which each fall pitched their tents in the verdant forest that encircled Kleinburg. During one night's performance for the drunken residents of the village, Falcona danced for the men in the crowd, as she did every night, collecting coins from them in exchange for allowing them to leer at her undulating body, barely concealed behind sheer scarves and metal bangles that encircled her waist.

Falcona spied a handsome man at the rear of the torch-lit crowd. He looked conspicuously more refined than any of the other men in attendance, so she weaved her way to him like a snake upon pond water. Though she was adept at the art of seduction, her charms and finger cymbals failed to arouse the response for which she had hoped from the finely dressed gentleman. Instead, he introduced himself as Dr. Aldo Zorn and proposed to her an offer of employment, as a housekeeper at his castle in the area. He explained that he required absolute privacy, therefore he did not want to enlist help from Kleinburg's villagers; anyone with links to the local social circles would likely fall victim to the human frailty of spreading gossip about his most important experimentation. That, he could not afford. Falcona was intrigued by Zorn's offer, as life in a traveling caravan was beginning to wear on her, but she would only accept his offer if he also took on the services of her brother, Estevan.

The doctor was pleased by the prospect, as it alleviated his immediate concerns; his search was for two household staff members, so the alluring woman's suggestion fit perfectly with his needs. That night, Falcona excitedly discussed the proposal with her brother, and the next day the two eagerly accepted the positions. Their new jobs would pay much more than the meager wages they earned as scantily-clad dancers working village crowds for coins during the torchlight performances of the troupe of vagabonds.

Only a few days after Falcona and Estevan had begun working for the doctor, Zorn's sister Freeda and her husband made a brief sojourn at Castle Zorn. She had come to settle some minor family business regarding the stately abode that she had co-inherited along with Aldo and her sister, Agatha. Although the stopover lasted a mere hour, Freeda took an immediate liking to Falcona and was quite congenial with her. Out of curiosity, the young woman asked Freeda about the recent events in her brother Aldo's life, to gain a better understanding of the man who now employed her. Freeda privately confided about the passing of their mother and the unfortunate illness and sudden death of Aldo's wife Magdaline one year hence.

But now, just over one year later, something Freeda said on the afternoon of her visit was nagging at Falcona's subconscious and had been since that day.

"You remember what she told me, Estevan," Falcona continued. "I asked her just what caused the death of Dr. Zorn's wife, what disease it was, and she didn't know. Dr. Zorn never told her, he just said it was a terrible degenerative illness, that it disfigured her. He performed the diagnosis. He kept her hidden away throughout her illness. No one saw her. No one even saw her after she died. He signed the death certificate and prepared her for burial. And the funeral was a closed-casket ceremony. Freeda said that Dr. Zorn said it was because the disease had ravaged his wife physically, that she was hideous and he wanted no one to see her face after she died... But after she died from what?" Falcona concluded ominously.

Estevan was silent, for he knew not what to say. Falcona voiced her distrust of Zorn more often than he did, but he reasoned that if he spoke too frequently of his misgivings, it would erode his sister's confidence in him, and he wanted to be strong for her. But his silence did not mean that he was any less suspicious of the doctor, or any less concerned than Falcona about their safety and well-being inside the walls of Castle Zorn.

Falcona's demeanor was one of stone. "If some man told you that I had died and he had buried me, and no one else had witnessed it, and he gave no concrete explanation about what happened to me, what would you think?"

Estevan gave her a smile of reassurance. "We need to know what he's doing down there," he said.

A devious smile animated Falcona's lips, for she had already been formulating a plan to find out just that.

Dr. Zorn excitedly checked the mercury thermometer mounted to the wall. It was still a sweltering thirty-seven degrees Celsius in the stone room, just above the average temperature of the human body. The great cauldron of boiling water in the chamber below the lab had maintained that exact climate for the past hour.

Zorn's periodic examinations of the corpse dangling at the center of the room confirmed that the chemical bath in which it had been immersed had sufficiently saturated the flesh, enabling the body's temperature to reflect that of the air in the steam-shrouded laboratory.

Although it was coated with ambient moisture, the skin manifested signs of the dehydration of the excess fluid in which it had been cured; the epidermis was increasingly less unctuous, and the pulpous subdermal muscle was becoming progressively firmer to the touch. At last, after years of theorizing and material preparation, it was time for the experiment to proceed to its final stage.

Into the center of the room, Zorn wheeled a cart bearing a meter-long cylindrical metal device. To each of its ends was fastened a thick black cable, and extending from a slot cut into the top of the device's casing was a series of interlocking trays, each embedded with a flat, ebon magnet. Zorn positioned the cart beneath the feet of the corpse and attached the rubber-encased black cables to the circular metal plates sewn into the harness, one at the body's chest, the other in the center of its back. The head hung limply, its face obscured by the voluminous red hair that was now beginning to dry into wild waves and curls. His heart beat wildly as he weighed every nuance of both the corpse itself and his complex scientific endeavor as a whole, but he took a moment to gaze upon the hideous angel suspended in the air before him and steadied himself for what was to come.

With great care, Zorn rotated a crank that fed the magnet-bearing trays into the cylindrical body of the strange device, but after the first two trays disappeared into it, the mechanism greedily devoured the entire length of magnets and pulled them within itself. The magnetic fields projected from the trays were repulsed by other magnets installed in precise locations around a central axle, resulting in an automatic churning of the rotor composed of the interlocking trays. The result was the generation of an electric current that sped through the black cords and fed into the metal plates that lay upon the chest and back of the corpse. Immediately, Zorn toggled a lever on the madly vibrating device, resulting in an isochronous dispersal of the electric current and the low hum emanating from the scientist's invention assumed a rhythmic cadence.

With each surge of voltage into the chest—and heart—of the corpse, the body spasmed slightly, the back straightened momentarily and the head bobbed, its crimson mane swaying and brushing against the pale breasts. Zorn was mesmerized by the mechanical dance of the flesh marionette, anticipating each jolt and its resulting physical movement of the body. Though it was not alive, it was moving of its own accord, each jolt bringing the macabre experiment closer to its climax. Behind the network of silk stitches and incisions that embellished its flesh, the female corpse was breathtakingly beautiful in form, each piece specially selected as a representation of the doctor's ideal of physical perfection. He retrieved a chair and sat next to the pulsing dynamo, watching the grotesque performance with rapt attention. He was an audience of one for the grim burlesque.

Zorn wiped his forehead. The room's oppressive heat made him feel light-headed, but still, he kept his attention on the female body. The electric current made it convulse, then the head came to rest against its chest. It convulsed again seconds later, and again it rested. Each throbbing, rhythmic spasm evoked memories of the thrusts of his pelvis against the inner thighs of his wife, Magdaline. How her small but firm breasts would undulate in measured synchronicity with his impetus. Again, the corpse twitched, and he felt his penis begin to lengthen and harden as he stared at the nude form before him. Now freed from his pants, his cock bobbed against his lower abdomen as he displayed it to the dead form. The body twitched, and so did he, and though he did not commune with a living being, he felt the need to share with it his most intimate and primal emotions. He and the object of his creation would enjoy this moment as one.

Zorn gripped himself tightly and worked his fist up the shaft to expel a drop of crystalline lubricant, which he spread over the head of his cock with his palm. Again, the body twitched, its breasts swaying. He spread his legs wider, panting audibly. A surge of electricity, a spasm. How long it would take, he did not know.

The hand of the scientist moved in cadence with the electrical surges that made the corpse dance in the air. Steam continued to rise from the cold stone floor, creating a cocoon of heat and moisture that enveloped Zorn and his patchwork creation. With his other hand, he adjusted the lever on the dynamo to increase the frequency of the surges of electricity that penetrated the body, and so, too, did he mimic that frequency with his vigorous strokes up and down the length of his manhood. So rapid were the electric impulses that the corpse veritably vibrated; jerking, spasming again and again in rapid succession. He could feel it welling within him as he watched, the tip of his cock beginning to tingle; its thighs tightened, and its hair swayed. Zorn stroked faster, his grip tightened, so close; the breasts jiggled with each jolt, the nipples seemed to harden from the infusion of electricity, pulsing, pulsing, impossibly hard...

His own body spasmed as cum erupted from his cock in a thick white stream.

And in that same instant, the eyes of his creation snapped open.

Life!

Zorn's hand flew for the device and threw the switch that would cease the electric current being fed into the body. The eyes were open! It lived!

And behind the deep red hair that fell in ringlets across the visage, the face of Magdaline, his wife, stared out at him for the first time since her death.

The body was a composite of limbs, internal organs major and minor, viscera, skin, and even blood mined from innumerable corpses over the past year, but the face... the face belonged to Magdaline. The being stared as if it saw right through him, beyond the room, beyond the infinite. He had accomplished that for which he had dreamed throughout the entirety of his medical training and research. It was an achievement never before realized in the history of science, as the exploration of the very foundation of his research was without precedent. Yet, though he prepared for this moment his whole life, the gaze of the creation froze Zorn to his core.

CHAPTER EIGHT
MAGDALINE

The body hung inertly from the ceiling as the shroud of steam embraced its feminine curves, but the eyes still did not blink. Zorn quickly washed his hands in a basin, then excitedly detached the black electrical cords from the harness. He gazed up at the flesh and blood Aphrodite of his construction and cupped one of its hands in his. The flesh was warm, but the hand was unflinching, which caused immediate concern in his mind that he pushed back for the moment; he did not want to process the full weight of its implication. With the operating table now beneath the figure, Zorn unlocked the winch and lowered the body onto the silver slab. His hands trembled as he unbuckled the harness across its breast, but no matter how he jostled the prone form, the eyes did not blink.

Something was not right.

With two fingers, he pressed on the artery of one wrist, then the side of the neck. Frantically, he placed an ear to the damp chest, listening, listening for something, anything. There was no pulse. The heart was not functioning. But the eyes remained open. A harsh realization washed over him: All that had been achieved was an involuntary muscle contraction of the muscles of the eyelids. The creation did not open its eyes of its own accord. It was not alive.

In silence, he gazed upon the composite being, and though the climax of the experiment was not as he had feverishly anticipated, he did not consider it an abject failure. Zorn assessed that the calculations he had meticulously made and the conclusions that he had reached were not in error and such a supposition was an impossibility. Some unforeseen element had interjected itself into the process, an obstacle that he could surely surmount with additional research.

The yellow-green fluid in which the body had been stored was one of the crowning jewels of Zorn's scientific genius. In multiple research trials, it had proven to do exactly as he had theorized. The aqueous solution, whose base was formaldehyde, would logically best serve as a preserving fluid, but when infused with the precise mixture of elemental compounds and rigorously oxygenated, the result was a chemical that not only preserved human flesh but activated and energized the red blood cells present in once-living tissue. Incredibly, those cells proceeded to repair any damage that had been done to the tissue.

Even more astounding, two disparate pieces of flesh that were sewn together and immersed in the solution exhibited a most unprecedented result. The volume of collagen produced during natural biological healing was amplified to the extent that the skin and muscular tissue of two separate structures coalesced; two pieces of flesh from two different donors became one, growing independently of a living human host.

There was no error in the formulation of the solution; of that, he was certain. Numerous trials had all met with success. That was not the cause of the failure. It was something else, something that would remain intangible, for the moment.

The face stared ceilingward and something about the open, expressionless eyes of the death mask induced unease within Zorn. He closed the eyelids, but that did not erase their accusatory judgment of him and his work, or so he imagined. It was the exact look he had seen on Magdaline's face so many times in the past when he eluded her questions about the direction of his research.

Not that many years ago and while immersed in his graduate studies, Aldo Zorn was a brash young doctor who considered his devilishly handsome features to be a stumbling block to his success. Being attractive was a burden, plain and simple, as he wanted nothing more than to be left alone to pursue his studies, but it left him in a quandary due to a basic human desire for companionship. That weakness of character, as he viewed it, often got the better of him and to his recurrent dismay, he found himself attending one uncomfortable social gathering after another, during which he counted the minutes until the opportunity arose to escape to the solitude of the nearest laboratory.

It was during the social event commemorating the advancement of his class at the University of Prague, under the tutelage of the eminent chemist Professor Charles M. Rictor, that his eyes met those of a beautiful woman gaily draped in garments of ruby. She shone from across the banquet hall like a glittering star against the tapestry of the heavens. Their eyes at last met and the connection went unbroken for several seconds; they both knew in that instant that fate had brought them together in the candlelit chamber. The strains of the string quartet that played over dessert and the incessant chatter of his fellow graduates disappeared behind the beating of their two hearts.

Magdaline Ruzika was born into wealth, as was Aldo. Unlike the detachment he experienced with his parents and siblings, she maintained a closeness with her family, which seemed to be the hallmark of the Ruzika family. Although she was twenty-three years old, as was Aldo, Magdaline had thus far successfully avoided numerous offers of marriage from multiple suitors, none of whom—while well-intentioned—rang the chimes of true love within her. Despite Aldo's aloof demeanor and calculating mind, her physical attraction to him could not be denied and although conversations with him were always strained because of his single-minded pursuit of scientific studies, she fell head-over-heels for him. After only two months of courtship, she happily accepted his proposal of marriage.

As she would eventually learn, Magdaline did not live up to either Aldo's or his mother's stringent and unreasonable physical expectations. Yet, she did fulfill his emotional needs and the two were wed one year later. In his scrutiny, he found that her nose was not quite straight enough, her breasts were not quite as full as he would prefer, and she would be much more attractive if she possessed red hair to which he was singularly attracted. Unfortunately, there was nothing he could do to physically mold his wife into the ideal of which he felt he was worthy. To Magdaline's dismay, Aldo's callousness knew no bounds as he shared with her all of his misgivings, without the consideration that his remarks would be injurious to his wife's self-esteem.

The couple resided in a comfortable Zorn family holding on the west bank of the Vltava River, where Aldo dedicated an entire wing of the estate to his scientific studies, the nature of which he kept secret from his conventionally-educated wife. It was as if they spoke two different languages, but during times of intimacy, the way he would run his fingers against the side of her cheek as he marveled at her classically-proportioned features made her bury her misgivings about his true intentions. He loved her, she was sure of it. But as one year turned to two, and two to four, Aldo and Magdaline began to drift apart. All of Aldo's attention was focused upon some secret experiment, the nature of which, Magdalin was assured, she was much too poorly educated to attempt to comprehend. His condescending attitude and his avoidance of any discussion about subjects that interested his wife cut deeply and as the years passed, the distance between their philosophies grew ever wider.

Upon occasion, her thoughts ran contradictory to what Magdaline considered were the duties of a devoted wife. At times, she even entertained the notion of packing a bag and returning home to her mother and father. She had never told her parents of her misgivings about her marriage, but considering the social standings of the Zorn and Ruzika families, she felt that the act of leaving her husband would attract unwanted attention in social circles and most certainly appear scandalous. Still, due to an infection she had suffered in her youth, Magdaline was unable to bear children, so if a separation from her husband were to occur, it would only be she who was burdened by the subsequent upheaval of her life and reputation. She weighed her options daily, but never did she speak her thoughts aloud. Aldo remained oblivious to the foundation of her displeasure; all he knew was that

Magdaline's behavior was becoming increasingly distant and he concluded that this was due to her deep-seated jealousy of his work.

One stormy October night, just months after the passing of the Zorn matriarch Catherine, a corner was turned in the silent stand-off between Magdaline and Aldo. Since nearly the first day of their wedded life, she had endured uncountable nights alone while he toiled behind the locked door of his laboratory. When at last he would come to bed, his clothing and hair smelled of acrid chemicals.

But no matter the hour at which he would retire each night and slip beneath the covers with her, he immediately reached for Magdaline, wrapping his arms around her and pressing his erect penis between the cheeks of her behind. Always, she would feign sleeping, until the rhythmic grinding of his cock against her ass and his groping of her breasts inflamed her own suppressed passions and she willingly submitted to his sexual overtures. Strangely, it always seemed to her that it was not her body that excited him so, but rather some other activity that stoked his desires long before he entered the bedroom each night.

How could it be her body that aroused him in such a manner? After all, did he not always drop subtle hints that her physical appearance did not live up to his high standards of perfection? On those nights when he would place his palm over her breast and squeeze the entire soft globe, she could not help but recall the numerous times he made comments on how feebly she was endowed. For a man who was so disinterested in her bosom because it did not meet with his approval, it did not stop him from pleasuring himself by groping her at every opportunity. Each night, she would push those thoughts aside momentarily as he took what he wanted from her. Always, within minutes, it was over. He would roll to his side of the bed and without a word he would drop off to sleep, while she lay in the blackness, staring at the ceiling, wondering how her life had come to this.

After their first six months together as man and wife, she gave up trying to pry from him the content of the research that dominated his life. All he would tell her was that it was groundbreaking, and when completed, he would surely be awarded the coveted Rictor Prize in Chemistry. Magdaline could not care less about awards and accolades; she wanted companionship, attention, and respect from the man to whom she had pledged her love and her life.

So it was on that night that, as the rumble of distant thunder rolled through the halls of the mansion, she decided that enough was enough. He entered their dark bedchamber shortly after midnight, but as he held the lantern aloft, he found Magdaline standing before him in her nightgown, her arms folded across her chest. How long she had stood waiting for him in the dark, he did not know, but her unexpected appearance gave him a start. Her eyes blazed with unwavering intent.

"Aldo, we've been together for five years," she spoke in a measured tone, "And I deserve answers. I want to know exactly what it is that you're doing in your lab. Everything. The subject of your experimentation, why it demands so much of your time, and when it will finally be completed." She left no room for doubt; her statement was an ultimatum and Aldo could only guess to what lengths she might go if he failed to satisfy her curiosity.

He composed his thoughts, then calmly intoned, "Come with me." If he was ever to have peace and escape her suspicious badgering, the truth must be told. "You want to see what I've been doing? Fine. I'll show you everything." Magdaline donned a peignoir to cover her thin dressing gown and followed her husband into the blackness of the hallway that led to his laboratory.

A flash of lightning threw their shadows against the door of his inner sanctum as Aldo slid a key into the lock. In the early days of their marriage, Magdaline found it quaint that he had a private chamber, and while he was still the man of the house and dictated the rules by which she would live, she teased— as one would speak to a child—that in her kindness she had allowed him to have his own playroom. But as the weeks and months passed, Magdaline began to feel a growing resentment of the locked door and what lay behind it; the laboratory transformed from a workspace for her husband's genius to a symbolic wedge that had driven the two of them apart, perhaps irreparably.

Magdaline's first barefoot steps into the large room were tentative, as what she saw when the lantern's light fell upon the chamber's interior was not what she was expecting. She had envisioned a laboratory that was as methodically organized as Aldo's precious protection of it, but instead, she surveyed an unorganized assemblage of bottles, chemicals, and strange mechanical devices, with every flat surface blanketed by open books, rags, and papers on which had been scrawled mathematical and scientific equations. Interwoven throughout a thin metal framework, glass condensers and flasks dominated one table, with rubber tubes snaking about, tying together the various cork bottle stoppers and distributing liquids from one flask to the next. Most notable, though, was an odd, acrid chemical odor that filled the room, the same scent that permeated all of Aldo's clothing.

The scientist lit a second lamp to better illuminate the lab, then held his hands wide. "There. Now you've seen it," he said, his voice dripping with sarcasm. "I don't know what you expected, but as you can see, there's nothing nefarious afoot, if that's the path down which your mind has wandered."

Magdaline nodded an acknowledgment, but the way she puckered her lips to one side of her mouth spoke of other curiosities not yet satisfied. To her surprise, rather than asking the questions that had burned in her mind for months, something else entirely came from her lips. "You don't have to be afraid of me, you know," she offered.

The scientist scoffed. "'Afraid?'" he repeated with contempt. "What a preposterous statement. Why in the world would you say such a thing?"

"I don't know. It's just your secrecy," Magdaline explained. "Let me be clear. I'm not accusing you of any wrongdoing. It's just been my experience that when people shut out others, it's because they don't want to have to explain their actions, and more often than not, it's because they don't want to face any repercussions for what they might be hiding." Her voice softened. "It's foolish, I know," she said. "But if you don't offer me any information, all I can do is make assumptions."

Aldo reassured his wife. "You have to understand, Magdaline, the scientific research community is rife with thieves who have no qualms about stealing the work of others, warping it to meet their criteria, and claiming it was their intellectual brilliance that was responsible for their scientific achievements. What I'm doing here in this lab is unprecedented. Even the slightest hint of what my work entails outside of this room could have disastrous consequences on the preservation of the purity of my theorem."

"You can trust me, my husband," she assured him, placing a hand on his arm. "But what is it? What do you hope to achieve?"

For a few moments, Aldo considered his wife analytically, then turned to a square metal case that sat on the floor in a very conspicuous position in the room. The case stood waist-high, with all edges heavily reinforced and riveted. On its top surface was installed a hinged door bearing a polished chrome handle, and the entire square hatch was skirted by a thick, rubber gasket. The case vibrated slightly, but shaking more vigorously was a smaller mechanical engine. It was cylindrical in design and fueled by steam transferred through a thick canvas tube attached to the lid of a boiling vat of water sitting atop a cast-iron stove.

"Come here and put your hand on this," Aldo directed his wife, referring to the metal cabinet.

Magdaline did as he instructed, but upon placing her palm against the metallic surface, she withdrew it immediately with a start. "It's freezing cold!" she exclaimed with bewilderment. "What is it?"

"I call it a regelation chamber," Aldo explained. "I'll not go into the specifics of its operation, as it's much too technical for you to understand, but within this box, I've created a sub-zero environment that can be maintained indefinitely. But the chamber must go through an extended trial period to ensure its viability before I can apply for a patent. You see why I've guarded it so fervently;

no one must know the direction of my studies, because if they did, it would surely send one of my unscrupulous colleagues down the same path. I cannot allow someone else to spring from my initial theory and possibly reach the same conclusions as I and take the credit for themselves."

Magdaline smiled, in full understanding of Aldo's fears. As she hugged him in a show of fealty, something lurking on a table against the wall caught her attention. It was something rectangular, the size of a hatbox, and draped with a sheet. A low hum purred beneath the veil. Whatever was under the sheet emanated a sickly yellow-green aura that fluctuated in intensity like the reflections of moonlight upon the surface of the Vltava River.

Aldo gently gripped Magdaline's upper arms and pulled her into a kiss. She complied, but her gaze was transfixed on the yellow-green glow behind him. She genially drifted from his embrace, then turned to look about the room, but not in the direction of the strange box. It was purposeful misdirection.

"It's an incredible accomplishment, Aldo. You should be proud," she said politely.

"I am," he replied. "Immensely."

Magdaline was impressed by what she had seen but she knew in her heart that he was hiding something from her. "Is there anything else you'd like to share with me?" she queried playfully, as she examined the intricate maze of scientific glassware on the table.

"No," he said flatly. "It's late," he stated, making plain that he had nothing else in the lab that he wished his wife to see that evening.

Magdaline affected a mien of naiveté as she made her way toward the draped, glowing object. Unless she moved quickly, she would probably never again have an opportunity to uncover what was concealed beneath the sheet.

"What is this?" she asked, quickly lifting the fabric covering. She exhaled sharply in disgust, first from the chemical fumes that she had smelled every night on her husband's clothing, then from what she saw within the glass tank.

Filling the rectangular aquarium was a green liquid that was illuminated by some form of mechanical apparatus that also swirled about the chemical contents and emitted air bubbles that streamed to the surface. To her shock, something floated in the tank: It was a severed human hand, suspended within the emerald, aqueous material. From its slender nature and the length of the nails, it was clear that it was the hand of a woman, with curious silk stitches that encircled the ring and smallest fingers. Anemic, blue-white arteries protruded from the stump, and a loose layer of skin extended far past the lacerated musculature. The flap of skin looked as if it was attempting to seal off the offending injury. She gulped hard and placed a hand to her mouth, suppressing her urge to vomit.

Magdaline knew that her husband would construe her behavior in only one way; it was impulsive, but most revealing was that it displayed a clear distrust of his word. To her surprise, however, it did not send Aldo into a rage. Rather, he stood silently, breathed slowly, and exhaled in one protracted sigh before blowing out the flame in the nearest oil lamp. In that instant, Magdaline realized that the enemies her husband so feared now included her among their number. She was not his wife; she was an intruder.

"Aldo, for the love of God, what is this?" she asked, more fearful of his answer than she was of the anger her question might provoke within him. He blew out the flame of the lamp he had carried into the lab. The room was now enveloped in near-complete darkness, save for the yellow-green glow that emanated from the horrific display. "Whose hand is that?" she quavered.

"It doesn't matter one whit," he said indifferently.

"But why? What are you doing to it?"

He casually took the sheet and draped it again over the tank, obscuring the grisly contents. "You've done enough damage for one night. And you've shown me exactly the kind of person you are. Petty. Jealous. Ignorant. I extended to you a courtesy that I have given to no one else in this world, and it wasn't good enough for you."

A streak of lightning over the estate briefly lit the room. What more was he hiding? "Whose hand is that, Aldo? Tell me!" she demanded, her voice rising an octave as panic began to grip her.

"Whoever she was, she's dead now, isn't she?" he shouted. "Life for her is over, isn't it? That's what we all believe, that life ends when the heart stops beating, isn't that so? No! It is not so," he said with a smile. "I have proof. In that tank is the hand of a cadaver, but two of those fingers are from another body."

"What are you doing to it," she whispered in utter disgust.

His delivery was clipped. "Five fingers. Two donors. And now, they've grown together into a single hand. After death!" he added with joyous enthusiasm. "Can you comprehend what I'm saying? Through my genius, I have developed a process in which I've sewn together dead flesh and rejuvenated it. It lives! It has healed itself! Even now, the skin attempts to seal over the severed end to make itself whole."

"No," Magdaline croaked. "What are you saying?"

Aldo took a step closer and she took a step backward. His was an act of restrained menace. "I have unlocked the key to life after death, isn't it obvious?" he bragged in complete self-absorption.

He took one more step forward and she again took one step in retreat, but her back was now against the lab table. For the first time since she had known him, Magdaline feared that he might harm her. She had never seen this side of him before and it shook her to her core. She was alone. In the dark. With a man who now seemed like an absolute stranger to her. Her mind went immediately to how she would need the help of one of the household staff to retrieve the large steamer truck that was stored in the attic. She would need a case at least that large to take enough of her clothing and personal belongings down to the river, where she'd arrange passage on a ferry across the Vltava. Her sister always told her that she had enough room at her residence if Magdaline ever felt the urge to pay an extended visit. Now was that time.

But Magdaline's sister would never see her again, alive or dead.

Shaken from his reverie by the steam hissing around him, Zorn averted his gaze from the creation that lay on the metal slab. It was a thing of beauty, but until its breast rose and fell of its own volition, it was simply a mass of organic matter and nothing more. There was nothing left to do but retrace his steps and repeat the process from the beginning. He would return the body to the tank to ensure that any damage done to it by the electrical surges repaired itself, recheck his calculations, and begin again in the morning. But first, he needed to attend to the vat in the room beneath the lab, as the heat created by the steam was making it difficult to breathe.

Holding a lantern aloft, he descended the stairs and threw several buckets of water onto the white-hot embers beneath the vat, the blackened pine planks hissing in protest. When the last of the embers were extinguished, Zorn ascended the stairs to both the laboratory above and his temporarily unsuccessful experiment.

As he climbed upward from the stairwell and glanced at the dissipating vapor in the lab, he beheld a sight that sent a jolt up his spine and made his heart pound wildly in his chest.

On the metal operating table, the composite being that he had so meticulously constructed over the past two years was sitting upright, its back to him, the crimson curls of its head spilling down a supple back crisscrossed by a network of silk sutures.

Aldo Zorn froze. At that moment, years of mad dreams coalesced into a living reality, but it was an impossibility for the creation to have moved by self-locomotion unless the heart was now beating.

He had succeeded!

So captivated was Zorn by the unexpected sight that he unconsciously whispered, "Are you alive?" As the words left his lips, the head of the creation lifted and straightened on its neck, then slowly began to turn in his direction.

CHAPTER NINE
BEYOND THE DOOR

It was the moment of triumph for Dr. Aldo Zorn, and a flood of emotions rushed through him in a wave of euphoria. On the operating table, the creation sat upright, as motionless as a cathedral gargoyle. Although its head had moved only moments before, it sluggishly stopped it fully faced the doctor. Zorn cautiously approached his creation, not wanting to startle it.

The extraordinary aspects of which he had theorized had been resoundingly verified but there was still one great unknown to which he could only guess: What would be its mental capacity? He had taken great care in the implantation of the brain into the creation and he had labored for days without sleep or sustenance to safeguard the delicate integrity of the cerebellum. Damage to the brain's ingrained mastery of motor skills would have been disastrous. However, he did perform a series of extensive surgical adjustments to the neocortex, as personal and intimate memories of the brain's donor needed to be erased from the organ. To achieve ultimate success, the personality must be a blank slate, devoid of the personal experiences, knowledge, and emotional remnants that it had held when still within the skull of its previous owner. Only onto a pristine cerebral template would it be possible to inscribe the personality of his choosing. The being's current intellectual capacity was unknown, so until he was certain that it retained no recollections of a past life, he needed to proceed with systematic caution.

He approached with slow and measured steps, and once he was within two meters of the naked being, he spoke in a calm, non-aggressive manner. "Hello," he said.

There was no reaction. The head did not turn and not a muscle twitched in response to his utterance. It sat upright, stark still, unmoving. Zorn drew closer to better view the living construct face-to-face, but still, the creation did not respond to his presence, the blank eyes staring straight forward. Even when he reached out a hand to stroke its shoulder, it did not move. The body was warm, which was a good sign, but the possibility existed that the trauma of transplantation had some adverse effect on the brain that would coalesce into cognizance, with time. It might be an extensive journey until his ultimate objective was achieved, but he was prepared for the arduous task that lay before him.

He leaned close, waving a hand before the eyes, but there was no reaction from the creation. Zorn held the lantern higher, resulting in the contraction of the pupils of the eyes which he had so deftly transplanted into the hollow sockets. The natural response was encouraging and indicated that the orbs were functioning, but the being acknowledged neither the light nor the heat of the lamp. It was all so fascinating, a puzzle of his construction, and one that would be solved eventually. Thorough physical examination and cognitive testing would be the first steps toward unraveling the mystery.

Zorn gently ran his hand over one of his creation's forearms, then up to the shoulder, testing the firmness and elasticity of the muscle beneath. The rest of the body—the thighs, the breasts, the feet, the neck—all responded to his squeezing and prodding exactly as living flesh should. The sutures themselves, some years old, all retained their structural integrity, although they were now unnecessary, as the skin and muscles of an unknown number of donors had grown together into a single unit. Weaving beneath the sutures were indentations in the flesh, reddened depressions that delineated every slice of Zorn's scalpel, but those, he reasoned, would fade with time.

As he looked upon his handiwork, he was torn between his scientific objectivism and his primal urges as a man. The being was a thing of absolute beauty, a statuesque expression of perfect posture and symmetry. *Dear, sweet Magdaline had never looked so beautiful*, he thought, but in truth, the thing that sat on the operating table was not Magdaline. It only wore her face. This being was not his late wife by any stretch of the imagination. But in time, it would take her place.

If only it would speak, or at least acknowledge his presence. He then realized that in the minutes since it sat upright on the table, his excitement had gotten the better of him and he had not checked for a pulse, nor had he seen the chest rise and fall. He looked upon the magnificent, full breasts, but as he watched, they did not move, nor did the ribcage expand. As he lowered his face to its upper torso to listen for a heartbeat, he hesitated as he noticed that a single, pale bead of fluid had been expressed from one nipple and had traced a path down the gentle curve of the breast. He paused; never had he considered that any of the women from whom his creation was composed were mothers who had left behind children. As with every other uncomfortable truth in his life that he did not want to acknowledge, Aldo Zorn pushed the notion of an orphaned child from his mind as immediately as it had been conjured. He listened intently, his ear pressed against the chest, but still, there was nothing. No heartbeat. Again, he waved his hand before the eyes. There was no reaction.

"Can you hear me?" he whispered. "Are you alive, or aren't you?" The eyelids did not flutter and the being remained as stone, just as it had after the initial infusion of electricity, yet since then it had moved of its own volition, even with no pulse or respiration. It was completely perplexing. A different tactic was in order.

Zorn commanded in a measured tone, "Lie back." To his astonishment, the creation began to slowly recline, as if in some somnambulistic state. He thrust his hands under the back to ensure that the head did not collide with the table and the being lay flat once more. It responded to his direct command! By all scientific measures, the thing was not alive, yet it could move, and to his delight, the brain functioned and was able to process audible signals.

The scientist was beside himself, emotions rushing through him in a torrent of self-congratulation, outright astonishment, and befuddlement.

"Lift your right arm," he asked. In response, the fingers twitched upward, then the palm, then the entire arm raised from the table. He ordered the arm down and the command was obeyed. "Sit upright, please," he asked gently. The creation lifted its torso upward from the table, the head steadily balanced upon its straight neck.

Zorn rushed to retrieve his journal and began feverishly writing notes, recording every single event that had occurred that night in the damp basement laboratory. No matter its gravity, the young scientist documented every step he had taken throughout the day, hoping that somewhere within his writing might lie the shadowy and unanticipated impetus for the scientific phenomenon that sat before him.

When he was satisfied that he had captured every moment on paper, Zorn straightened in his chair and stretched, then ran a hand through his thick, blonde hair. Across the room lay his creation, resting silently upon the lab table. He could not tear his eyes away from it, the amber glow of the room's lantern deepening the crimson hue of the figure's red hair that spilled from the cold table on which it lay.

He looked down upon it, the body that he had assembled from corpses, the body that was capable of obeying simple commands. Incalculable hours of work lay ahead, but there would be no way to achieve his dream until it breathed and its heart beat; until it spoke and learned all that he needed it to know to be perfect, in his eyes. He placed one hand against its cheek, feeling the soft curve that he had sculpted, then ran his fingers over its full lips, Magdaline's lips, now a bit plumper due to the implanting of fatty tissue beneath the flesh. The eyes were now a haunting green, unlike the dull brown of Magdaline's. He was never fond of her eye color, but that was no longer a concern. He straightened her nose and gave her a new jawline, taken from the skull of a nameless woman. Onto the jawbone, he fused the facial musculature that he had carved from Magdaline and had stored in his deep-freezing unit until the time was right for transplantation.

Dr. Aldo Zorn was a man of many talents, all of which were displayed like a musical crescendo on the slab before him.

He did not know how it would react, or if it would react at all, but he could not restrain himself as he admired the entirety of the being. The thing before him did not live, yet it was with stuttered timidness that his hand found one breast, then the other. He squeezed them lightly, rolling the nipples between his thumb and index finger. As he did, he imagined the response such actions would have on a living woman. His hand traced the stitching down the rib cage and over the belly, firm and muscled, unlike Magdaline's softness in that area, then his fingers run through the soft, dark hair of the mons pubis.

He looked to the face, but there was no reaction, no indication that it felt anything at all as a result of his touch. It was disheartening, but the lack of response felt like a challenge. His fingers moved ever downward. Separating the labia, he found the clitoris, which he had specially selected himself. He lightly rubbed the tip of his finger over the pale pink jewel. Ever harder he pressed as he made small circles around it, but the inert body remained motionless. It felt nothing, apparently; either that or it was unable to respond to sexual arousal. Zorn recalled times when Magdaline did not respond to his touch and the frustration he felt then quickly resurfaced. With renewed intent, the scientist rubbed downward, his fingers brushing over the velvet-smooth lips. Slowly, with romantic intent, he penetrated the vagina, and with the slow, smooth strokes and curling of his fingers that Magdaline had taught him in the early days of their marriage, he attempted to arouse the fire within the living—yet unliving— creation. The vagina was warm and wet, but when he looked upon the face, he was crestfallen.

He pulled his fingers roughly from her. "Damn you!" he shouted. Zorn took a breath, then laughed. He could shout as threateningly as he liked, but the being was not going to respond. However, that was beside the point; he was not angry with the creation, he was simply the victim of his sexual frustration, along with a vivid imagination. He realized, too, that the many hours he had spent in the lab that night and the intense feelings of anticipation that had consumed him for hours had exhausted him. It was quickly decided that he would retire to his bedchamber and resume his examination at dawn.

As a precaution, Zorn employed leather straps and buckles to secure the creation onto the lab table. He did not know if it was even capable of walking but he thought it best to take measures to prevent it from doing any unexpected nocturnal wandering in his absence. He secured the arms and legs, then in a vaguely parental gesture, he placed a sheet over the body. "Close your eyes," he directed, and the golemesque creation obeyed.

The wheels of the table shrieked as he pushed it to a small, dark alcove in the lab, opposite the spider-like furnace, then he collected the lantern and locked the door behind him.

If sleep came to him at all that night, he knew that his dreams would be haunted by the tantalizing mystery of where the experiment had taken a wrong turn. It was the culmination of his life's work, but it was achingly flawed; something was missing, but he knew not what. What he did know was that his libido had been stoked after his sexual groping of the thing that now lie alone in the darkness.

Zorn climbed the steps in the curved stairwell, whose stone walls bore white calcite deposits that fairly glowed in the lantern's light. As he rounded the curve, he was surprised to find Falcona descending the stairs toward him. She carried a single candle, one hand cupped before the flame, and she was dressed in her sleeveless sleeping gown, a sheer, white dress that brushed the floor at her bare feet. Her raven hair was not tied up, as she wore it while performing her housekeeping duties around the castle, and it flowed freely over her shoulders. The candlelight danced in her dark eyes.

When he first encountered her at the carnival just over one year ago, Zorn could not help but be intrigued by the dark, Mediterranean beauty, and even now, as she stood above him in the stairwell, he was similarly fascinated. Through the diaphanous material of her nightclothes, he could see the full roundness of her hips, the same hips that had transfixed him so on the night that he extended to her his offer of employment. Her striking physical appearance was not why he considered her suitable for hire, but it was certainly not a drawback.

"What are you doing down here?" he asked. It was unusual that Falcona was still awake at this late hour, and even more unusual that he would find her creeping about the lowest level of the castle.

"I hate to disturb you while you're working," she said coyly.

"I'm not working. I'm on my way to bed. Why have you come down here?" he asked firmly.

She scrunched her nose just a bit as she spoke. "Something's been bothering me for the past week," she explained. "I've had a pain in my side. I haven't mentioned it to you because I don't like to complain and I know how busy you are, but it's keeping me from sleeping. I thought you might…"

Zorn interrupted. "Falcona, I might be a doctor, but you know I'm not a general practitioner."

"I know, sir," she said in a low tone, "But maybe you could just look at it?" As she explained herself, she rubbed one hand slowly over her stomach, pressing the material against her skin, so much so that he could see her navel through the material. Her hand then moved to the indentation at her waist, just above her pelvis, and she lightly massaged the area. She winced as she touched the spot, but in truth, there was no pain, and there had never been any pain. Her physical malady was nothing more than a façade, an excuse to meet with him alone. Her eyes met Zorn's, a look of smoldering intensity on her face that could have been discomfort, or it could have been something else.

"Maybe if you just looked at it," she repeated in a sultry whisper.

"Very well. Come with me," the doctor replied.

On the nearest workbench in his laboratory, Zorn pushed aside the books and papers that cluttered the surface and placed the lantern upon it. A medical examination would be best performed on his operating table but since that was currently occupied by his grotesque creation and hidden away in the alcove, the wooden countertop would have to suffice. "Sit here and I'll have a look," he instructed Falcona. The housekeeper did as he said and sat before him, her back straight and her gaze intent. It was the first time she had been beyond the door of his laboratory and she tried to mentally catalog everything within her view for later review. Somewhere among all of the clutter and mechanical gadgets and scientific equipment lay a clue to the subject of his research. She just had to find it but not let him become aware of the ulterior motive of her midnight visit.

"Now. What seems to be the problem, exactly?" Zorn asked with professional detachment.

"It's a pain when I bend or lift things," she said, rubbing her hand over the inverse curve of her waist. She reached out and took the doctor's hand and placed it upon her warm side, pressing his palm against her. He looked at her curiously as she continued to exert pressure on his hand as if to keep him from removing it.

"It's too high to be the appendix," he concluded. "Have you recently suffered any kind of injury? Any scrapes or bruises?"

"No," she responded. "I'll show you." With that, she released Zorn's hand and adjusted her weight back and forth from one side to the other so that she could pull her long nightdress up over her thighs and buttocks. She held it teasingly just above the bottom curve of her firm breasts, almost exposing her nipples, but not quite. It was readily apparent to the doctor that Falcona's reason for seeking him out that night had little to do with any physical malady she might be experiencing, confirmed by the faint aroma of bourbon on her breath.

Aldo had never seen Falcona unrobed. She was indeed a finely sculpted young woman. As a result of his earlier examination of his naked creation, his sexual urges were already piqued and as he glanced down to her thighs, the sight of the silken black hair that peeked from between her closed legs caused a tingling along the underside of his penis. There was already a slippery wetness within his pants, the result of his earlier arousal that had gone unfulfilled but now his cock was pulsing in anticipation. Falcona's exotic beauty and unexpected lust for him had overwhelmed his senses, just as she had planned.

The silence in the room was palpable. Zorn wondered if his unanticipated patient could hear the excited pounding of the heart in his chest. She looked into his eyes and smiled, then widened the spread of her legs so that he might admire the rich, cocoa hue of her beckoning labia. With slow, teasing intent, she slid the dress upward to reveal her nipples, now achingly hard, then placed her hands on the sides of Zorn's face and pulled him toward her, crushing her full lips passionately against his. The scientist did not resist. He put his arms around her back and pulled her toward the edge of the table so that she could wrap her legs around his waist. The kiss was long and deep, as both released their repressed passions, not for one another, but in a ravenous display of basic human need.

Without breaking their kiss, Falcona unbuckled his belt. She slid her hand into his pants and firmly gripped his cock with her slender fingers. The doctor was likewise fondling her, one hand squeezing her ass as his other hand slid between her parted thighs and rubbed upward across her chocolatey lips, already slippery from anticipation. He wet his fingers with her sweetness and slid two of them inside of her. She gasped in pleasure. In absolute abandon, she slid from the table and dropped to her knees in front of him, roughly pulled down his pants, and took the entirety of him into her mouth. Her tongue played teasingly up on down the underside of his penis, just below the opening, then she swallowed him again, flattening her tongue and thrusting it forward and back against his shaft as she increased the suction in her mouth. Zorn flung his head rearward in ecstatic approval as the dark beauty continued alternating between licking and sucking, and when he could stand it no longer, he roughly pulled her to her feet and turned her. She willingly bent forward over the workbench and spread her legs, offering every intimate part of herself to him.

Zorn reciprocated Falcona's previous stance and got on his knees to worship the perfect, firm roundness of her derriere, into which he pressed his face after he gripped both of her cheeks and spread them. She smelled glorious, a combination of the natural scent of her sex and the fine French bath soap he had given her on her birthday that past October. He extended his tongue and ran it down her entire crack, ending at her puckered opening, where he flicked and darted teasingly, then stiffened his tongue and inserted it into her ass. Falcona bucked as a shiver rushed through her and she purred as he continued to fuck her tight ass with his tongue, her muscles tightening around it each time he slid it inside of her. She had never experienced anything like it or the waves of pleasure that it created within her and she pressed her hips back into his face as he continued to suck and tongue her.

"Dr. Zorn..." she panted, "Fuck me...fuck me now...Fuck me in my ass."

The words startled even her, as she had never before experienced the sensation of a man inside that most intimate part of her but her request was uttered in a moment of absolute candor and sexual abandon. Zorn was more than willing to comply with her randy request.

A swirl of conflicting emotions whirled through Falcona's mind in that instant. It was her full intent to seduce her employer in an attempt to gain access to his laboratory. That plan was going along swimmingly. But what she had not anticipated was how quickly she could be swept up by the repercussions of her covert actions. She had to keep in clear sight the true intent behind her flirtatious pretense. Quickly retracting her impulsive offer for him to sodomize her, she spun to face him and pressed her lips against his, sucking on his lower lip as she playfully pushed against his strong chest with both hands. Her breasts crushed against him and she used her own body to move him away from the counter with his back to the rest of the darkened laboratory.

"Lay down, sir," she cooed, "I want to ride you like a stallion." Her dark eyes burned into his. The scientist did exactly as she asked. Now on his back on the cold, stone floor, Aldo's heart pounded as she lifted her long nightdress and squatted over his hips, grinding her clitoris against his rock-hard cock in slow, rhythmic motions, like the surf lapping against the sands of Playas Las Arenas in her former home of Valencia. Zorn closed his eyes as she continued her dance upon him and Falcona took full advantage of his momentary distraction to quickly look all about the room, to take in everything that she could about the contents of the laboratory.

The scientist's breaths now came in short pants and he moaned in ecstasy. Falcona was also in the throes of passion and within seconds she began to feel pulsing tingles that flowed down from her clitoris into her silken lips, now dripping with her slippery wetness. She thrust her hips harder and faster against him and his cock grew even more rigid as it slid back and forth against her pussy. He was ready to explode and so was she.

Throughout the entire encounter, Zorn focused not on the dark-haired woman who was grinding her pussy against his cock but on a mental vision he conjured in the haze of passion. In his mind's eye, he fantasized that the one urging him so close to ejaculation was the crimson-haired thing under the white sheet, hidden away among the cobwebs in the alcove. Yes, it was her who rode him, her skin no longer bearing the stitch work or scars of his multiple surgeries, her perfect, perfect form in his arms as he gripped his creation's hips to hasten her thrusts...

With an exclamation of release, Aldo's entire body stiffened as his thick cock released a stream of cum that spurt through Falcona's silken pubic hair and onto his shirttails that lie across his lower stomach. The sight of his explosive ejaculation sent Falcona over the edge, her entire body convulsing as pulsing contractions rippled through her vagina. All around her blurred as the intense orgasm surged through her and it was at that exact instant that she saw something in the dark, in the back of the laboratory. The form's true identity evaded her as orgasmic spasms overwhelmed her senses but it looked almost like the barest hint of a woman's face staring out at her from a black recess in the wall. If it was a face, where there should have been eyes were pooled haunting, dark recesses. If it was a face. She had only glimpsed it for a fraction of a second, so she could not be certain what it was. Falcona refocused her eyes and looked again to the alcove, but there was no haunting vision discernable to her lurking within the shadows. It was only her overactive imagination, she assured herself.

Falcona was shaken from her transfixion by Aldo's firm grip on her hips and his timorous apology. "I'm sorry. I didn't mean to..." She laughed congenially, then bent and kissed him on the lips.

"It's okay," she consoled him gently, not wanting to bruise his masculine ego. "I didn't mean to either. But that was fun anyhow, wasn't it?"

Falcona rose from him as he sat upright. "How is your side?" he asked with a smirk. Still a bit shaken by the ghostly white face she thought she had seen a moment earlier, she hesitated as if confused by his question but she quickly recovered her wits. A smile crossed her lips. "It's better, thank you, Doctor," she giggled. "How much do I owe you for this visit?"

He laughed and reached for her, shaking her hand politely as a physician would a patient, his pants at his feet and his penis still semi-erect.

"No charge," he chuckled. Zorn pulled up his trousers and straightened his clothing, while Falcona pretended to have no interest in her surroundings. She had in her mind that if she queried him about his work, he might react like a startled hare and retreat; however, showing absolutely no interest in the lab might lead to the dropping of his defenses, and thus he might offer information that he normally would not if he did not consider her a threat to his privacy. She would tread lightly, taking any breadcrumb that she could, but all the while her mind was on that dark alcove and the spectral visage that she probably imagined.

Although minutes earlier he seemed quite intent on retiring to his bed-chamber, Zorn now seemed in no hurry to call it a night. He offered her a glass of water, which she gladly accepted, and the two stood silently, watching one another. Zorn seemed to have something on his mind and it was as if he was struggling to find his voice. At last, he spoke.

"Falcona, I'd like your opinion about something. Concerning the nature of life and the human condition. Would you be interested in hearing me out?" he asked politely.

She had no idea if what was on his mind had anything to do with his secret experiments but she sensed that this was the breaking of the ice for which she had been waiting. "Of course, Dr. Zorn," she replied with a smile.

He crossed his arms and chose his words with great care. "In your opinion, what is it that constitutes life in a human being? In other words, why are we alive? What differentiates a living being from a cadaver?"

"I suppose the beating of our hearts?" she answered as if she had been quizzed by a school teacher.

He shook his head in mild approval. "Yes. And the brain? Does it not work in concert with the heart?"

She thought about it and responded, "From what I know, yes. Doesn't the brain tell the heart to beat?"

"Indeed," Zorn said. "But is that it, in your estimation, that it is just the brain and the heart that provide the spark of life, or is there something else to be considered?"

Falcona had no idea why he asked the questions but she was enjoying the first real conversation she ever had with him, one that did not revolve around washing his clothing or making his dinner. In the year that she and Estevan had been in his employ, Zorn had never spoken to either of them as friends, rather than servants. She was suspicious of why he would suddenly respect her opinion, or at the very least ask for it, but it was a pleasant experience nonetheless.

She considered the doctor's question, then an answer occurred to her. "The spirit. The soul. That is also what makes us what we are" she concluded. "At least, that's what the church tells us."

"As a man of science, I've been taught to preclude such nonsense. But you've got me thinking, so let's consider all options. Let's say that the soul is indeed a reality. Along that line of thinking, without a soul, what would we be?" There was an intensity in his voice as if he was deeply interested in what she might say next.

"I don't know, exactly," she conceded.

Zorn displayed a curious anxiousness, as if on the brink of an epiphany and he exuberantly continued his questioning of Falcona, shaking a finger in the air as he hypothesized. "When someone dies, we're told that their soul leaves their body and the pious ascend to Heaven to receive their final reward. But consider this: What happens if someone dies, their soul departs their body, but they are revived by a skilled physician, through surgical or chemical means? Such things are theoretically possible now, you know." Falcona was intrigued by the disclosure and continued listening intently. "If a body is brought back to life, would it not be bereft of its soul? Would the Lord our God receive a member of his flock into his eternal kingdom, then banish them once again to the hellish conditions that mortals endure on this Earth? That would be a callous act of a loving God, wouldn't you agree?"

"If such a thing was possible, to bring someone back from death," she replied, "then I'm afraid I would agree. They would have no soul. It's a horrible thought. But I cannot imagine that we could exist without a soul. It is who we are. Without it, we would be...lost," she concluded.

"Lost," Zorn repeated. "Yes. Lost."

Falcona's eyes widened as she recalled something that she hesitated to reveal but the casual atmosphere stimulated by their conversation encouraged her to speak. "When Estevan and I were with the carnival, the Romanis talked about an old woman, one of their kind, who lives in Kleinburg. She owns a cartomancy shop. Madame Sabina is her name."

"Next door to the tobacconist. I've seen her shop," Zorn said with interest. "Dreary little place. But proceed, please."

"That's the one. They say," she hesitated, "they say she has powers. Magical powers. Not like the kind of magic performed by professional illusionists or carnival magicians, card tricks, things like that, but actual supernatural abilities." Falcona finally looked up to see what expression was on Aldo Zorn's face. Rather than disparagement, he exuded only intrigue.

She continued without inhibition. "Well. One of the stories I've heard is that Madame Sabina is believed to have a divine relationship with the elemental forces of this world. Earth, wind, fire, water…" she paused, "And spirit."

"Is that so?" Zorn spoke with reverent fascination.

"At least, that's what the Romanis say," Falcona added. She avoided committal to whether or not she believed the tales of Madame Sabina, as she did not want to look foolish in Zorn's eyes if he found her story preposterous. "But what they also say is that Madame Sabina can commune with souls after death and she can freely associate with them, even to the extent of pulling them from the other side into our world. Naturally, it would be sacrilege to even entertain such a notion," she demurred.

"Naturally," Zorn replied gently. "Have you ever met this Madame Sabina?"

"I have not," she admitted.

Zorn unfolded his arms and slid his hands into his front pants pockets. "Well. Perhaps I'll resume this topic with her one day. I've enjoyed this talk, and it's given me a lot to think about but it is late and I am exhausted."

He motioned toward the door and Falcona followed, taking one last furtive glance at the dark corner while the doctor wasn't looking.

I didn't see a ghost, it was my imagination, she assured herself. She also noticed for the first time a doorway in another corner of the room, hidden behind the grandiose, blackened furnace. Whatever lay beyond the forgotten portal was barred by a wrought iron gate. The frame of the doorway was marble, whose light hue stood in stark contrast to the dark stone of the laboratory walls. But for all of its beauty, the threshold appeared to be in disuse and forsaken.

In the dark passage outside the laboratory, Dr. Zorn locked the door behind them. The sexual encounter that they had just shared was still fresh in her mind and had been quite exciting, but still, Falcona wanted to set some boundaries and clear the air. "Dr. Zorn, I would like you to understand what just happened in there, what we..." She paused in embarrassment. "It will not happen again. I know it was frightfully forward of me but it was a moment of human weakness. It changes nothing between us. I hope you understand. I'll not expect it again, nor will I view myself as anything other than your hired housemaid. I just want you to understand that I had a basic human urge. You helped me to satisfy it and I thank you for that."

Zorn was relieved to hear what was on Falcona's mind, as he did consider the negative aspects of fornicating with the hired help and how it might create the illusion that the status quo of the household had changed. It would not, he had already preordained, but it was reassuring to know that the Spanish beauty simply used him to satisfy her drunken sexual impulses and had no designs on him as a paramour.

"When I hired you to keep my house, I had no idea how intelligent you were." He smiled warmly, and the two ascended the curved stairwell leading to the main floor of Castle Zorn.

Falcona quietly shut her bedroom door, cautious not to rouse her brother whose room was just down the hall from hers. What had transpired in the basement laboratory would be her secret, as long as the doctor behaved like a gentleman and never spoke of it to anyone. She would be absolutely mortified if Estevan learned to what lengths she had gone to try to unlock the mystery of the scientific work being performed in Zorn's laboratory, but in truth, she feared that her sibling would think less of her for the extreme measures she employed to gather information.

She did not sleep soundly that night.

CHAPTER TEN
THE CONSULTATION

On the following day, the early morning weather was exceptionally pleasant and the air was filled with birdsongs as Aldo Zorn steered his carriage down the worn, dirt road into the quaint village of Kleinburg. It was on rare occasions that the scientist left the seclusion of his castle; in fact, this would be only the second time he had ever visited the hamlet, the first being when he made the necessary financial arrangements for Ivonette's accommodation at the boarding house. As far as he could see, nothing had changed in the past year since he was last there; but then, life rarely differed from day to day, year to year, in sleepy towns like Kleinburg. The carriage rolled over the relatively smooth cobblestones of one of the two main thoroughfares that wove through the village and he tugged at the reins to steer the horse toward the avenue on which was nestled the tiny cartomancy shop of Madame Sabina. As he passed, a few curious villagers tipped their hats respectfully when they realized that this was the master of the ancient castle upon the hill, the revered Dr. Aldo Zorn, about whom they knew practically nothing. He was an enigma to the residents of Kleinburg, a reputation that suited him just fine.

As his carriage slowly rolled past the building that housed the rathskeller in its basement, Zorn noticed the old, black buckboard wagon of Leuthar and Hugo resting in the alleyway to one side of the two-story dwelling. A light tug on the reins brought his horse to a halt. He had not come to Kleinburg to seek out his two associates of questionable reputation but considering the phenomenal events of the previous day, it was now mandatory that he take advantage of the situation, track them down, and have a few words with them. Zorn had no difficulty locating them, as they were in the very first place he thought to search. It was only ten o'clock in the morning but Leuthar and Hugo were already drinking ale at a table in a dark corner of the rathskeller.

"Welcome, sir," the burly bartender exclaimed, cheerfully greeting the doctor. "It's nice to see you in Kleinburg! What can I get for you?" he asked, pulling the hand towel from his shoulder to wipe down the bar in front of Zorn. The doctor quietly surveyed the dank interior of the drinking establishment, his silver-handled walking cane over one arm.

Though he had never met Zorn, the bartender immediately knew the identity of the man before him; who else in Kleinburg would wear a lavender blush top hat that perfectly matched his finely tailored long coat of identical pigment? Yes, this must be the noble man of science who arrived one year hence, whose presence was gossiped about in the village.

"A cup of tea, please," Zorn replied. When asked if he would like to be shown to a table, the doctor demurred, stating that he would only be staying long enough to drink the cup before moving on. After being paid, the bartender departed down a flight of rickety wooden stairs to attend to the changing out of the beer kegs in preparation for the day's business. Zorn looked to the darkened back corner of the drinking establishment and found that Leuthar and Hugo were doing their very best to not acknowledge his presence. Casually, he took a seat at the table next to theirs, his back to them.

There was no one else in the room, as the bartender had not returned, and judging by the cursing that was coming from the cellar, he had encountered some form of dilemma relating to tapping a keg and would likely be absent for some time. Even so, Zorn did not turn to face the two men as he spoke.

"I'll no longer need your services for the time being," the doctor whispered over his shoulder.

Leuthar raised an eyebrow as he wiped ale from his mustache with a cloth napkin. Zorn's two associates had been anticipating this conversation. "Success, is it?" the tall man asked quietly.

"Nominal, but yes," Zorn replied. "In the future, if I should need you, I'll seek you out. Until then, no more deliveries are required," he said with finality.

Hugo downed what remained in his wooden cup and narrowed his eyes at Leuthar. The man with the creased forehead did not speak but his companion knew what was on his mind. "Hugo's wondering," Leuthar whispered, "what we're going to do for money until you need us again. If you ever do need us again. There's no other work in Kleinburg for two gentlemen of our aptitude. We might not hear from you for a year. If we don't want to starve, we'll need to move on," Leuthar warned.

"Then move on," Zorn said flatly. He sipped the last of his tea, placed his top hat on his head, strode to the stairs, and departed. Behind him on the table sat a small silk bag of silver coins. Leuthar quickly slipped the purse into his pocket. It was severance pay for Leuthar and Hugo, and the money the doctor left behind would sufficiently float them until they found other paying work, reputable or otherwise. Additionally, the payment would ensure their silence, or so Dr. Zorn hoped.

If he was being honest with himself, Aldo Zorn would have to admit that his visitation to Madame Sabina's cartomancy shop was an embarrassment. That a man of science would be seen setting foot in an establishment of that kind was unthinkable, and if his scientific contemporaries knew that he was there seeking consultation with the owner, he would be the laughingstock of the medical community. Yet, there he was. He tapped his cane on the wooden counter to alert the old woman of his presence.

Wearing a deep green hooded cloak, Madame Sabina parted the beaded curtain. Zorn eyed her cautiously, acutely aware that those in her profession possessed the unique talent for discerning facts about others with but a glance and could present those subtle observances as revelatory psychic phenomena. But upon seeing the slow, awkward gait of Madame Sabina, and how she squinted her cloudy eyes as she assessed him, he would be surprised if there was any sharpness at all about her presence of mind.

He spoke quietly, so as not to startle her. "You're Madame Sabina, I presume. I'm pleased to make your acquaintance. My name is..."

"Dr. Aldo Zorn," she said with a smile that threatened to crack her weathered face. "I know who you are, young man."

The doctor was slightly taken aback that she knew his name, but why would Madame Sabina not be able to discern his identity? Though they had never met, there was nothing supernatural about her pronouncement. The way he dressed could have given him away, or she could have heard his physical description from someone else in the village. Perhaps Falcona had lied to him and she did know the old woman and had gone to the cartomancy shop that morning to let the old Romani woman know that she could expect a visit from the doctor. Perhaps it was all a plan to lure him into…*No. That made no sense.* Zorn's bedroom was at the front of the estate where he would have heard the departure of the carriage if Falcona had gone to the village that morning before he rose. It was not magic. There was a logical explanation, but he could not be trifled with uncovering it.

The old woman approached the wooden counter and placed both hands upon it as if the steps she had taken from the back room had been taxing. "You're not here for an oracle card reading, are you, sir?" she said with assurance.

Again, she made a lucky guess, he determined. "You seem to know everything about me, Madame," Zorn snickered. Just then, something furry and black shot along the bottom edge of the wood counter and flew beneath the beaded curtain. It was a cat, a beautiful sleek animal that was none too pleased with the doctor's presence in the shop.

"Maybe I do know everything there is to know about you," she said slyly. "Or maybe I don't. Maybe I'm just an old fool who pulls the wool over the eyes of other fools to get my hands on their money. Would that be your professional assessment of me, Dr. Zorn?" she chided.

Before he had entered the shop, Zorn wasn't exactly sure how he would broach the subject of his visit but her words encouraged him to proceed with his questioning. "I am not here to pass personal judgment upon you. I am here because I was told you might be able to help me with my scientific research. I would be very interested to hear about the special abilities that others say you possess."

"I see," she said with a smile. "And what have you heard, Doctor?"

"It's my understanding that others believe that you have, shall we say, a *connection* to those who have passed from this world. They say you can snare the energy that some people call the soul."

Madame Sabina eyed him carefully. "If that was the truth, how would it be relevant to the work you do in your vocation, Doctor? Do educated men of science not dismiss the existence of the super-natural—like the soul and the afterlife—and proclaim it rubbish?"

"They do, Madame. But I'm asking you in all sincerity," he said evenly, "is what they say about you true? And if it is, can you prove it to me?"

Madame Sabina grew quiet beneath her hood, thought a moment, then turned her gaze to the wooden countertop before her. "Look here. What do you see before you?" she asked, referring to the items on the counter.

"A ledger. And a candle," he responded, looking upon the unlit object in a brass holder to his right.

She smiled. "Yes, a candle, but what is it really? A handful of wax, shaped into a cylinder. That is what it actually is, am I correct?"

"If we're speaking of its material composition, then yes, it is wax," Zorn responded, unsure where she was attempting to lead the conversation.

"And as it stands, it really doesn't do anyone much good. It's just a lump of wax," she repeated. Zorn furrowed his brow and smirked, as he was certain that this was all part of some confidence game, but where she was going with it was perplexing.

With a smile, Madame Sabina spoke again. "And now what is it, Dr. Zorn?"

The doctor sighed, then looked to the candle. To his astonish-ment, a flame danced upon the tip of its wick. Beneath her hood, the old cartomancer smiled as she saw Zorn's eyes grow wide.

"Now, it is not just wax, but a candle. It provides light when it is dark. It provides heat when it is cold. It is now so much more than our original, disparaging description of it, isn't it?" she said.

"How did you…" he sputtered.

Madame Sabina leaned forward against the wood as if preparing to reveal a great secret. "How it happened is not as important as the fact that it did happen," she imparted coldly. "Those who speak of me will tell you many things, depending on who you ask. Their views are based not on facts but on opinions and even if they had facts in front of them, they would still refuse to see the truth. They would say I practice witchcraft, or that I do the Devil's work. In my many years, I have heard what people like yourself, Dr. Zorn, have said about people like me. You proclaim that the world of spirits is without merit. You say that some things are impossible, such as the magical conjuring of a flame to light a candle. Yet, it was magic that transformed it from useless wax into a tool that can help others, a tool that even a man of science can use to illuminate the medical journal he is reading on a dark night, perhaps. And from his reading, he might learn how to heal a sick child, all thanks to the magic that ignited the candle. What does it matter how it happened, as long as it did happen and that those in need will benefit from it?"

Zorn rolled her words around in his head, repeating them over and over to himself. She made quite an interesting point that was certainly open to debate, but as a basic premise explaining the existence of the supernatural, her passionate and surprisingly eloquent theory hinted at enlightenment he had not anticipated. Perhaps her speech was nothing more than a dramatic reading that she had perfected over her decades of life, a pre-prepared hook that easily slipped into the mouths of those in the waters in which she fished because of its seemingly coherent and logical foundation. However, the crux of her argument was strikingly similar to what he knew to be the truth, based on his own experience and research. What he had accomplished in his castle laboratory had never before been achieved by modern science, and his contemporaries would adamantly refute the science behind his principle as preposterous. But the living—or non-living—proof of his success lie covered in a white sheet in the bowels of Castle Zorn. He had succeeded in the impossible, the reanimation of dead flesh. It could not be denied. What had once been considered witchcraft or the Devil's work was now scientific fact, and it could be that the magic Madame Sabina was rumored to wield could be proven to exist, once the same light of awareness was shined upon it.

"I see I've given you pause, Doctor," Madame Sabina cooed in a raspy voice. "But why exactly have you called upon me today?"

The handsome scientist gathered himself, and with a renewed outlook, he spoke. "In my castle upon the hill, I have a very special patient who suffered a horrendous accident. I have done all I can to mend the injuries, but..."

He paused, as his next words would reveal all he had hidden for the past few years. It would be a revelation that he had never spoken to another, and his mouth grew dry as he warily prepared to share his groundbreaking discovery, not with the world-renowned scientific board at the University of Prague, but with a woman whose stock in trade was deception.

Madame Sabina exuded an aura of calm and understanding. She read Zorn's inner turmoil and offered to him what would most soothe him at that moment. "I see you are in great need, but there is one who is in greater need. It is on her that we must focus," she imparted wisely.

He did not know how the old Romani discerned that the patient of whom he spoke was a woman, but the doctor fearlessly plunged forward with his explanation. "As I said, I have a patient who suffered severe bodily injuries, and was—for a brief period—deceased." There was no way he was going to disclose the absolute truth about his horrific creation, so some slight modifications to the facts were in order. He continued, "Through a medical breakthrough of my invention, I was able to pull the patient back from death, but she is not as she was before her brief time beyond the veil. She responds to verbal commands, but she does not breathe, nor does her heart beat. Yet, she lives. I have evaluated the malady and in my estimation, her condition is due to one piece being missing from her physical form: A soul."

"I see," the old woman whispered.

"But the situation is much more delicate than retrieving her departed spirit," Zorn continued anxiously. "The circumstances of her life, and her death, were of such horrifying magnitude that to invigorate her body with her former soul—and memories—would be a most unbearable burden, and cause her unimaginable grief. I seek to bring life back into her body by infusing the energy of the spirit so that her heart once again beats, but in the interest of humanity, I hope to bless her with a new life devoid of the horrors of her past."

"Five hundred Thaler it will cost you," Madame Sabina demanded solemnly. No longer did she wear the warm grin with which she had greeted the doctor.

"Done," he said quickly. Within minutes, the shop was locked and four black cats watched from the storefront window as the iron shoes of Zorn's horse beat a tattoo on the cobblestones as the carriage carried the doctor and their mistress out of the sleepy village of Kleinburg.

CHAPTER ELEVEN
ORACULUM OBSCURA

One hour earlier, Falcona watched her employer's carriage disappear into the maw of the wooded lane leading to Kleinburg. When he was out of sight, she bounded into the stable where Estevan was replacing the old, rusted hinges on one of the stall gates. Her sudden appearance surprised the strapping young man and he fell backward with a start. "Estevan! Come with me, quickly!" she shouted.

The young Spaniard wiped a bead of sweat from above one eye, unknowingly wiping onto his forehead a smear of orange iron oxide dust from the old hinge on which he was working. "You scared the hell out of me, Falcona!" he chuckled. "What's wrong?"

"You have to come see this!" she said with an air of mischievousness. Estevan retrieved his shirt from a post, threw it over one of his strong, tanned shoulders, and followed his sister into the castle.

Within minutes, the siblings stood on the landing of the wide stone staircase that hugged the interior surface of the outer wall of the castle between the second and third floors. The landing was situated at the juncture of the eastern and southern walls and hosted an access door that appeared to have not been used in decades.

"So, what is it?" he asked his sister, using his shirt to wipe the sweat and rust powder from his forehead.

She turned to face him, exhaled sharply, raised her eyebrows then lowered them as she narrowed her eyes in concentration. He knew what the motions meant: She was about to tell him something. He was going to laugh and dismiss her, and she was going to get angry with him for not taking her seriously. She would then curse at him, call him a colorful name, and not speak to him for the rest of the day. To avoid all of that, he straightened his stance like a star pupil before a headmaster and prepared himself for what was to come. But he also smiled at her, to let her know that he was aware of the well-worn pattern that might play out over the next minute.

Falcona slapped his bare chest and laughed. "Just stop it and listen to me, alright?" Estevan nodded in agreement. She proceeded to tell him the details of the previous night, demurely leaving out the more scandalous aspects of her encounter with Dr. Zorn, but she did recount the ghostly face that she thought she had seen in the darkness of the laboratory.

"A ghost? You're certain it wasn't the bourbon?" he chided his older sister.

But she would not be a party to his teasing. "No, it wasn't. Now listen. I wasn't able to figure out exactly what he does down there, but there were papers and books, with notes everywhere. It would have been too obvious if I had tried to read any of them, but he's gone now, for who knows how long."

"The door to his lab is locked," he reminded her.

"I know, but in one corner of his lab is a doorway blocked by an iron gate. It's in the southeastern corner of the property. Directly below where we're standing right now. And," she pointed toward the door before which they stood, "the frame was exactly like this one. The same design, everything. I'll bet you a Thaler that they're connected. If we can get in here, we can get into his lab through that old door."

Estevan smirked. "I noticed you said 'we.'"

"Well? Aren't you curious?" she asked.

"Not as much as you are. Not enough to get us thrown out on our asses with no money and nowhere to go if he returns home and catches us in his lab," he cautioned her.

Falcona was focused and completely ignored his misgivings about her plan. She pulled on the door handle several times, but it did not budge. Estevan then gave it a try and was successful in breaking the seal of caked dust and rust that had been deposited over the years along the hinge edge of the door. To their encouragement, his efforts to pull on the handle resulted in partial success, as the handle assembly parted from the door frame enough for them to see that it had not been locked when last used decades ago.

"I'll be right back," Estevan said excitedly, then bolted down the stairs and out to the stable. Within minutes, he had returned with an oil can and rag, and being cautious that his efforts would not be detectable, he oiled the hinges and worked the door back and forth enough to pull it half-open. Inside, the pitch-black abyss was painted with copious and delicate cobwebs. "Do you see anything in there?" Estevan asked his sister.

Falcona peered into the blackness. "A wrought iron, spiral staircase. This is what I thought it might be. It's the inside of the southeastern tower."

"I'll get a lantern. You watch out the window," she said with an excited smile. She skittered up the staircase and within minutes had returned with an oil lamp from her bedchamber.

"There are probably hundreds of thousands of spiders in there," Estevan said warily.

"My brave little brother," she snickered. "If you see the doctor coming back, yell, alright?"

"I will," he assured her, before jovially imparting one last thought. "Don't let the ghost get you," he laughed. She did not find his chiding humorous.

Falcona used the edge of her palm to chop down through the barrier of abandoned spider silk, clearing a path to the spiral staircase. The ancient framework squealed even under her light frame as she descended into the darkness, holding the lantern aloft. She continued downward, chopping with the edge of her hand and taking one cautious step after the next, testing each stair before putting her full weight upon it to be sure it had not rusted through. But all of the steps were sturdy enough to bear her passage and within minutes she stood upon the timeworn flag-stones of the castle basement. Falcona was momentarily disori-ented from her spiral walk, but after a pause, she regained her bearings. The glow of the lantern revealed only one exit from the small room at the bottom of the tower. She tested the latch on the door, and after some pounding, she was able to open the ancient wooden portal, thickly draped with a sticky coating of cobwebs and dust. The hinges protested with an ear-piercing wail and resisted as best they could, but she was able to open the wooden door just enough to squeeze through. Falcona found herself in a short, two-meter-deep alcove, terminating at the wrought iron gate she had seen the previous night. Beyond loomed the foreboding darkness of the laboratory of Dr. Zorn.

Fortune smiled upon her, as the iron gate was likewise not locked, but it too had been frozen in place by rusted hinges. As she had done with the wooden door, the young woman pushed and pulled until, at last, it offered her admittance to the lab.

Falcona held the lantern high. After she had seduced Zorn to gain legitimate entrance to the chamber the night before, she maintained strict self-consciousness of her demeanor in front of him, as she did not want to express any outward sign of interest in his work. Now that she was alone, her eyes ravenously scanned the room, taking in one wonder after the next. What functions the marvelous apparatuses performed was unknown, but it was all quite astounding nonetheless. But she needed to work fast. Dr. Zorn would surely only be gone an hour or two; a casual ride into Kleinburg usually took half an hour, so she knew she at least had thirty minutes to gather what she could from the doctor's notes.

With awe—and just a touch of nervousness—Falcona began reading every scrap of paper she could find, carefully returning each piece to the exact position as she had found it. Much of what she read was beyond her comprehension, lists of chemical agents and scientific formulas worked and reworked, and to her frustration, the secrets that the formulas unlocked were unfathomable.

Out of the corner of her eye, her attention was caught by a gleam of the lantern's light playing off of the copper surface of the great upright tank. She examined the tall vat and ran her hand over the cold, studded exterior. Why did it have a round porthole in its face? It seemed like an odd feature for something constructed to hold chemicals, an assumption confirmed by the fumes which completely permeated the area around the vat. Fetching a wooden chair, Falcona stood upon it, held her breath, opened the shutter over the porthole, and peered inside. As she had guessed, the tank was filled with liquid, yellow-green in color, but she beheld nothing else within the dark vat. She closed the shutter and returned the chair to its original resting place.

Thus far, she had been completely unsatisfied by her covert exploration, as nothing that came to her notice could identify the nature of Zorn's experiments. Then she saw it, lying on a wooden counter across the room, the same counter on which she had sat during the doctor's examination of her the previous night. How ironic it was that the object of her search had lain right next to her the whole time she seduced her employer. With haste, she floated across the room, snatched up the leather-bound journal she had spied, and began to read in earnest.

After leafing through the pages, her eyes grew wide with horror. Falcona lost complete track of time as she turned page after page in astonishment.

While his sister investigated in the basement, Estevan kept diligent watch from a second-floor window overlooking the front courtyard of the castle. His heart skipped a beat: Zorn's carriage was now pulling up the drive toward the estate. With great haste, Estevan ran up the perimeter stairwell to the landing where his sister had entered the tower and called to her, but there was no answer. Falcona was deep within the bowels of Castle Zorn and could not hear the frantic shouts of her brother. He called again, but she did not respond.

Estevan ran back to his surveillance window, but the carriage had not pulled to the front of the castle; instead, he saw the tail end of it disappear around the corner tower. Zorn was going to use the side entrance to return to his laboratory. Again, Estevan ran to the door he had pried open and called to Falcona, but again, all he heard was the echo of his own voice as it resounded through the dark tower. He did not like it one bit, but she was on her own.

Within the lab, Falcona fell back against the cluttered worktop as the gravity of Zorn's written words sank ever deeper into her mind. It was then that she heard the key in the lock, and panic shot through her. She replaced the journal and flew for the wrought iron gate, glancing only once at the dark alcove that she had thus far refused to investigate since her surreptitious entry into the laboratory.

Last night, she was sure that she had seen a face in the darkness. Now, after reading Zorn's journal, she knew that she had not imagined it.

She slid past the iron bars and pulled the gate shut behind her, melting into the darkness between the two doors just as Zorn opened the laboratory door and ushered Madame Sabina into his dank workspace. But Falcona could go no farther; the wooden door that would afford her escape was open only enough for her to squeeze past it, but the barest movement of it would produce a loud, metallic screech. She concluded that it would be best for her to stay where she was, concealed by the blackness, and wait for Zorn and his guest to depart before attempting to make her way past the squeaky door. She extinguished the lantern's flame and was enveloped by darkness.

Madame Sabina moved slowly through the lab, drifting away from the scientist and taking in the entirety of the room with a suspicious eye. Zorn did not speak as she examined the intricate glassware used in his experimentation, nor did he comment as she ran her fingers over everything within her reach. Her odd behavior was a bit unsettling to Zorn. Whether or not the old Romani woman possessed supernatural powers was immaterial; her actions were implicitly overt and it was readily apparent that she wanted him to believe that she was attempting to read the secrets of the room with her fingertips. Zorn laughed to himself and let her go about her showmanship.

Madame Sabina stopped and looked upward at the thick wooden beams that supported the main floor of the castle above them. "I'm surprised this place is still standing," she scoffed. "I knew the widow who lived here before your father assumed ownership of the estate—along with all of her belongings—after her untimely death," the old woman revealed. Oddly, the mention of the former owner of Zorn's home generated a pang of nervousness that noticeably crossed his face.

Madame Sabina continued, "Her name was Isadora, you know. A lovely woman, she was. Spanish, as is your young house staff. An odd coincidence, don't you think?" she said with a sly smile.

"And irrelevant," he spat contemptuously. Zorn was uncomfortable with the direction of the ancient cartomancer's seemingly superfluous rambling, and so flustered was he that it failed to dawn on him that Madame Sabina possessed information about his hired help that she should not have known.

"Is this where you tend to your patient, in a dark basement that reeks of chemicals?" she asked, loudly sniffling a few times. "I would think that the atmosphere down here would not be conducive to health and vitality," she postulated.

Everything that the doctor had anticipated before his first meeting with Madame Sabina was borne out. She possessed exactly the type of devious disposition and theatrical flourishes he had expected, but to his dismay, she seemed much sharper of mind than he had predicted. Something about her, even her manner of speech, hinted that there was much more to Madame Sabina than met the eye.

"Where would you like this?" he asked, referring to the heavy traveling case that he carried for her.

"Right at your feet would be fine, thank you," she replied. Before leaving her shop, Madame Sabina had hurriedly packed the trunk with bottled elixirs, herbs, and magical accouterment, none of which was immediately identifiable to Zorn, and he watched her prepare the case without judgment. The least that would happen was he would pay for a private carnival act performed by the old woman, but if there was even a shred of truth in her claims, his dream might soon be realized. However, he needed to cement the terms of his agreement with Madame Sabina before revealing anything further to her.

From his coat pocket, Zorn produced a small, silk bag of coins. He displayed it to the old woman while giving her a very stern look. "As I promised, five hundred Thaler will be yours *only* if you produce for me the results I desire. Should I detect that you're trying to deceive me in any way, or if it is apparent that you are employing sleight of hand misdirection or some other carnival foolery, you will find yourself back in your shop in Kleinburg with your purse as empty as it probably is right now. Do you understand me, Madame?" he asked adamantly.

The corners of the old woman's mouth turned upward. Her smile was sarcastic, as was her response. "Oh, I understand you perfectly, Dr. Zorn," she whispered knowingly.

Frustrated with her odd behavior and her apparent attempt to make him feel ill at ease, Zorn pushed ahead with the purpose of Madame Sabina's presence in his laboratory. "Please stand here," he instructed her, "and I will bring out the patient." He paused as if to reassure himself that the coming revelation was the right thing to do, then walked to the dark alcove and wheeled the sheet-draped operating table to the center of the room.

Since the night the young couple had visited her shop, Madame Sabina had dealt the oracle cards and performed multiple personal readings for herself in an attempt to ascertain the hidden meaning of the message that they were trying to impart. With each reading, no matter how she shuffled the oracle cards, the result was the same: The phrase "unholy creation" was conveyed by the deck time and time again. Before Zorn had entered her cartomancy shop that morning, Madame Sabina had consulted the oracle deck, and as she expected, the message was again "unholy creation." But this time, the surface of the card was not black as it had been over the past dozen readings. This time, the murky surface shifted and swirled, and coalesced into a visage that stared out at her from the dark face of the card.

The face on the oracle card and the countenance of the body that lay on the surgical table were identical.

"What is her name," Madame Sabina whispered.

"I have been asked by her family to keep that information strictly confidential," Zorn explained, concocting a story as he spoke. "As I said, she lived a most unfortunate life, filled with grief and torment. When she died, her burden was lifted, and her family—while devastated by her loss—was happy that she had at last found peace."

"But then you got involved," the old woman quipped pointedly.

"I did as is dictated by my profession: I used my knowledge and training to save her life. But as you can see," he said solemnly, "she is not who she once was. I have spoken with the custodians of her affairs and they agree that her soul should not be disturbed. It should remain where it is. However, they have permitted me to continue with my exploration of her incredible condition."

"May I see her entire form?" Sabina asked.

The doctor had no idea if the old woman was buying into his story and he feared that her perceptive nature might disclose the lies he was concocting, but he was in too deep. He did as Sabina requested and pulled back the sheet to reveal the full, hideous extent of the surgeries that he had performed on the body.

"What on Earth could have caused such injuries?" Her weak voice faltered slightly, the first time she had appeared to be on unsound emotional footing.

"I would rather not go into such gory and indelicate details. Suffice to say, the accident she suffered was ghastly." It was without any apparent compassion that he changed the subject. "How do we proceed?"

"Slow down, boy," she warned. "You can't reassemble a shattered vase without first gathering all of the pieces, can you? I will know what I need to do for her once I know her."

The proclamation generated great unease within the doctor. What he had done, what he had created, while it was unprecedented and perhaps even unethical, was not illegal. He had convinced himself that his groundbreaking work was legitimate medical research, but he still did not want the spiritual medium to know the true genesis of the body on the slab. That was his secret, and he would guard it jealously. But he also needed the cartomancer's help.

"Proceed, then, Madame. Do what you must," he offered with a strained smile.

"My case, please."

Zorn pulled a short table to the center of the room and hefted the case upon it. The surface of the small trunk was as dry and weathered as the skin of its owner and the ancient hinges creaked as she opened the lid. From within, she extracted five white candles, which she lit and placed on the floor in a wide circle around the table, two on each side and one at the foot of the slab.

From the case, Madame Sabina next removed a white mortar into which she poured the ingredients of three of the small bottles she had packed, then opened a leather pouch and emptied its dried contents into the marble bowl. Once the pungent ingredients were thoroughly mixed and ground with the pestle, the old woman held the bowl over the body with both hands and voiced an indiscernible chant in an unknown, sing-song language. Zorn watched with great interest, still skeptical of Madame Sabina and her dramatic performance.

She could feel the unspoken disdain emanating from him and rolled her eyes in the direction of the doctor at her side. "If you have a good book, I suggest you fetch it," the elderly visitor cajoled. "This might take a while."

With that, Madame Sabina dipped her bony fingers into the mortar and thoroughly rubbed the liquid she had prepared over both hands, taking great care to ensure that every surface of her parched skin was covered. Then, with the intense focus of a surgeon, she placed her hands one upon the other and pressed them to the chest of the still figure on the table before her. Time within the laboratory seemed to stop, and a deathly silence filled the chemical-laced air. The old woman did not twitch or sway, and seemed frozen in place as she seemingly absorbed something, some form of ethereal, otherworldly information that only she could fathom. At least, that is how it appeared to Zorn.

The deep lines around her eyes softened as she looked down upon the scarred and stitched countenance, and as one would comfort a newborn kitten, she gently placed her hands on the sides of the face. With that, both eyes of the creation opened and stared blankly at the ceiling, as if incognizant of the woman who stood over her.

Madame Sabina inhaled slowly, then expelled the air in one long, measured action. Zorn could only guess what might be swirling through the old woman's mind but he surmised that she was quelling all stray thoughts to bring her psyche into tune with that of the unresponsive body that lay on the table.

In truth, that is exactly what she was doing. Steadying herself against the side of the surgical table, Madame Sabina leaned forward and looked deeply into the unblinking green eyes. For a long moment, she gazed into the orbs, then closed her own eyes and stood upright.

The doctor watched respectfully as the ancient diviner set about touching every inch of the body with her dry, cracked hands. The stitchwork laid a path for her; upon each section of mended flesh, each reattached limb, each piece of the puzzle before her, her hand lingered for a moment before moving on. At length, her old hands had touched every part of the body and when her task was completed, she stepped back and looked as though she was weighing in her mind what she had learned.

"Well?" Zorn asked, impatiently. "What is your assessment?"

It was then that she felt it, like a feather lightly stroking the back of her brain, a tickling sensation that flowed upward over the top of her head, then down into her arms, raising the hair on them beneath her cloak. The tingling ebbed and waned, and beneath the strange aura was a voice, weak but distinct, drawing her attention to one dark corner of the room, as if something called to her from the shadows. The old seer froze, absorbing the entirety of the sensation and the spectral words that were whispered by something from the beyond.

Madame Sabina slowly turned her head, and as her gaze met Zorn's, the entire atmosphere in the room changed precipitously. No longer did she have the flippant air of jocularity about her, and her penetrating gaze sent a shiver up the spine of the doctor. It was as if she knew every intimate detail about Aldo Zorn and his work. Rather than clear the air and reveal what she had learned, she spoke not a word.

It was just more theatrics, Zorn assured himself.

Nervously, he turned to the subject at hand. "As you can see, the eyes open, but there is no heartbeat. Can you do as you profess and reinvigorate the body with the spark of life?"

"Have a seat, and let me do my work," she croaked.

Zorn anxiously shifted in the wooden chair as he watched Madame Sabina perform her arcane magic over the body. She leaned in and asked it to close its eyes, then placed one palm against its forehead, her fingers spread through the rich, crimson hair. Her other hand was raised in the air over the form as if beseeching a higher power to hear her overture, and just as a spider's spindly legs deftly manipulate strands of its web, so did her fingers wave and undulate, palpating the very energy within our reality, and the energy beyond. A whispered song escaped her lips as she worked, a haunting melody rife with disconcerting chord changes and ominous dissonant notes. Zorn was expecting theatrics and Madame Sabina did not disappoint.

The thin voice of the elderly cartomancer grew in both temerity and volume. Beneath the dark emerald cowl, her head rose and fell repeatedly as her hand manipulated the empty air above the body. Her fingers gripped and pulled at the nothingness, a pantomime that suggested the capture of forces unseen within her grasp. With each clasp of her hand, her other hand gripped tightly the forehead of the body. If Zorn was reading the motion correctly, the old woman was trying to convey the improbable action of pulling energy from some other dimension, sending it through her own body, then infusing it into the female form on the table. The drone of her chant continued, her voice growing stronger with each iteration of a single repeated phrase spoken in an unknown tongue, her whole body now swaying in unison with the clenching of her hands.

Then, without a crescendo, it was over.

The old woman ceased her motions, lowered her arm, then looked upon the scarred and stitched face. The eyes were still closed. The breast did not rise and fall. Nothing about the disposition of the undead corpse had changed. Madame Sabina bent forward to place her face against the body's cheek, and it looked to Zorn as if she might be kissing it. What he could not see was that the aged mystic had put her lips to the ear and whispered a single, barely audible word.

"Remember," she said.

It was as if a mighty ripple of electricity tore through the reposed form on the table. The eyes snapped open once again, the back arched, its hips thrust upward from the operating table, and the entire form spasmed as its hands clawed desperately at the air. The long shapely legs kicked uncontrollably against the surface of the metal table, creating cacophonous bangs that resounded off the walls of the laboratory. Dr. Zorn rose to his feet, absolutely astonished by the horrifying sight. Madame Sabina gripped the shoulders of the body to offer a reassuring touch and to prevent the being from injuring itself, but the lashing of its arms sent her tumbling backward to the unyielding stone floor.

It was then that the lips parted and an ear-shattering scream erupted from deep within the core of the being. It was unlike anything either Zorn or Madame Sabina had ever heard, a terrifying—and terrified—wail that encompassed the celestial essences of both life and death in one dreadful and primal aria of manifest pain.

From the floor where she lay, Madame Sabina observed the hideous phenomenon in shock and dismay, fearing that the supernatural manipulation she had just performed had doomed the pitiable creature to an eternity of unimaginable torture. But just as suddenly as the scream ushered forth it ceased, and it seemed as if all life was siphoned from the form as it dropped to the table like a corpse upon a mortician's slab.

"What have you done?" Zorn screamed, pulling the old woman from the floor by one arm. "What have you done!"

"I risked my life for this poor creature is what I've done, you fool," she hissed. "I did exactly what you implored me to do," she explained, as he gripped her arm tightly. "I reached through the veil to the other side and extracted the essence of being. I allowed it to flow through me into that body. I have given it life."

Zorn seethed with anger. "No! I had given it life and you have destroyed that! That scream was the scream of death, the scream of utter destruction!"

Madame Sabina broke from his hold with far more strength than he had imagined the elderly soothsayer could possess. She turned her back to him, intent on maintaining her focus on the still body. Zorn's ears still rang with the hideous scream, the scream of the being he had built with his own two hands. He was certain that Madame Sabina had done irreparable damage to his creation. His dream was shattering around him and his vision became a haze of unbridled rage. Years' worth of research and toil and excruciatingly intricate surgeries were obliterated in the blink of an eye by a common charlatan.

The enraged scientist reached for her back, his hands trembling with unbridled frenzy, but his fantasy of throttling the Romani woman was interrupted when she slowly turned her head toward him. Madame Sabina's face was now a placid mask, awash with tranquility, and her cracked lips drew into a faint smile. She raised one cloaked hand and fluidly motioned to one side as she drew away from the operating table, evoking the image of a carnival barker introducing her star attraction.

Zorn's eyes grew wide and a gasp escaped his lips. Sitting upright on the table with her legs thrown over the side and supporting herself with her arms, his creation looked about the room in confusion and wonderment.

"Help me," she whispered in a raspy voice, looking first to the cloaked woman who gave her awareness, then to the man who had created her.

CHAPTER TWELVE
THE SOUL AWAKENED

Despite the mournful quality of her words, the voice brought tears of joy to the eyes of Dr. Aldo Zorn. At last, his creation spoke!

Madame Sabina contemplated the nude woman who sat upright and lost on the surgical table but what thoughts swirled through her mind remained her own. After a few moments of silence, the cartomancer turned and held out her hand toward Zorn.

"That will be five hundred Thaler," she said.

The doctor was overwhelmed with emotion and scientific fascination, and could not take his eyes off of his creation, even as he thrust the silk coin purse into the palm of Madame Sabina.

"Thank you," he stammered, his mind immersed in the myriad tasks that now lay before him. His creation at last lived; she had been imbued with the divine spark of which she had been devoid. He was anxious for the departure of the ancient mystic so that he could pursue a thorough evaluation of the patchwork woman.

Zorn flew to the door, unlocked it, then shouted down the dark hallway. "Estevan! Come quickly!" he implored, then he pulled on the cord that fed up through the ceiling, twice ringing the servants' bell in quick succession, the code that he required assistance from one of his staff. Within seconds, Estevan hurried down the spiral stairwell, fearing the doctor had discovered that his sister had secretly entered his laboratory. The young servant found him and his elderly guest in the dark hallway, standing before the closed laboratory door, and was relieved to discover that Zorn simply wanted him to return Madame Sabina to her shop in Kleinburg.

In the dark alcove behind the monstrous furnace and concealed by the wrought iron gate, Falcona trembled. Her heart still raced after witnessing the ghastly spectacle that had played out before her wide eyes moments before. Since Zorn had stepped from the room to give some kind of instructions to her brother, now was her opportunity to escape the tiny, cobweb-shrouded chamber. She pushed past the stubborn wooden door and managed to secure it against its frame without the hint of a squeak, and quietly climbed the crumbling iron stairway that corkscrewed back to the portal that led to the interior of the castle.

"It would be my pleasure to escort you back to Kleinburg, Madame Sabina," Estevan said with pride, bowing respectfully. The old woman uttered not a word as she followed Estevan up the stone steps to the iron gate at the exterior entrance to the basement. After securely stowing Madame Sabina's trunk of magical paraphernalia behind the driver's seat of the coach, he opened the door and helped her up to her seat. The old woman made herself comfortable, clutched her cloak beneath her chin, then placed a weathered hand upon Estevan's shoulder.

"I hear the traveling Romani carnival is still camped in these woods. I'm sure they'd be delighted to have you and your sister rejoin them." Estevan raised an eyebrow, not immediately understanding the intent of the old woman's statement, but even more puzzling was her knowledge of his sister and their past. With a gravity that would make it impossible to misinterpret her sentiments, she imparted a thinly-veiled warning to Falcona's brother. "At least among them, your safety would be assured."

He did not know what she meant and he did not ask, but he nodded in acknowledgment and closed the carriage door. He took his seat and drove the horse on through the pines, his mind preoccupied with thoughts of Falcona, who he had not seen since she descended into the black shadows of the abandoned southeast tower of Castle Zorn.

"Hello," Dr. Zorn said with a soothing voice as he slowly approached his creation. Because of the confusion written on the woman's masterfully sculpted face, he made no overt movements, nor did he reach out to her for fear of frightening her. She looked upon him, the blank deadness of her emerald eyes now replaced with the intensity of fear and confusion, but those emotions were not as important to Zorn as was one overriding aspect: Those eyes—which he had surgically implanted into her skull himself—now expressed genuine emotion. It was a remarkable advancement from her nascent corpse-like presence.

"Do you understand my words?" he asked.

She gazed around the dark chamber, contemplating the array of mysterious apparatuses that crowded every work surface, then turned her attention to the man who spoke. "I do. I understand you," she hoarsely replied. "Who are you?" the patchwork creation uttered with a strain of confusion.

For a multitude of reasons, Zorn knew that he must carefully select every word that he spoke, the foremost reason being that he had to proceed under the assumption that despite the intrusive surgical adjustments he had made to the brain he had implanted within her, some memory of her previous life might remain. If any recollections of her former mental incarnation were accessible by her psyche, things could get very awkward very quickly.

She asked again, "Who are you?"

Rather than provide an answer, Zorn echoed her query. "Who are *you*?" he asked inquisitively.

The creation contemplated the scientist's question. Zorn watched as she appeared to wrestle with the conundrum. She must have been searching through her memories—or searching for any memory—to recover the answer to the tantalizing question. After several moments of silence, she responded with a look of composure, as if accepting of the absence of information within her mind. "I do not know who I am," she said with assurance.

"You do understand all that I say to you?" Zorn inquired.

"I do."

He held up one hand and pointed to it. "Do you know what this is?"

"Your hand," she replied.

He held up his leather-bound journal. "And what is this?" he asked.

"A book."

"What is two plus two?"

"Four," she quickly responded.

"And nine plus three?"

"Twelve," she answered.

Without hesitation, he asked, "What is twelve multiplied by nine?"

It was similarly without hesitation that she replied, "One hundred and eight."

"If you placed your hand over a flame, you would feel cold?" he speculated incorrectly.

"No, I would be burned, wouldn't I?" she noted suspiciously.

Zorn was pleased that she recognized simple items and her rudimentary reasoning skills seemed to be unhindered. It also appeared that the many intricate and painstaking surgical manipulations he had performed on her brain tissue had not resulted in the loss of learned knowledge ingrained upon it, yet it appeared that he had succeeded in wiping away only the intimate, personal memories of the woman who once possessed that most vital organ.

He asked one more question. "What is the opposite of hate?"

"Love," she emotionlessly replied.

He moved toward her slowly, his hands held before him in a friendly gesture. "I understand that there may be some confusion in your mind. My name is Dr. Aldo Zorn, and I am here to help you," he said with a smile. "I would like to physically examine you," he stated with clinical detachment, and she permissively nodded. Dr. Zorn took her hand and pressed his fingers against the inside of the wrist.

There was no pulse.

A spontaneous chill tingled along his hairline as panic swept through him. He adjusted his fingers on the wrist, but still, he felt no throbbing of blood through her veins. She did not flinch when he placed his hand against her chest, nor did she recoil when he thrust his head against her and pressed an ear to her pale, stitched skin, just above her breasts.

There was no heartbeat within her chest.

Zorn pushed away from the table and began pacing erratically, as dozens of puzzling questions screaming for answers bombarded his mind. How could it be possible? She sat upright, she conversed with him; by all appearances she was alive, yet the body, the woman, the thing he had created was still nothing more than animated, dead flesh.

He dashed back to her side. "Take a deep breath," he commanded. She complied, but there was no subsequent expelling of air from her lungs. The befuddled doctor watched her for several minutes but there was no movement of the chest, no exhalation, and no further inhalations. Not only did her heart not beat, but she also did not breathe.

Zorn rubbed a hand through his hair, his mind ablaze with uncertainty. He crossed his arms and gripped his face. It was baffling, absolutely baffling. But he could not let his creation know of his exasperation; regardless of his bewilderment, he needed to assert his dominance of both the situation and the woman. He calmed his mind, retreated several steps from the operating table, and issued a command. "Please step down from the table and walk to me." He beckoned to her with both hands.

She looked to the floor with uncertainty. It was an indication of hesitance as if she needed to recall how to perform the function he requested but within seconds, she slid from the table and placed both feet on the stone floor. Her full weight was now upon her legs. Her posture was slightly slouched but she quickly straightened her back as a full recollection of how to walk returned to her. With several slow, graceful footfalls she moved toward him.

Never in his life had he seen such elegance. She moved like a jungle cat, an intensity in both her gait and her gaze that spoke of single-minded purpose. Her hips swayed with each stride and she came to a stop just inches from the doctor.

Despite the hideous scars that encircled her body like an abandoned spider's web, the beauty of the crimson-haired woman of Zorn's creation was breathtaking to behold, even though she was indeed a walking corpse. She looked down upon the doctor, as she was slightly taller than him, and though she was completely naked, she either did not recognize her undraped state, or it mattered not to her that she was nude. Zorn noted the movement of her eyes as they scanned the room. It appeared that she was desperately trying to find anything familiar to her. At last, her lost and forlorn gaze fell upon the face of the well-dressed blonde man who stood before her.

"What is this place?" she asked, her voice beginning to clear from its initial huskiness.

In the center of the room, Zorn placed two wooden chairs, each facing the other, beneath the harness apparatus that hung from the chain in the rafters above them. "Sit," he implored her and the creation complied. "As I said, I am a doctor. This room is where I treat my patients. What do you know of your condition?" Zorn asked as he took a seat.

She closed her eyes. Her head tilted slightly to one side, then she straightened her posture and opened her eyes once again. "I remember nothing. Nothing at all." She seemed to be grasping for the right words to explain the nothingness at her core. "I awoke in blackness and was suddenly surrounded by light and colors...intense light...it hurt, hurt so much...I was pulled into it, into the light and the colors...they burned..." She paused, lowering her chin to her chest, the wild curls of her hair covering her face, Magdaline's face. Her head began to sway slowly from side to side and her voice grew to a whisper. "I screamed. And then..." she paused, lifting her head, "and then it was gone. The light. The colors. The pain. It was all gone. I saw the old woman. And you. That is all I remember," she voiced sadly.

Zorn patted her lightly on the knee, then put a reassuring hand on her shoulder. "Everything will be alright. There is nothing for you to fear. I am here to take care of your convalescence and I assure you, you will be in the very best hands. My hands."

The long shadows cast by the timber frame residences across the cobblestone avenue crept toward the door of Madame Sabina's cartomancy shop as Estevan helped the old woman from Dr. Zorn's carriage. She moved stiffly, keeping her eyes on her feet to avoid stumbling on the uneven surface. With Estevan supporting her by one of her spindly arms, she made her way safely to her door.

"Thank you, young man," she said with a smile.

"You're quite welcome, Madame," he replied. "You know, I am curious about something," he added.

"As are all handsome young men your age," she chided. "Continue," she gently implored.

"I don't know how well you know the doctor," Estevan said, carefully choosing his words.

"I don't know him. I've never met him until this morning," she interjected.

"I've been in his employ for over a year. I have to say, I don't think I know him, either," he admitted.

Madame Sabina narrowed her eyes. "Something troubles you about the doctor?"

"It's mostly my sister, Falcona," he said. "Yes, I admit Dr. Zorn's a bit eccentric but Falcona is very anxious around him. She's certain that there's something…evil, as she says, about what he's doing in his laboratory."

"And you want to know why Dr. Zorn brought me to the castle today."

He nodded sheepishly. "If you can tell me anything, just so I can reassure Falcona that…"

"There's no need to hide behind your sister's insecurities, Estevan. No man should feel shame for misgivings about things of which he knows nothing. It's alright to be frightened," she said soothingly.

"But *should* we be frightened? That's what I want to know," he pleaded.

The old woman was silent as she gathered her thoughts. "Let me ask you this," she offered. "Have either of you ever had the feeling that you are not alone in the castle?"

"What do you mean?" he asked.

"What do you think I mean?" she parried.

"Usually, when people say that, they're talking about," he paused. His face lit up as he discerned the meaning of the old woman's words. "Just this morning, Falcona told me she thought she saw a ghost in the doctor's laboratory. Is that why you were there? Is there a ghost?" he asked, anxiously.

Madame Sabina placed a reassuring hand on his arm. "The longer you tread this Earth, the more you will learn that what lies in the realm of the unknown far outweighs what is known. People like me are looked upon as witches or charlatans because that of which we speak cannot be proven by those brilliant men of science who sit in drawing rooms extolling the virtues of their intellects. But what they will not confess is that every one of life's mysteries those men eventually come to explain through their vaunted scientific investigation was once considered supernatural. Or magic. Or madness. And one by one, the mysterious aspects of life are revealed to be irrefutable truths. The supernatural becomes the natural."

It was an interesting observation but Estevan was unsure where her soliloquy was leading. Still, he was enraptured by her words. "You're going to tell me that there's a ghost in Castle Zorn?" he asked.

"Estevan," she said, "there are ghosts all around us but we must learn to listen to them. I listen to them and I heed their words. You are not alone in Castle Zorn but that was not why I was requested to visit. I cannot speak of Dr. Zorn's work, nor why he called upon me. It is not for you to know. It is not for anyone to know. It is something that should not be, yet it is, and the repercussions of his work will fall upon all those who surround him." Her voice grew even more sallow. "All I can tell you is that there is more to fear from the living than the dead."

"I understand," he said with a gracious smile. In truth, he did not understand, but it was at least comforting to know that the misgivings he and Falcona felt about the doctor were justified, and those feelings were shared by Madame Sabina.

"See to your sister," his elder urged. "She is going to want to talk to you about what she witnessed today in Dr. Zorn's laboratory."

Again, Madame Sabina spoke of something that she could not possibly have known unless she was aware that Falcona had secreted herself away in the abandoned tower that led to the laboratory. "How do you know my sister was watching? Did you see her? Did Zorn see her?" he asked frantically.

"No. She was not discovered. She is safe, for now. Return to her, my boy," Madame Sabina imparted firmly. Estevan warmly hugged the frail old woman, then sprang to the driver's seat of the carriage and urged the horse to carry him back to the castle at a swift gallop.

CHAPTER THIRTEEN
A GHOSTLY VISITATION

Falcona stared upward at the deep crimson canopy luxuriously embroidered with gold threading. Late afternoon sunlight streamed through the window onto the bed and her body was comfortably confined within the brilliant patch of warmth in her otherwise dark bedroom. It was little comfort to her tormented mind. Try as she might, she could not help but recall again and again the horrifying tableau she had witnessed in the lab. Before secluding herself in her bedroom, she had slipped unnoticed from the southeast tower and a fleeting glance from the second-floor window revealed that a carriage bearing her brother and Madame Sabina was departing the castle grounds. She was now alone, with no one else in Castle Zorn save the doctor himself.

But there was also the woman. The undead woman whose bone-chilling shriek continued to reverberate through the fear-stricken memory of Falcona. The creation of Dr. Zorn, sewn together from the corpses of an untold number of women, a being who now wore the face of the doctor's deceased wife.

It was all too much to digest and her valiant attempts to ascribe some form of benevolent intent to the doctor's experiment did not result in solace or satisfaction. It was madness and it was unholy.

As she awaited Estevan's return, the young Spanish woman gazed impatiently around the room. The deep hues of the mahogany paneling that concealed the castle's crumbling gray skeleton reflected the darkness she felt encroaching upon her soul. The room was lushly decorated, as was the entire castle, all part of the estate that Aldo Zorn's father had acquired after the death of its former owner. From her prone position, her eyes fell upon the exquisitely detailed oval mirror mounted just above the tall, oak chest of drawers. To divorce her mind from the unsettling events of one hour past, she mentally traced the filigree curls that adorned the mirror's frame, up one side, across the top, and down the other side.

As her focus lingered on the gold frame, she became aware of a darkness that fell over the face of the mirror. It first appeared to be a dim shadow but the anomaly increased in opacity until the entire face of the mirror was black. Falcona squeezed her eyes shut, then opened them again, refocusing on what was likely an odd illusion created by the setting sun outside the windows and the shadows cast upon the far wall. To her dismay, the mirror still appeared as dark as obsidian. She sat upright to view it from a different angle, yet the odd effect remained.

Despite sitting on the bed in warm sunlight, her entire body was overcome by a sudden chill that reached inward to her bones. She gripped herself, her arms crossing her chest, and she felt the blood within her throb in the sides of her neck when a gray ghostly face appeared in the ebon blackness of the mirror. It was the same countenance she spied in the dark alcove of the laboratory beneath the castle.

Now it was within the sanctity of her bedroom.

It was the ghost and it had come for her.

She sat immobile on the bed, too afraid to move and too terrified to speak, and she watched as the face drew closer to the mirror's surface. It was as if the specter dwelled within a stygian chamber cordoned by the glass surface. There was nothing else discernable beyond the ghastly visage; no body, no hands, just a white face of feminine composite, its eyes hidden within deep wells of darkness. Falcona's own eyes widened and she inhaled sharply when the lips of the specter slowly parted and called out to her with a hollow, echoing intonation.

"The boy," the specter moaned, "the boy, the green bottle. The boy did this."

By that time, Falcona's nerves were shredded and jumbled emotions roiled inside of her gut like a burlap sack full of snakes. She wanted to turn away from the mirror, she wanted to run, yet her eyes were transfixed on the face. The longer she looked upon it, a creeping sensation of sorrow began to overtake her senses, an aura that seemed to emanate in waves from the haunting apparition behind the glass. Falcona feared that initiating any interaction with the specter might invite disaster; if it was a demon, her words might pull it forth from the other-realm and forge a bridge over which it could invade her soul. But so overwhelmed was she by the anguish the spectral form exuded, she felt compelled to reach out to it with compassion and empathy, even though her instincts screamed for her to flee the castle and never return.

"Can you tell me your name?" Falcona asked, her voice trembling concurrent with the involuntary shivers that rippled through her slender frame.

Curiously, the ghost behind the glass voiced the same cryptic message. "The boy, the boy, the green bottle. The boy did this."

The terrified house servant cautiously stepped down from the bed with one foot, then the other, her eyes transfixed on the ghastly white countenance that floated behind the surface of the mirror. She did not know if she would attempt to reach the bedroom door, or if she would instead approach the mirror to express a desire to decipher the words of the ghost, but the adrenaline rushing through her made it impossible to simply sit and talk casually. She had to do something. Anything. Falcona stood, and bravely took a step toward the visitor from beyond.

"There is no boy here, madame," Falcona sincerely admitted. "Of what boy do you speak? What is the green bottle? Can you tell me..."

"Below," droned the spirit, "both are below."

Just then, a rhythmic clopping outside the window reached Falcona's ears. The familiar sound increased in volume as it approached the castle. Falcona's heart leaped; Estevan had completed his task of returning Madame Sabina to Kleinburg and was now steering the carriage up the stone drive to the castle doors! She knew that he would never believe her incredible tale unless he saw it for himself. Her eyes on the window, Falcona excitedly spoke aloud to the ghost in the mirror behind her.

"Madame! Could you please…"

But as she turned to face the gilded looking glass, she found the spectral form floating before her, no longer confined behind the surface of the mirror. The phantasm reached out with icy fingers and gripped her slender shoulders.

"The boy! The green bottle! They are below!" it screamed into her face, so close to her lips that she could feel the chill of death upon its breath.

Every nerve in Falcona's body fired at once, and she shrieked in fear as she fell away from the wispy trails of ectoplasm that exuded from the feminine ghost's form. She hit the floor hard and quickly rolled to scramble on her hands and knees away from the horrifying apparition, but her long dress hindered her attempted escape.

She glanced over her shoulder to see if death was upon her, but to her relief, Falcona discovered that she was once again alone in the dark bedroom, grown even gloomier as the sun now hung below the stately pines that surrounded the castle exterior. It was over. The ghost had departed as mysteriously as it had appeared.

Falcona realized that her entire body had broken out in a cold sweat. She burst into cleansing laughter, even as tears welled in her eyes, fomented by uncontrolled emotional release and mental exhaustion. She could not wait to tell her brother of the events she had beheld since her descent into the blackness of the southeast tower. She threw open the bedroom door and descended the marble staircase to the first-floor foyer three steps at a time.

Estevan pulled sharply on the reins to halt the trot of the horse when he saw Falcona rush toward him from the front doors of the castle. Fifteen years ago, he had seen that same pained look on her face. They were both children at the time, on a lazy summer day. As was his daily duty, he was tending to the flock of sheep on their parents' ranch, in the wide pasture on the other side of the hills that separated the grazing land from the hacienda.

Falcona had dashed across the meadow toward him, her eyes brimming with sorrow and tears. Through her sobbing, she informed Estevan that an accidental fire had overtaken the stable, an inferno that had taken the lives of their mother, father, and one cousin. He would never forget the anguish written on her face that day, a pain that was echoed in his own heart, and he prayed that he would never again see Falcona in such a grief-stricken state. This was not quite that, but it was close.

She rushed to the black coach and in a flurry of half-sentences, disjointed thoughts, and exclamations of horror and fear, Falcona tried to relate all that she had discovered and seen. She blurted about the secret of Zorn's research, the patchwork corpse brought back from the dead, Madame Sabina's magic, and the ghost that confronted her in her bedchamber. All of it came out in a jumble that left her brother dazed as he looked down at her incredulously from the driver's seat of the stately carriage. Falcona was sure that Estevan must have heard the scream from the creature, but he told her he had been down by the road, putting a new padlock on the front gate as his employer had directed him that morning. Since Falcona had gone to the bottom of the southeast tower to spy on the doctor, Estevan figured that there was nothing for him to do but await her return and go about his daily duties to not raise suspicions in the mind of Dr. Zorn.

But before Estevan could attempt to make heads or tails of Falcona's impassioned revelations, the stern voice of their employer barked from behind them. "Estevan! Falcona! I need your assistance immediately!" He stood in the open doorway, a sense of urgency about him that exceeded that of his emphatic utterance.

Estevan's dark eyes met Falcona's and an unspoken message was instantly relayed between the siblings. Moments before, he had been skeptical of his sister's outlandish statements, but after seeing her cringe at the sound of Zorn's voice, the notion that there could be some truth to what she had told him was substantiated in Estevan's mind. He knew his sister well, and she had never been prone to exaggeration or fantasy. At least, not after that warm summer afternoon back home in Valencia. The tragic fire had transformed the siblings forever, for both of their childhoods came to an abrupt and heart-wrenching end that day.

Estevan hurried to remove the bridle from the horse and led it into the stable, then made haste to the castle. He found Zorn and Falcona in the long hallway whose walls were lined with oil paintings and which terminated at the door leading to the basement stairwell. There, Zorn was instructing Falcona to re-trieve one of her nightgowns. She was also to prepare a serving tray containing a small loaf of bread, a fork and knife, a napkin, a pitcher of water, and a drinking glass, and deposit the items outside the door of his laboratory.

The task Zorn assigned to Estevan would require physical labor. He was to carry to the lab a mattress from one of the many unoccupied bedrooms in the mansion, along with a blanket, a sheet, and a pillow. Likewise, he was to leave them outside the laboratory door. Zorn explained that there was a woman with an extremely rare and puzzling affliction who would be staying at the castle for an extended period. Since her condition required his constant medical supervision and analysis, she would be confined to his laboratory. He hoped to make her stay as comfortable as possible while conducting an extensive medical evaluation of the vexed patient.

Estevan shot Falcona a knowing glance from the corners of his eyes to let her know that, yes, he did believe her story. Zorn's confession about the woman's presence in the castle now confirmed at least part of what Falcona had shared with him but whether or not he believed her fantastic story about encountering a ghost remained undetermined.

The tall Swiss grandfather clock in the main study on the first floor of the castle chimed six as Estevan finally succeeded in carrying the mattress down the spiral staircase, with Falcona's help. She had already completed Zorn's requests of her, and the tray of bread and water and a freshly-laundered and folded white gown lay just outside the locked laboratory door. Together, the siblings carried the mattress down the dark stone hallway and propped it against the wall. Falcona lightly tapped on the reinforced wooden door. "Everything is as you asked, Doctor," she spoke through the barrier.

"Thank you," came Zorn's reply from within his sanctum. "You both may retire for the evening. I'll need nothing more from you tonight."

The finality with which he spoke made it clear that he was not to be disturbed again that evening. Falcona and Estevan were more than happy to comply and gingerly made their way up the spiral granite staircase to the main floor of the castle.

CHAPTER FOURTEEN
DARK COMMUNION

The laboratory was an eerily silent vacuum, save for the occasional high-pitched *plicks* of water droplets striking a standing puddle in some dark corner of the basement. The rain that drenched the mountaintop estate several nights past had finally managed to seep through the limestone that blanketed the top of the hill and had stubbornly found its way into the subterranean chamber through fissures in the castle's foundation. Something as unassuming as a droplet of rainwater would not be denied from pursuing its course, even when faced by a seemingly impenetrable barrier. It would find a way.

And so it was within the mind of Dr. Aldo Zorn. With diligence, he would eventually unravel the baffling condition of his creation.

He watched her attentively as she adjusted her position on the mattress that lie on the floor of the laboratory as innumerable questions assailed the unbound curiosity within her. She desired neither the bread nor water that was offered to her, nor did she express the slightest inclination to rest. Dr. Zorn had done his best to make her comfortable in the moldering underground vault but her disinterest in the most basic of the human necessities of life was perplexing, as were the results of his periodic testing of her pulse and respiration. Neither produced the results that indicated that the woman with whom he interacted was a living being.

Masking his frustration, Zorn stood from the chair and stretched, stiffly making his way to the work table installed against the longest length of the cold basement wall. Over the many months that he toiled in the covert acquisition of internal and external human body parts, and the prolonged periods he endured performing intensive surgeries to stitch them all together, he wrestled with the conundrum of whether to concoct a previous history for his creation or to be truthful about her inception. He weighed all that he had thus seen of her astute mental capabilities and dichotomous lack of biographical knowledge and was certain the answers to the questions that plagued him would become more clearly delineated with time.

The creation watched Zorn as he examined a small wooden clock on the tabletop and slowly wound its internal spring with a brass key. "There is something that we need to discuss, of a very delicate nature," he said soothingly as he checked the proper time on his pocket watch, then made a slight adjustment to the minute hand on the wooden clock. "I want you to think and concentrate deeply. Throughout all of the memories and knowledge that you possess, do you see any faces, or recall any names? Family members? Your home? Your childhood?"

She rolled from her lying position to her knees, resting her buttocks upon her heels. Her head dipped and her eyes searched the room, focusing on nothing, her hands unconsciously toying with her white nightgown's tie strings that lay beneath her collarbone. She twirled the two strings between her fingertips as her head swayed from one side to the other. After quiet introspection, she spoke with an emotionless intonation.

"It's as I told you before. There is nothing. I simply don't remember anything about my life," she uttered with finality and sadness. "You said you can help me," the living corpse reminded him.

The doctor returned to the chair at the side of the mattress and sat facing her. It was time.

"I am a man," he began. "I was born of woman, as are all humans. That you understand, correct?"

The crimson-haired woman was naturally confused by the odd question and knew not how to answer. Of course, all humans are born of women, everyone knows that, as it is basic biology. But why would this man, who calls himself a doctor, ask such a ridiculous question of her? Was her condition such that her brain possessed some devastating deformity and she must be talked to as one would interact with a child? She spoke not one of those words, but the expression on her face painted each one in clearly defined brushstrokes.

"You were not born of woman," Zorn revealed in an even, compassionate tone, "and you are not the result of normal human reproduction. You are the masterwork of my scientific genius."

Utter perplexity was written on her patchwork face. "I don't understand," she whispered.

"You began life by natural means, but not as an individual woman. You were once many women who met untimely deaths. Women who were taken from this Earth much too young," he explained. "I am a doctor and a scientist. Over my lifetime, I have devised a process by which I can reanimate dead tissue and revitalize that tissue, allowing it to live on after death. Even more astounding, I have unlocked the true secret of life. True life is not the simple act of existing. True life is growth and it is growth that I have instilled in you." The creation sat silently, absorbing each word.

"Within you is the pure spark of life. Examine yourself, your hands." She did as he requested. "Those sutures and scars bear out the truth. Your body is a composite of innumerable women, whose dead flesh was sewn together to create a being unlike any other in this world. You are a woman who was not born of a woman. You were born of science and the spark of life that I have instilled in you has rejuvenated every organ, every limb, every muscle, every bone, every ligament, and every inch of skin. That spark has encouraged them to grow together as one. You are now one woman, whereas before you were many. I have given a second chance at life to those women from whom you are composed."

The crimson-tressed creation sat motionless for several minutes as she absorbed Zorn's revelation. At last, she voiced an acknowledgment that was both profound and accusatory.

"If what you say is true, and if your genius is such that you can mimic the work of God himself, why did you not simply revive those dead women instead of disassembling them? Why would you do such a thing?" Her emerald eyes burned into his contemptuously. It was an off-putting, momentary flash of primal emotion that the doctor had not anticipated. To his relief, what appeared to be barely-repressed anger was swiftly replaced by uncertainty. "Why have you done this?" she implored. "Who am I?"

"I have brought you from nothingness and shaped a life from death," Zorn reminded her. "What I offer to you is the most wonderful gift any man could give to a woman. You and I, together, will shape you into who you shall be. You have a lifetime of learning and knowledge, but you are unencumbered by adverse experiences or the negative effects of an uncultured upbringing. You can be whoever we wish and I will mold you into the perfect woman." Zorn's gaze lowered to take in the fullness of her breasts, then continued to her hands, which the creation was still studying with uncertainty. "Even those ugly scars upon your skin will disappear with time. You shall be perfection but do not forget, you would be nothing without me. I am your creator and you must obey me if you are to achieve your full potential."

She was a lost soul, a forlorn figure untethered to the man who spoke, the mattress upon which she sat, and the stone room that surrounded her. In that instant, the panic tied to her inner emptiness ebbed, leaving behind the nothingness that was her soul. She voiced her crushing desolation in the only way possible. "I will do whatever you ask," she acquiesced.

Zorn lowered himself to his knees on the mattress beside her, then gently embraced his creation with nurturing tenderness. She did not react in any discernable fashion, her cold rigidity unmoved by his overt gesture. Without question, it would be a prolonged and arduous process to win her unwavering compliance. However, the doctor was heartened, as there were telltale signs indicating her unbalanced emotional composure would be easily sculpted and in all likelihood, his deft manipulation of her delicate psyche could produce the desired result of her absolute psychological and emotional obedience to him.

He held her closer and placed one hand on her knee. The skin was cold but supple. His heart began to pound in his chest. He could not help himself. His hand slid upward, across her sutured flesh, his fingers running along her inner thigh toward her womanhood.

Aldo Zorn could never have anticipated the effect his touch would have upon her. As his hand began to creep upward between her legs, the creation felt a tingle within her stomach, a butterfly flutter just under the skin near the heart-shaped birthmark to one side of her navel. The sensation grew and spread as if igniting her entire nervous system before coalescing in the deepest recesses of her mind. A warmth spread like a wildfire throughout her brain, accompanied by a wave of needle-like pricks that blanketed the top of her head under her voluminous red hair. Her vision lost focus, the dark room blurring into a glowing green fog, and suddenly, from somewhere, a name echoed in her mind: *Ludwig Hertz.*

Then another name. *Gina.*

Flashes of recollections began to explode in bursts of light at the core of her memory. She saw the shadowy interior of a barn bathed in moonlight. A man roughly taking her as she bent against bales of hay. A gleaming silver dagger concealed within the handle of a walking cane plunged viciously into her stomach. And from somewhere else, a haunting voice, two tones layered one upon the other, one ancient and hoarse, the other youthful.

The voice intoned a single word. "Remember."

The body of the creation stiffened with a start, and as she pressed her hands against Zorn's vest a concussive force flowed from her fingertips and against the chest of the doctor. Tendrils of blue-white electricity arced from her hands into the air between them and Zorn was forcibly thrown backward until he lie on his back halfway across the chamber.

"Never touch me like that again," she warned darkly, before collapsing upon the mattress in apparent mental exhaustion.

Zorn rose stiffly from the floor and rushed to the side of his creation. His chest ached even as his exasperated mind was flooded with questions. What had just occurred was yet another scientific impossibility. Somehow, through some arcane means, the creation generated an electrical charge within her of such measure as to manifest itself as Newton's second law, but from where had the charged particles been generated and how could they have converted from a current to a physical force? It was another baffling conundrum, an unfathomable manifestation of his accidental contrivance.

The creation watched him cautiously as he stood over her. He hesitated to lend her a hand for fear of another attack and struggled to find the words to reassert his dominance over her mental state.

A haunting composure crossed the creation's features. It spoke of confidence within the chaotic storm of confusion. Her quickly-shifting mien gave Zorn pause. Even more unnerving to the doctor was her seeming indifference to the shocking ability she had just displayed. At last, she spoke, but it was not to voice another threat as Zorn had anticipated.

"Do you have a mirror?" she asked.

How typical of a woman, he internalized. Concurrently, he theorized about the origin of the unseen force that had sent him sprawling seconds before. He could not let her know that he was baffled and unnerved by the display, for that would convey weakness on his part and must be avoided at all costs. Zorn determined that it would be prudent to dismiss altogether what had happened and focus his attention on her apparent insecurity.

From amongst the beakers and bottles cluttering his workstation, Zorn retrieved a rectangular mirror used in the observation of sediments at the bottom of a rack of test tubes and handed it cautiously to the scarlet-haired woman. She rose, stepped away from the mattress, and moved toward the most illuminated area of the darkened laboratory.

The face that returned her gaze appeared to mean nothing to her. As a woman might scrutinize her appearance before leaving for an evening at the opera, she examined her face from all angles, then turned to the doctor. "These scars. Will they indeed fade as you suggested?" she mused.

Zorn thought it odd that with all of the concerns he assumed one in her position would have about the very foundations of her humanity, a characteristic as frivolous as vanity would take precedence over substantive issues. His response was condescending.

"Don't worry, my dear. One day your beauty will be unequaled," he balked.

The creation was cold and direct. "Do not assume that I am so vapid that my only concern is a pretty face, Doctor. What I desire is to appear unobtrusive."

Zorn noted that the more she talked, the greater was her self-confidence. It was a positive indication that the logic center of her brain was functioning normally, but it was clear that to maintain control over her psyche and shape her into the obedient woman he desired, he would need to closely monitor her defiant spirit, and if necessary, break it. But something else about what she had just said struck him and needed to be immediately addressed.

"You need to have a clear understanding of your place in this world," he lightly scolded. "Even after your scars disappear, you will unfortunately not be welcomed into social gathers. You'll not be shopping at the market, or attending gala balls. Those interactions are for the living, which you are not. Your heart does not beat, you do not breathe. You do not appear to require food or sleep, as do living things. In essence, you are the antithesis of what you once were, of what the multiple women were whose bodies were cobbled together to form the woman you are now. You are an oddity. A scientific experiment. A ragdoll that was sewn together not from cloth but flesh. You are to be studied and probed, and I will do everything in my power to make you comfortable. You might even feel loved. But you are not alive, and therefore will never be a party to social engagements outside this castle."

Without turning her head to face him, she held out her hand to return the mirror. As Zorn took the glass from her patchwork hand, he felt a momentary ringing in his ears, followed by a slight blurring of his vision. The past few days had been quite strenuous, and his sleep had not been all it could be. He simply needed rest, he concluded.

But as he shook off the brief spell of dizziness and his eyes refocused, he was witness to a most astonishing sight. The supple hand that still lingered beyond his reach was smooth and unblemished, with not a trace of the scars and sutures that were the remnants of his surgical handiwork. Her arm, too, was clear and evenly toned, no longer displaying a variety of skin shades, dependent on the derma of the various donor corpses from whom she was constructed. Likewise, her face, when she turned to look upon him, was devoid of the incisions that he had surgically carved across her forehead, down the sides of her nose, across her chin, and down her cheeks, and which had encircled her eye sockets.

Aldo Zorn was shaken to his core.

"All you say is true, Doctor. I understand. I am dead," she said sadly. As fallen leaves are moved about by the autumn breeze, the mournful quality of her voice shifted and took a decidedly self-aware and resolute inflection. "But it seems that we have differing aspirations."

In the hamlet of Kleinburg, as the shroud of night began to blanket the uneven cobblestone streets, Madame Sabina sat quietly in the old wooden chair, the candlelight in the darkened back parlor barely illuminating the oracle card held close to her lips. The face of the card bore an ornate illustration of a hauntingly beautiful woman, with skin of alabaster and hair of crimson, her body draped in a network of scars and sutures.

"Remember," the cartomancer whispered to the mysterious image. "Remember."

CHAPTER FIFTEEN
A MIDNIGHT STROLL

A soothing, ambient drone filled the air, emanating from the golden wheat fields that stretched between Kleinburg and the pines of the highlands that encircled the valley. Not unlike the sound of ocean waves in perpetual motion, the natural melody resulted from the warm April breeze weaving through the chest-high stalks whose unmistakable earthy aroma signified that harvest time of the winter crop was nearly upon the village.

The residents of Kleinburg walked a little more briskly and chatted a bit more congenially than they had in the past few months; the long winter was at last over and the anticipation of warmer days filled even the cantankerous village elders with optimism. Birds sang in the trees and splashes of color dotted the countryside, and the rich green of hearty seedlings pushing their way through amber blankets of pine needles filled the forest. Life was renewing itself all around the village and everywhere there was work to be done. Pitched rooves required repair after the past season's heavy snowstorms. Fields needed to be fertilized. Potholes in Kleinburg's cobblestone streets demanded to be filled. Even at the village's sedate boarding house, the landlord was busy posting a sign that read "Room available." The previous month, the young female tenant named Ivonette had returned to her home in Braumstadt, according to a message delivered to the hostel by her employer, Dr. Aldo Zorn. Her meager belongings, he explained, were to be given to charity at Ivonette's request.

High atop the hill crested by the brooding Castle Zorn, Falcona also felt the lure of nature that urged her to breathe deep the spring air outside the stale confines of the dark manor. At every possible opportunity, the young Spaniard assisted her brother with his outdoor chores, whether it was shoveling stable stalls or trimming the creeping ivy that threatened to overtake the castle on every front. It wasn't that Estevan needed help or that Falcona did not have enough responsibilities within the household to keep her occupied; she simply looked for any excuse to escape the stifling grip of the cold stone walls. But each time she stood in the sun and basked in its warmth, her thoughts were immediately pulled into the recesses of the castle basement, to Zorn's shadowed laboratory and the unfortunate creature that he kept secluded in darkness.

Dr. Zorn became a phantom within his own home, his presence felt but rarely seen. He rose each morning before dawn before his two servants had begun their daily duties and disappeared into his lab, taking with him food for three meals to last throughout the day. When Falcona and Estevan did see the doctor it was for only moments each night as he made his way through the main hall and up the staircase to his room, seldom if ever speaking to them.

So it had been for the past fifteen days and nights since Madame Sabina visited the castle, the same day that Falcona had watched in secret the awakening of Zorn's creation. It was also the day that she had her brush with the supernatural specter that dwelled behind the surface of her bedroom mirror.

The first few nights after the encounter, Falcona occupied Estevan's bed while he grudgingly slept on the floor, but within a week he succeeded in bolstering his sister's courage by ensuring her that it did not sound as though the spirit wished her any harm. Estevan slept in Falcona's room the first night she returned to it, but there was no spectral visitation. The following night, she resumed sleeping alone in her bedchamber. Outwardly she appeared to have overcome her fear of the ghost, however, a sheet concealed the room's mirror and she used the one at the top of the staircase in the main hall to arrange her hair before beginning her household duties each morning.

In the basement laboratory, the unknown could not be so easily hidden or dismissed. Each day, from dawn to well into the night, Zorn sat with the creation, performing every conceivable test that he could upon the woman who was a mere facsimile of life. He was met with nothing but frustration, as every attempt to construct some reasonable hypothesis that would explain her unnatural state bore only the bitter fruit of failure. His achievement was an unprecedented scientific accomplishment. He had succeeded in developing a procedure that rejuvenated dead flesh. He had pieced together various corpses and animated the piecemeal human and that creation now walked and talked and reasoned. All of it was astounding and his detailed notes illuminated the scientific methods by which those previously unheard-of outcomes were attained. But try as he might, he could not explain how the creation could exist without the need to breathe or eat, and it had no functioning heart to pump blood throughout its frame. Likewise, he still could not account for the physical electrical force that had erupted from her fingertips.

As for the miraculous disappearance of the scars and stitches that enwrapped the body of the creation, Zorn's sensibilities could not accept that the event was of supernatural origin. He chastised himself each time his mind conjured the possibility as the only resolution to the puzzle. The first morning after the scarring had vanished before his eyes, his examination of the creation revealed that although her flesh appeared smooth and unblemished, his fingertips could feel the scars and sutures that had bound her limbs together before they had grown into one. The sutures and scars were all there, yet invisible to the naked eye. His only assumption was that it was some form of psychological entrancement imposed by the creation upon those near her, but that phenomenon was relegated to the realm of seances performed in dark parlors by charlatans. Zorn's scientific training led him to immediately reject that conclusion.

One day, a satisfying explanation would be found, but there was another more important aspect of his research that held his intense focus. That aspiration was a complete mental servitude he wished to instill in the woman he had constructed. She was the perfect female companion birthed by his scientific genius and was destined, by his decree, to fulfill his obsessive personal and sexual needs. However, that facet of his work was conspicuously missing from his meticulous hand-written documentation of the past few years. Zorn knew that he would be hailed as the greatest scientific mind of the century once his experiment and its result were shared with the scientific community at large. But he was also aware that his professional reputation would be destroyed and the morality of his groundbreaking work scrutinized and immediately discredited if it came to light that he intended to copulate with the flesh he had brought back from the dead. That hidden desire would be his secret forever.

The days passed without incident or advancement, save for the discovery that the creation had a voracious appetite for reading. On the third day under Zorn's scrutiny, the creation grew restless and asked for something to read. The doctor granted her request, retrieving several carefully selected volumes from the dusty book-case in the upstairs drawing room. The tomes were once the belongings of the late widow Isadora, whose personal effects became the possessions of the doctor's family upon Wilhelm Zorn's acquisition of the estate upon her death. The creation was delighted by the materials supplied to her, even though embers of remembrance told her that she had read them all before in one of her past lives, or maybe several of her past lives. Her admission greatly intrigued the scientist, but it also simultaneously drew his caution.

As she quietly read, her vivid, emerald eyes absorbed the poetic compositions of John Milton. Zorn was touched by the indescribable beauty of a woman who yearned to enrich herself. He could have happily observed her in that state for the entirety of the day, but a gnawing question urged him to reluctantly interrupt her reverie.

"You know the work," Zorn asked.

"I do," she responded, not looking up from the bound pages.

"Do you recall anything about when you first read it? Where you were, what was happening around you? Perhaps even your state of mind at the time?"

The creation paused and turned the porcelain perfection of her face toward him. There was a long moment of silence, and in those few seconds, Zorn's heart began to race. Could it be that she was remembering something and if she did, had he unlocked Pandora's box by urging her to open the floodgates to past lives better left buried? The interminable wait ended with her words, "No, I remember nothing. Only the poetry."

Twelve days had passed since that exchange, and now the shroud of night enveloped the castle, the end of another day without a breakthrough for Dr. Zorn. One by one the lamps illuminating the estate's many glowing eyes were extinguished as Falcona and Estevan retired for the evening. Shortly thereafter, the doctor wearily made his way to his bedchamber and locked the door behind him, alone with his thoughts and burning frustration. But in the basement laboratory, sequestered in solitude, the creation sat alert, her mind searching through the dark corridors of her memory for any vestige of recollection that might tether her to the reality of her existence.

As she had done for weeks, she focused on two names that had haunted her: Ludwig Hertz and Gina. Somehow, those names meant something to her but she knew not what. She spent hours each night attempting to let herself be absorbed into the essence of their meaning, detaching her mind from all other distractions in the hope that the names would pull her into the light of understanding. As on the past fourteen nights hence, the two appellations remained without nuance.

During her long hours of isolation each night, the creation had analyzed every aspect of the scientific accouterment that leered mockingly from the shadows of the laboratory. She had memorized their every curve, reflection, and rivet, transforming the fascinating scientific apparatus into nothing more than the window dressing of her bleak lonesomeness. Tonight was no different.

Then it was that she heard it, a singular sound that resembled a slow, deliberate exhale that wafted from somewhere behind her upon the underground chamber's stale air. She rose from the mattress and peered beyond the reach of the single lantern that grudgingly lit the laboratory, but found herself alone. Something within her, some intangible wordless urging, told her that she was not alone.

"Hello?" she whispered, as her hand ran over the moist stone walls. There was no response. Farther from the lantern she ventured, her bare feet leaving prints on the damp surface of the flagstone floor. "Is someone there?" she asked.

Again she heard it, again from behind her. There was no fear in the mind of the creation, only fascination. Her eyes widened in anticipation of any discovery that might blossom into some-thing—anything—to bring meaning to her insufferable existence. She attuned all of her senses to the vacuum of silence and was drawn to one black corner of the chamber, behind the tall copper vat and the ebon furnace with its spiderlike tubular appendages. Upon investigation, she found against the wall behind the furnace an ancient rusted gate that barred passage to a small alcove beyond. It was a doorway to a much larger world; for her, it was a world undiscovered. Was she prepared to accept the cascade upon her senses that what lies beyond would unleash? She paused and pondered the tantalizing decision that cried out for a response.

From her basic, ingrained knowledge of the human condition, the creation knew that it should be impossible for her to see anything in the pitch blackness of the alcove, yet somehow she could see as easily as an owl spots its prey hiding in the blackest shadows of the night. As she peered beyond the barrier, through the pitted metal bars within her clenched hands, something began to coalesce in the air, a pulse of lightness against the dark. It was a shape, a form of almost human proportions, and within that form congealed dark pits that sculpted themselves into a semblance of a human face. It was a woman, she was sure of it, and her assumption was substantiated by a sullen female voice that seem-ed to surround her.

"This way," the voice said. Upon the utterance of the words, the phantom held up one beckoning hand to urge the creation to follow her.

Effortlessly, the crimson-haired being pulled open the rusted gate and followed, as the specter floated above the floor and away from her, receding deeper into the stygian alcove. The creation followed the visage through the thickly cobwebbed tunnel, then both ascended the iron, spiral staircase. The ghostly apparition stood before a wooden door at the stairwell's head and looked down upon the creation as she stepped upon the landing.

"Unlike me, you are not bound to this place. Pursue your destiny," the ghost imparted, then dissolved into nothingness.

The ancient door to the castle's formerly sealed southeast tower creaked open. Down the stone staircase, the creation descended and she moved silently to the front door, driven by a purpose even she did not understand. Then, as a birdsong is heard from across a grassy meadow, it came to her. It was a voice, at once raspy and silken, but it was not the same voice as that of the now-departed specter. This was someone else.

"Remember," the voice sang.

With that, a floodgate opened within the mind of the creation. Her body stiffened, then relaxed, as a wave of absolute composure and enlightenment washed across her soul, painting every soft curve of her features with tranquility. It was a moment of stark crystal clarity and with that celestial breakthrough came a full decipherment of the names Ludwig Hertz and Gina.

Now she knew. Now she must act. Her conscious mind was gently ushered to one side as another more dominant personality asserted itself, one with a very explicit agenda that would not be denied.

She removed her nightgown, covered herself with Falcona's hooded cloak that hung from a hook near the front door, and ventured out into the moonlit night. Her bare feet carried her across the castle's portico and down the steep drive that led to the shadowed lane leading to Kleinburg, but that was not her destination. Instead, she walked in the opposite direction, toward the hamlet of Inglestadt.

The inn at Inglestadt was indistinguishable from any other in the valley. Its confines were packed nightly by the men of the village and never was there a complaint about the cloying aromas of pipe tobacco and stale ale that permeated the stained, wood plank floor. This night was like every other, and like every other night, the attitudes of the patrons were decidedly more belligerent upon the inn's closure than they were when the clientele first entered the drinking establishment hours before. To the landlord's relief, all had now departed without argument, except for one. Everyone else had voluntarily left and now wove their drunken ways down the cobblestone street away from the inn, but Ludwig Hertz was not convinced that the night had come to an end.

"It's time to go home, sir," the landlord gently urged yet again. His patience was at an end, having already reminded the well-dressed young man four times that he needed to leave. Still, Hertz ignored him as if he owned the place, and that set the landlord's teeth on edge. Enough was enough. "Herr Hertz, you leave me with no alternative but to call for the Bürgermeister and have you removed from the premises."

An arrogant sense of entitlement seeped from the man named Hertz. "Ha! I own the Bürgermeister, you idiot," he laughed as he stood from his table. "I leave you now of my own volition. And tomorrow night, I'll again remain in your shabby establishment as late as I'd like." With that, he paced his tophat upon his curly, black locks, kicked open the door, and strode out into the night.

Hertz's pompous air of superiority over all other men was like a sickening stench that offended all who crossed his path, and tonight, that path would be crossed by a shabbily dressed and unshaven old man, begging for a handout. As Hertz approached his carriage and driver, the elderly vagabond crept from the shadows and extended a tin cup held in one gnarled, arthritic hand. "Master Hertz, sir," he slurred, "the wife and children are deathly ill. If you could find it in your heart…"

Startled by the bum's sudden appearance and his senses dulled by tavern ale, Hertz immediately lifted his walking cane over his head. But when his eyes could at last focus on the perceived threat, he spat out a laugh. "Heart? I have no heart, you stinking rabble, and I couldn't give a damn about the family of a beggar!"

In a frighteningly violent move, Hertz swung the cane down upon the shoulders of the old man as he venomously shouted, "Don't you dare crawl to me again, you decrepit old bastard or I'll not think twice about killing you where you stand!"

The old man yelped and gripped his shoulder. Unconvinced that his message had been received, Hertz thrust out his boot and knocked the beggar onto his back. "Take me home," he commanded his driver, and with that, the aristocrat climbed into the black carriage and it was pulled into the night by twin black horses.

Ludwig Hertz was a man hated by all. His stature was assured by a healthy endowment he had inherited upon the passing of his father three years prior. It was an inheritance that he would share with no one, thus becoming not his good fortune, but his curse. As the coachman silently ushered his master up the wooded road leading from the hamlet of Inglestadt, the encroaching shadows on the dark lane seemed to thicken and reach inward, but Hertz was oblivious to anything other than his uneven equilibrium brought about by the evening's drink. The carriage lurched into a blackness as pitch as the heart of its owner.

A sickening crack resounded over the clatter of the horses' hooves as one of the rear wheels of the carriage split upon a large rock. The vehicle took a frightening dip backward, throwing Hertz against the upholstered seat and nearly hurling the driver from his loft. Acting quickly, the carriage man heeled the steeds and brought to a stop the conveyance whose damaged rear wheel had cut a deep rut into the dirt drive behind it.

Hertz screamed from the carriage's cabin. "Driver! I'm in no humor to be jostled about. I'm far too full of tavern ale to…"

Before he could complete the sentence, he realized that the driver was not on his perch and was already standing at the rear of the disabled carriage. "Damn it, man! Is it your intention to have yourself dismissed from my service tonight?" he shrilly shouted.

"I'm sorry, master Hertz. A rock in the road is what did in the back wheel," the driver explained. "I'm afraid we'll…"

"Perhaps you would like to rephrase your statement," Hertz scowled. "I will do nothing, while you will walk all the way back to Inglestadt and retrieve a replacement for the shattered wheel. And I won't be kept waiting here all night, is that clear?"

The constant browbeating that the driver endured from his insufferable master was nothing new. Without a word, Hertz's servant retrieved his top hat from the grass where it had tumbled during the accident, straightened his jacket, and marched back toward Inglestadt. But it wasn't until he was out of earshot of the carriage that he mumbled through his thick white mustache, "Go to hell, you arrogant bastard."

Hertz settled into his seat, gripping his walking cane and fuming about his bad luck, but the driver had only been absent for scant minutes before the nobleman realized that he would not make his wait in the blackness alone. A casual glance toward the surrounding woods revealed something unusual that caught his attention.

There was movement in the trees, or so he thought. He narrowed his eyes to focus them. Something was there—or more accurately, someone—and they walked slowly from the dark foliage. The face of the stranger was obscured, but the form beneath the hooded velvet cloak was feminine. As she drew closer to the carriage, Hertz could see voluminous crimson curls spilling from the hood and onto the ample bosom of the woman.

"I am Ludwig Hertz. Who goes there?" he called. There was no response, but the figure continued to approach with a measured but leisurely pace.

A man of his wealth—and particularly of his temperament— had nothing to fear, he assured himself, but he still held tightly to the curved-handled walking cane upon his lap. The figure came to a halt before the carriage door and slowly reached for her hood. As she revealed herself, Hertz inhaled sharply. She was the most astoundingly beautiful woman he had ever seen in his life.

"Do not be concerned, sir," the woman heartened. "I had no intention of startling you."

Hertz scoffed. "Startle me? I think not, girl. What do you want and why are you sneaking about in the woods at this hour?" he gently demanded.

A smile crossed the lips of the redheaded beauty. "By your indulgence, kind sir, I'd ask for your assistance."

Although her intent was yet to be revealed, the emerald eyes of the stranger convinced him that he would be a fool not to try to take advantage of the situation. "Let me offer you the comfort of my couch while you explain your plight." With that, he unlatched the door and swung it open as a spider might lure an insect into its web.

She sat quietly across from him as he assessed her from head to foot in a most lascivious manner. After a few moments, as if suddenly awakened from an impromptu nap, he snapped his head upward and straightened his posture. "If it's transport you're seeking, I'm afraid I'm temporarily waylaid by a broken wheel. I've sent my man to Inglestadt for a replacement, but it could be several hours before we're on our way again."

She did not seem concerned by the revelation. With a curt smile, she offered an alternative to waiting silently in the dark. "Perhaps we can just sit here and converse—just you and me— until you *can* make that offer."

"That would be delightful," he leered. "Warm company on a cool night, hmm? What is your name, my dear?"

She paused. "I would prefer to remain an anonymous passenger if you would not mind."

"You're in some kind of trouble, then, perhaps with the authorities?"

"That will remain my secret as well," she teased, before quickly changing the subject of conversation. "What a beautiful cane handle," she gushed, in admiration of the walking instrument that lie across the lap of Hertz. "Is that gold?"

"Solid gold," he bragged. "An heirloom that my father acquired in Portugal. But enough about me. Tell me about yourself and why you're so underdressed for a midnight walk in the woods." Hertz bent forward and glanced at the bare feet of his guest, her pale skin glowing in the moonlight. "Your lack of footwear does have me wondering if you wear any garments at all beneath that cloak." The statement wasn't so much of a question as it was a thinly-veiled inducement of seduction. His drunkenness was apparent, but he made every effort to gather his composure and convey an air of superiority, which usually led to him getting whatever it was that he wanted at the moment.

The woman smiled demurely. "You have me at a disadvantage, sir, and I suspect that I will have to confirm your suspicions before you will assist me further." With that, she leaned back and opened the cloak before him, just enough to reveal the twin inner curves of her breasts and her stomach. She teasingly pulled the cloak closed once again before he could fully digest what he had just seen.

Ludwig Hertz had long since learned that an aloof disposition often attracted the attention of the opposite sex and seeming disinterested in female companions occasionally spurred the objects of his momentary affection to pursue him. It was a game he quite enjoyed but his unexpected companion that evening was so physically striking that he had to remind himself of the rules he had written.

Even so, he felt that he must comment on what he had just seen. "Such lovely skin," he slurred. "Such a fine belly. What you've shown me—and some other quality about you—reminds me of someone I once knew."

The red-haired stranger leaned forward playfully, placing a hand on his knee. "I see in your eyes that you have a story to tell me about this girl," she suggested. "To pass the time until your driver returns, please honor me with your last recollections of her and do not leave out a single detail."

Hertz raised an eyebrow. It was an odd request but his mind was on only one thing at that moment: the lust he felt welling within him as he sat opposite the vivacious wanderer who fell from the darkness to within his reach.

"Every detail?" he asked.

"Every detail, no matter how intimate," she replied. Her response was exactly that for which Hertz had hoped. She had given him an open invitation to tell her a randy tale and he was certain that by its end she would be naked and grinding upon his lap.

He chuckled and looked deeply into her eyes. "Very well, my lady. I will tell you everything. Not a detail missing, as you request. But be warned, the memory is quite explicit," he cautioned.

"Everything," she repeated coyly.

And so, he began his tale. "As you must know, I am a very wealthy man. Wealthy and powerful. And I am accustomed to getting exactly what I want. In contrast to my assets, I own a modest estate near here, willed to me by my dear, late father. Since acquiring my wealth, it has been my belief not to waste money on people or possessions, for both will eventually turn to dust. Adhering to that philosophy, I will never take a wife, who would eventually squander all that I have amassed. I employ only my carriage driver and one maid. Her name was Gina, a beautiful blonde girl, another of my father's acquisitions, who I retained after his death. Aside from the most mundane of household chores, her charge was also to supply me with anything that I desired, at any time."

"One night, this past fall, I had returned from the inn at Inglestadt. As I passed the stable I noticed a lantern burning within. I investigated and found Gina at the pitcher pump over the well. She was filling a bucket with water. It was an unusually warm night for September—I believe it was September—and the stable stank of animals and manure. Perhaps that's what makes my remembrance of that evening so much more vivid."

"I approached her, and we had a conversation," he continued, deep in remembrance. "She wore a simple dress with the neckline pulled loose and falling past both shoulders. She was radiant and I wanted her. I put my arms around her from behind and kissed her neck as she re-locked the pump handle, and I remember telling her that the sweat on her skin smelled repulsive. She laughed and said, 'It repulses you or excites you, sir?'"

"Gina and I had a mutual understanding, you see, but that did not extend to the charity of allowing her to disrespect me. I reminded her of her place. I told her, 'Watch your tone, girl. I'm not some drunken peddler down in the village,' and as I did so I pulled her blouse down to her waist to reveal her glorious breasts. Her nipples were hard in anticipation. That sent a chill of excitement through me." He thought for a moment, recalling another detail. "Her only physical failing was an ugly, heart-shaped birthmark, dark pink in color, to one side of her navel. Anyhow, I had taken to my knees before her, and I ran my hand up the inside of her thigh, beneath her dress. Her mouth was open and she threw her head back in ecstasy as I slid my fingers between her lips. I felt her warm wetness."

Ludwig Hertz paused, as a more fully realized recollection came to mind. "Now that I'm remembering the entire scenario, I do recall something else we discussed at the time," he confided.

"And what was that," the cloaked visitor queried.

"We discussed that she was a witch."

The woman who sat across from him in the dark of the carriage seemed not at all disconcerted. "*Was* Gina a witch?" she asked.

Hertz seemed adamant in his response. "I'm sure of it. I was well aware of the pagan rituals she performed in her bedchamber. My father had shared her peculiarities with me before his death. I told her, 'You practice magic and I will keep your secret, as long as you continue to fuck me when I demand it.'"

"What did she say?"

"She thanked me, naturally," Hertz responded smugly. "I had nothing to lose and she had everything to lose. But if you consider the barter, she was receiving far more than me. She was the chosen consort of Ludwig Hertz," he crowed, without any attempt to conceal his massive egotism.

The mysterious woman smiled. "Please, continue," she implored.

"Well, what happened next was I took her. I turned her around and she bent against the bales of hay. I took her from behind. She gripped my cock so tightly within her and her moans of pleasure were so arousing that it wasn't long before I was ready to explode. I ordered her to get on her knees. We regularly had sexual relations, so she knew what to do."

"Did she take you in her mouth?" the woman asked, feigning naivete, but Hertz was too enraptured by his recollection to recognize the sly disingenuousness of her question.

"She did. I pulled my cock from her pussy and she swallowed the entire length of me. It was an incredible talent. Just incredible. I gripped the back of her head and began fucking her mouth, then pulled from her and came all over her beautiful face."

The silence in the carriage engulfed both Ludwig Hertz and his unscheduled companion, broken only when a chuckle escaped his lips.

"You laugh," the cloaked woman said. "Do you recall something else?"

"It's nothing. As she wiped her face, she said, 'That was incredible,' or something of the like, but she used my name, Ludwig. I reprimanded her for that. She was never to call me anything other than Master Hertz. But how could I blame the girl for dreaming? Because of my kindness to her, I wasn't surprised by her inappropriate familiarity. I'm sure in her simple mind, she concocted fantasies of one day being my wife. But as I said, I will never share my estate with a woman, especially not one so far below my station."

The crimson-haired woman shifted her weight upon the seat, settling back as if to quietly process all that she was hearing.

"I know she truly loved me," Hertz continued, "but I could see that she confused my lust for respect, and I would have to set her straight. I knew that resentment would soon grow from my blind eye to her infatuation, so I promptly severed her service with me. It was for her own good."

The woman looked into his eyes, her own filled with innocence. "Such a bawdy story. I feel a bit flushed, embarrassed even, by your frankness, sir."

"You desired to hear the tale, I simply complied with your request," he reminded her.

Her response was immediate. "But I sense that there is more to your story, perhaps other details you left out?"

Hertz became noticeably uncomfortable, adjusting his grip on the cane across his lap, clenching his fists around it in a telling fashion. "I left nothing out. There's nothing else to tell," he avowed with finality.

"I think there is," she countered, her gaze intensifying. An air of sinister underpinning permeated her words and it did not go unnoticed by the drunken nobleman.

"What are you getting at?" he demanded. "Just who are you?" It was the first time in the past half hour that Hertz realized he was alone, in the dark, with a woman who had walked out of the blackness that enveloped his disabled carriage. Should she harbor ill intent against him, there was no one to come to his aid. "Well? Who are you?" He demanded an answer.

"There are many things that I know about you, Ludwig," she revealed with silken venomousness, "such as what else happened that night and what was Gina's true fate."

Hertz was livid as beads of nervous sweat began to form at his hairline beneath the thick black curls that covered his head. The woman did nothing but smile, the intensity of her gaze drilling deeper into his own and it was then that dizziness began to wash over him. He tried to snap himself from its grip but the sensation grew until he felt as if he was being held underwater and his hearing had warped into an unsettling echo chamber. Even on nights in the past when he had overindulged past his limit, never had he experienced hallucinations, for surely that is what this was. But try as he might, he could not move and was at the complete mercy of whatever imbalance was assailing him.

His eyes darted nervously about the interior of the carriage before once again locking onto hers, the emerald of her own eyes growing in intensity and brightness, not unlike white-hot coals. It was then that he realized that her voice had become oddly ethereal. But the words did not fall from her perfect lips. The words were inside his head.

"What happened then, Ludwig Hertz?" the ghost-like voice asked knowingly.

Hertz suddenly found himself outside of his own body, or perhaps within his mind. After a brief sensation of falling as if into the pit of Hell itself, he was back in the barn that past September. Before him was Gina, wiping the semen from her face and pulling her blouse upward to cover her breasts.

"As usual, my dear, you were enormously entertaining," he said to the young woman. There were other words the baffled Hertz wanted to say, but he was incapable of uttering anything beyond what had been spoken at that moment in the past. He was imprisoned in memories. "Now get back to your chores," he commanded harshly.

Gina was unmoved. "Yes, sir. But I wonder if it would be in your heart to…"

Hertz helplessly re-lived his annoyance with the servant he had just fucked. "Effectively maintaining an estate does not require a heart."

Gina was insistent that she be heard. "I must tell you, I'll need an increase in my wages soon. You see, I'll need additional money in the months to come unless you agree to marry me and claim the child that I carry in my belly. *Your* child, sir."

"I'll have none of it! Harlot! How dare you seek to coerce me into…"

"You know that the child is yours," she whispered most resolutely.

Once again, he could feel the fury burning within him, just as it had that night. "Enough! I'll not hear another word from you! As of this instant, you are no longer in my employ."

Hertz felt the sensation of rushing headlong into a hurricane-force wind. His vision blurred and to his relief, the interior of the barn was replaced by the luxurious confines of his carriage. The mysterious woman still sat in the shadows opposite him on the upholstered bench.

"And you remember what you did next, don't you Ludwig?" she asked as if she already knew the answer to her question.

"No!" he screamed in an absolute panic. "What is happening to me?" Again, he plunged into the past, and again he faced Gina in the lantern-lit barn. Hertz was helpless as he watched himself repeat his actions from months before when he slid the concealed, razor-sharp dagger from the confines of his cane handle and proceeded to butcher the girl.

With a jolt that shook him to the very foundation of his reality, Hertz was thrust from his horrible reminiscence to the present. The crimson-haired woman glared at him, only her eyes visible in the shadows of the night. "It was a brutal and vicious bloodbath for which you still feel no remorse. And all because of greed."

Hertz was now sweating profusely and his hands shook uncontrollably. "Then what did you do, Ludwig?" she hissed. "I'll tell you what you did. You sold Gina's hacked and bloodied corpse to two men of questionable reputation, with an additional bonus paid to them to ensure their silence."

"But how? Are you a witch?" he sputtered. "You're in league with Gina, is that it?"

Her response was as steely as her glare. "I am no witch, Ludwig Hertz. I am a woman." With that, she opened her cloak to reveal her entire body to him.

Despite the antagonism that was now shared between them, his heart still skipped a beat in anticipation of seeing her nakedness but his sexual fantasy was immediately dashed. As the cloak parted at the center of her body, it was as if her facial features were repainted before his eyes by some otherworldly hand to reveal a network of scars and surgical sutures that covered her face and flowed down over her neck and across her entire body. As his eyes fell upon her lower torso, the revelation of a heart-shaped birthmark on one side of her navel left his subconscious screaming in terror.

"That birthmark! You can't be…!" he cried.

"But I am, Ludwig Hertz," she glowered. "I am Gina. And I am so much more."

Frantic, Hertz's fists clenched not only in rage but in fear. He held them up before him, ready to strike out at whatever kind of hideous beast it was that had cornered him with knowledge of a crime that would surely send him to the gallows. "You can't prove a word of it!" he said in his defense. "Ghost or demon or whatever you are, you can't touch me! The law can't touch me, or shall I say they are paid not to touch me. Is that what you want? Money?"

The strange creature merely laughed. "What use have I for money?" she said, deflating his attempt to escape the exposure of his murderous act. "I want only to touch you, as Gina once did." His protests for her to keep her distance were ignored and she reached out both stitched hands toward his own, still raised in front of him. "One last touch, dear Ludwig."

The creation slid the fingers of both hands between his and pressed her palms against his own, and as he watched, she wrenched both of her hands upward, bending his fingers backward at an impossible angle. The sudden movement simultaneously dislocated all eight of his digits, separating ligament from bone.

Hertz screamed as her fingernails dug into the backs of his hands, cutting through flesh and knuckle. With one vicious motion, she ripped the fingers from both of his hands as he howled in shock, blood pouring from his mangled appendages.

As horrific as the damage was to his utterly ruined hands, she was not yet done with Ludwig Hertz. The full, terrifying toll of Gina's thirst for revenge had not yet been calculated.

A horned owl howled from somewhere in the forest as the driver at last returned from Inglestadt with a replacement for the ruined carriage wheel. The horses stood silently as did the carriage itself. The driver assumed that his master must have fallen asleep in his absence, which was all the better for him. Hertz would not be aware of the passage of time and it would be one less thing about which to berate his servant. As the carriage man rested the wooden wheel against the conveyance's frame, out of the corner of his eye he noticed something reflecting the moonlight beneath the carriage door.

To his revulsion, the driver found that blood had pooled on the ground below the door, and as he looked upward he found that the gore was dripping from the inner traveling compartment.

"Master Hertz?" wavered the driver's voice. "Are you in there?" he stammered. There came no response. His mind brimming with absolute dread, the driver turned the handle of the carriage door and slowly opened it. What he found inside the blood-splattered compartment was the corpse of Ludwig Hertz, his body violently mutilated, his shirt ripped open at his breast. The driver stepped upward to closer inspect his murdered master. His quivering hands separated the bloody shirt, then turned his head and violently vomited upon seeing the shredded flesh and broken ribs of the body, pulled outward from the chest cavity and the gaping hole wherein Ludwig Hertz's heart once rested.

It would be the next morning when the scene of the ghastly crime was investigated by the local authorities that the final punctuation to the previous night's horrific attack was revealed. In attendance at the crime scene was a young local lawman, Sergeant Klaus, accompanied with a British man by the name of Inspector Jason Pike. The detective was vacationing in the area and due to the short-staffing of the local constabulary, he was called upon by Klaus to assist in the investigation. Found conspicuously positioned atop the driver's seat was the carriage's emptied wooden toolbox. Through its lid had been plunged the prized solid gold handle and attached dagger once concealed inside the hollow body of the victim's walking cane.

Within the oak box lay the pale organ that had once pumped blood through the body of Ludwig Hertz.

REDEMPTION

PERCEPTIVE

PURIFYING

PROTECTION

CHAPTER SIXTEEN
REFLECTION OF THE DEAD

Falcona lay still beneath the sheets, watching the shadows of tree limbs and leaves play across the far wall of her bedchamber. It was well past two in the morning and once again her overactive mind was preventing a stroll through dreamland. Since the visitation of the ghost within her sanctum weeks before, the routine of falling fast asleep for two or three hours and then waking and remaining so for a similar period before again falling asleep was becoming tiresome. The sheet she had placed over the mirror glowed white against the dark paneling of the wall, but she made a concerted effort each night to not even glance in its direction for fear of invoking another visit from the specter.

Estevan and Falcona now led such simple lives in the employ of Dr. Also Zorn, but the mundane exterior of the castle hid unbelievable horrors that the unwitting villagers of Kleinburg could never have imagined. Those secrets were reserved only for the consciences of Falcona and her brother. It was a weight that was nearly unbearable, particularly when the shadows of the night encroached upon her as she lay alone in the quiet of her room. In her insomnolence, Falcona's mind traveled a well-worn path of inner reflection colored by uncertainty and self-doubt. This night was going to be no different.

Since the death of their parents and the siblings' departure from the family farm in Spain, Falcona found very little opportunity to develop personal relationships with anyone other than her brother. They were always on the move, from one job to the next, one town to the next, leaving little to no opportunity to generate any form of lasting connection with those around them. They were vagabonds, but at least they had each other.

Still, when her thoughts turned to the other young women she had known in her youth in Spain, a pang of jealousy rustled within her, along with a tinge of regret. By now, all of her childhood companions were happily wed and raising families of their own as she worked her fingers to the bone, all while being aware that at any moment she and her brother might once again pack their belongings and hit the road for parts unknown. Falcona recognized, however, that her independent streak relished that freedom but as the years passed she began to wonder if and when the call would come for her to settle down and plant permanent roots. And if she did so, what would become of Estevan? Since Falcona was older than him, he had always looked to her as his spiritual and moral guide. It would be selfish to presume that if she changed the course of her life he should do the same. Still, the two had relied on each other so heavily since the untimely demise of their parents that the thought of not having Estevan at her side was impossible to imagine.

So she lay, thinking, as the hours passed. In some other place, at some other time, she would have taken advantage of the quiet and solitude to pleasure herself but she was mortified by the thought that she might be watched by the otherworldly inhabitant of the castle as she rubbed herself to climax. It had crossed her mind, though, that the female ghost could have been an observer when Falcona paid the visit to Zorn's basement laboratory a few weeks hence and had witnessed the carnal behavior she displayed on the stone floor of the underground chamber. *But so what? Why be ashamed of being a woman with natural desires? Was the ghost not once a woman herself, possessing the same urges and needs?* It had been weeks since she last experienced release and the remembrance of Zorn's stiff cock rubbing against her clit as she slid along the length of his manhood evoked a tingle between her legs.

The unusual sound that broke her intimate reverie was distant but in the silence of the late hour, it was all too distinct. She heard, as clear as day, the unique sound made by the front door latch as it clicked into place.

Someone had either entered or exited the castle.

Innate curiosity overrode all as Falcona sprang from the bed, donned her peignoir, and silently crept from her bedchamber, a lit candle in hand.

Moving like a ghost herself, the young Spaniard placed an ear to the bedroom doors of both Estevan and Dr. Zorn, but only the sounds of sleep emanated from within. What she had heard was probably the result of an overactive imagination, or it might simply have been a squirrel or other rodent on a nocturnal mission. That was probably it. Still, to be sure, she stealthily made her way down the staircase to the marble foyer and the front door. The heavy wooden portal was closed and locked, and nothing seemed amiss, but as she prepared to return to her room, something caught her eye.

Hanging on the hook beside the massive door was Falcona's hooded cloak, which had hung there untouched since the last time she had worn it. But closer inspection revealed dark spots upon one portion of the crushed velvet. It was something wet. She held her fingers before the candlelight.

It was blood. Fresh, red blood.

She raised the candle high, looking all about her to the door and walls but it was on the floor that the yellow glow of the flame illuminated something that produced a clipped exhale from her lips. There, imprinted on the flagstones, were traces of moisture and dirt in roughly the shape of naked human feet. The tracks proceeded from the door, across the mansion's front room, and up the staircase that led to the southeastern turret of the castle. Falcona looked to the landing above the staircase and the long-ignored door to the secret passage to the basement laboratory.

There could be only one explanation: The woman of Zorn's scientific creation—the being into which she had seen Madame Sabina breathe life and who had since been locked in confinement in the laboratory—had escaped her imprisonment and was moving freely about the castle.

It wasn't a matter of whether or not she was frightened. In truth, she was. But Falcona could not resist reaching out in compassion to the creature in the basement. She thought of her own loneliness and what the unfortunate being in the laboratory must be feeling, and it was the only propulsion necessary to urge Falcona on, down the rusted spiral staircase to the castle's lowest level, and to the gated alcove that lie forgotten at the back of Zorn's laboratory.

With only the candle to illuminate the dark recess, she stood before the gate and held her breath. When viewed from the proper angle, the layer of moisture on the stone floor disclosed bare footprints that led from the bottom of the spiral staircase to the gate before which she now hesitated. Beyond the rusted barrier lurked the patchwork woman, alone in the blackness. The splatters of blood on her cloak upstairs lingered in Falcona's mind, but she buried her concerns about personal safety and pushed against the ancient iron gate.

The creation sat pensively on the mattress, swathed in the absolute blackness as Falcona cautiously approached from behind, her candle throwing a dim, warm light upon the room. The woman of Zorn's creation was nude, the nightgown once belonging to Falcona draped across her lap, and as the young housekeeper approached, she squinted to adjust her vision. What had looked to her like stitching and scars across the back of the creation seemed to melt and fade into fine, smooth flesh when the odd woman looked her way. *An illusion of the light as it pushed against the darkness. That's what it must have been,* Falcona assured herself.

The sitting woman seemed neither startled nor demure and the welcoming softness of her features soothed Falcona's frayed nerves. It was not only the fear of the unknown that weighed upon her but also the dread of how Zorn would respond should he find her in his forbidden inner sanctum. She would deal with that later if the situation arose. For now, her focus was on the welfare of Zorn's creation.

"My name is Falcona," she spoke softly. "I live upstairs. I keep house for the doctor." She could not know if the creation understood her words but she had faith that if she maintained an amicable demeanor the being would respond positively. "Can you tell me your name?" she asked, unsure if the question would be emotionally devastating to a being composed of multiple dead women.

The response was measured and unaffected by emotion as if the creation was completely unvexed by her ungodly state of being. "I have no name," she replied, before articulating in a more eloquent fashion than Falcona had expected. "It is my understanding that Dr. Zorn is acutely protective of this laboratory and would be angered if he knew that you've come here against his wishes," she warned.

"I don't care," Falcona snapped haughtily. "I am here for you. I want to help you. I don't want to disturb you and if you want to be left alone I will comply. But I want you to understand that if you have any questions, I'm here. I will be your friend if you would like."

The creation smiled warmly but for Falcona, there was something that needed to be addressed and ground that needed to be tread with the utmost lightness and sensitivity. "Do you...do you know why you are here?" the Spanish woman queried.

The creation cocked her head, her expression becoming a bit more sullen. "I do. But do *you* know why I am here?" she asked Falcona directly.

The Spanish woman brushed a strand of black hair from her face, gathered her strength, and admitted what she knew. As delicately as possible, she described what she had read in Zorn's journal and what she had seen the night that Madame Sabina infused the creation with consciousness. The nude woman nodded in affirmation. The prospect of learning more about the fantastic creation thrilled Falcona and her heart fluttered like a caged bird within her breast. Her eagerness was tempered by melancholy, however, for she looked upon the creation as a pitiable figure and inwardly wept for the unholy condition.

To reassure the woman of her goodwill, Falcona offered, "I'm very much impressed by your composure, in light of how you came to be."

The woman appeared introspective for a moment, then responded. "I suppose I am composed. If this is life, I must accept it. I cannot and do not feel jealous of what others know of our existence, because I have nothing to which I can compare my feelings. All I know of life is what I now feel in the moment."

"And what is that?" Falcona asked.

"Lost," was the morose reply.

Suddenly overcome by compassion, Falcona swept away all of her fears and dropped to her knees before the woman, then wrapped her arms around her in a warm embrace. It was an impulsive move, but one she could not contain, and Falcona's heart melted when the pale being returned her endearing gesture.

They sat in each other's arms for what felt to Falcona like an eternity and as she held the creation a shocking realization crept into her mind. Across the nude back of the woman, Falcona felt irregularities on the surface of her skin, like scars threaded with sutures, but there was nothing visibly amiss about the creation that she could see with her eyes. It didn't matter to Falcona one way or the other. Everyone has hidden scars that they conceal from others, whether they be physical or mental and she held the crimson-haired being even closer.

At last, they parted and as Falcona looked down at the creation's hands she found them smeared with dried blood. The dark-haired beauty looked deeply into the eyes of the pale woman with an intensity that spoke of an oath of secrecy. Whose blood was on the woman's hands greatly concerned her and why the creation had returned to the castle after her escape was perplexing but those were topics that could be addressed with time.

"Let's get you washed up, shall we?" Falcona chirped with a smile.

At Zorn's wooden workstation, the young housekeeper rescued a large sponge from among the scientific refuse littering the table, then pumped fresh water into a shallow surgical basin. She spotted a towel and as she reached to retrieve it, a collection of stoppered bottles caught her attention. One, in particular, piqued her curiosity. It possessed flat sides, with a white paper label affixed to its front surface. Inscribed upon the label were the words *Conium maculatum*. Distracted from the duty she had just offered to perform, Falcona lifted the dust-encrusted bottle and wiped one side of its surface.

The glass of the bottle was green and the words of the castle's specter rang through her memory. She whispered aloud the ghost's cryptic message from several weeks past. "The boy, the green bottle, they are below."

Falcona held the object aloft to observe its contents, and as she did the glass caught the reflection of the creation, now standing directly behind the young Spaniard. Her eyes widened in disbelief, for upon the polished surface of the bottle she beheld the visage of the being behind her, only now the face was covered by a series of scars and stitching. Falcona whirled in alarm but there was no threat evident from the red-haired creation, only a look of curiosity written by her perfectly composed features, completely devoid of the hideous surgical scars that Falcona has just observed in the reflection. The creation smiled and held out one hand.

"What have you there?" she asked, as Falcona nervously handed her the bottle. "*Conium maculatum*," the creation read from the label. "That is the scientific name for hemlock," she stated with self-assurance.

"How do you know that?" Falcona asked.

"I don't know," the creation confided. "But I am certain of what it is. It's a deadly poison." With that, she placed the bottle back on the worktable where it had rested for years, then rubbed her hands together and examined the dried blood that encrusted the cuticles of her fingernails.

Falcona soaked the sponge in the water, then took one of the creation's hands into her own and ran the sponge over its surface. "Maybe in one of your former lives you were a doctor," she conjectured, referring to her pale companion's identification of the deadly poison within the bottle. The other woman did not respond, she simply watched as the crimson water dripped from her delicate fingers into the basin. Soon, the nails, cuticles, and fingers of one hand were clean, and as Falcona ran the wet sponge over the palm she spoke what was foremost in her mind since the revelation of the green bottle's contents.

"In your time down here, have you ever seen a strange woman in the shadows of this laboratory?"

"Other than you?" The emerald eyes of the creation sparkled, a playful smile on her lips.

Falcona laughed. "Yes, other than me. What I mean to ask is, have you ever seen a ghost in this room? And if you have, has it ever spoken to you?"

"Falcona, do you believe in the supernatural?" the creation asked.

"Well, I believe in you, don't I?" Falcona cajoled as she began cleaning the woman's other hand. "Have you seen a ghost down here?" she repeated.

The creation revealed that she had seen the ghost, with the same indifference as one would express while describing seeing a robin alight in a tree on a spring day. As she continued her work, Falcona recounted the frightening story of her encounter with the specter and of the strange message it had imparted to her. Those haunting words pointed not only to the laboratory—the "below" portion of her warning—but also to the green bottle specifically. The only thing missing from the puzzle was the identity of the boy, to whom the ghost referred.

The creation dried her hands, noting the pained expression on Falcona's face. "I can see that the message from this castle's ghostly keeper greatly concerns you. This is a case that calls for deductive reasoning," she said soothingly, allowing Falcona to fit the pieces together for herself. The two stood in silence but it did not take long before the truth revealed itself to the young Spanish woman. She slapped the sponge down on the counter.

"The boy is Dr. Zorn," she said in epiphany. "And the ghost is that of Isadora, the former owner of this castle. Dr. Zorn's sister Freeda revealed her name to me on a visit she made here." Falcona let the theory thoroughly sink into her and the more she considered it, the more she became convinced that it was the truth. "Dr. Zorn had studied medicine since he was a child, he told me as much. And Isadora Luca died here—and the castle entrusted to the Zorn family—when Aldo was just…"

The creation was emotionless. "When he was just a boy," she whispered, completing Falcona's thought.

Dr. Zorn's bedchamber was decadent in its ornate beauty. When occupied by the late Isadora Luca, the room exuded the aura of a stately museum, every surface of the finely polished mahogany furnishings bedecked with treasures from around the globe, and exquisitely painted oils framed in gold dominated every wall. In the years since the chamber's original mistress departed the mortal coil, thick dust had settled upon every surface and the precious metals had lost their luster. Still, the austere ambiance of the chamber remained intact. Had Falcona been allowed to clean and dust the room, as she so meticulously did throughout the rest of Castle Zorn, the chamber would be remarkably pristine, but the doctor vehemently forbade her entrance to the room and kept the door securely locked. The housekeeper was perplexed by the command, but it was yet another idiosyncrasy of her employer to which she grudgingly but suspiciously acquiesced.

The secrets the doctor guarded within the chamber were not physical belongings, but rather his fragile twisted psyche. There was nothing discernably amiss or hidden within the room. But aside from his laboratory, it was the only place where he could be alone, away from the eyes of others, where he could obsessively dwell upon a lifetime of psychological repression and unbridled egotism. In that solitude, he also dwelt upon his frustrations, both sexual, and now, professional. The little time he spent in the chamber during waking hours was awash with introspection and anger, usually accompanied by masturbation as he fantasized about Magdaline and the numerous corpses of dead women who had been delivered into his possession. The bounds of his hidden depravity were grotesque beyond measure, and now, after being spurned by the mate he had constructed with surgical precision, the burning frustration began to eat at him from within, just as maggots devour an unattended cadaver.

The sheet beneath his bare back was saturated with acrid perspiration. Since retiring for the night, he had restlessly tossed spasmodically, his attempted slumber fraught by nightmares as it had been for weeks. Zorn had become a walking dead man, the lack of sleep taking a terrible toll on his concentration and focus, his mind beguiled by that he could not possess nor understand. The slightest inconveniences that presented themselves in the past fifteen days provoked unreasonable responses and he found himself smashing bottles and pounding his fists against solid wood out of frustration with even the most inconsequential of conundrums.

Sleep was his only refuge, but even that was met by abject failure and vexation. Even now, a scenario played before his mind's eye of the lovely Magdaline, perfect in her nakedness, tauntingly beyond his reach. She was there, upon his bed, her legs spread seductively to display her womanhood to him. Try as he might, Zorn could not reach her, as an unnatural force pressed against him and made impotent his attempts to advance toward her. She laughed at his struggle and mocked him as he screamed in anger. "You are a failure!" she laughed repeatedly, "A failure!" His teeth gnashed as he pressed forward toward the bed but the phantom wall that separated him from Magdaline would not be breached.

A wave of anger welled within him as he had never before felt and with one last Herculean effort, his dream self thrust forward successfully and fell toward Magdaline's naked form. But as he reached out to her, she dissolved into blackness, her body and the bed itself transforming into a yawning, ebon chasm into which he fell screaming.

Zorn awoke with a start, drenched in sweat, his heart beating wildly. Between his legs, his penis was engorged to its maximum, the rock-hard phallus bobbing in futility. He cursed its insistence. Something had to be done. Somehow, the torment had to end. His sexual fury must be unleashed, but the perfect copulation toy he had constructed from dead bodies might kill him if he again tried to seduce her. There was only one other option available to him.

The silk pajama pants he wore barely concealed his still-turgid member as he rapped lightly on the door to Falcona's bedchamber, making every effort not to be heard by Estevan, whose room was at the end of the hallway. Zorn and the housekeeper had only shared one sexual encounter but he reasoned that seeing him shirtless before her in the dead of night would kindle the fires of Falcona's passion and she would happily invite him to her bed. Again he lightly knocked but his attempt to rouse her went unanswered. The door was unlocked and he pushed it open. Falcona was not in her bed, nor was she anywhere in the room.

On the main floor of the castle, Zorn's search turned up nothing. Falcona was nowhere to be found, not even in the drawing room where he knew she would occasionally sneak sips from the bourbon decanter. The only other possibility was that she had gone outdoors, although he could not fathom what could have prompted her to make such an excursion in the dead of night. The impromptu game of hide-and-seek only frustrated him further, and he considered going back to his room but the remembrance of her firm breasts, her thin waist, the roundness of her hips...No. He would find Falcona, and she would submit to him that night.

Zorn opened the door and stepped into the moonlight, scanning the encroaching forest that surrounded the estate but could see nothing of the young woman. He turned and walked back through the ancient portal. Before he could close the door behind him he realized that he was not alone.

"May I ask what you are doing, Doctor?" Estevan snarled in the darkness. The scientist was startled by the sudden appearance of the young Spaniard but quickly regained his composure.

"How dare you question me," Zorn shot back, "and what business is it of yours?"

Estevan's glare was steely. "When you enter my sister's room in the middle of the night, it is my business," he snarled. " Now where is Falcona?" her brother angrily demanded.

Years of research, experimentation, and surgeries, weeks of frustration after his crushing rejection by the creation, and now the circumvention of his nocturnal quest all came to a crashing head within the mind of the scientist. Something snapped within him, but outwardly, he made no indication that anything was amiss. He simply smirked at Estevan, shrugged with his hands held wide, then looked down at his semi-erection, jutting defiantly against his thin sleep pants.

"If I knew where your sister was, I'd be fucking her right now," Zorn snidely quipped.

The fury of the young Spanish man was unbound by the doctor's crude statement and he thrust himself upon him, pushing Zorn violently to the wall. No words were necessary, as the action spoke for itself. Zorn rose his hands in defense, but Estevan already had his forearm pressed firmly against the scientist's throat, his other hand balled into a fist. For his entire life, Estevan had protected and defended Falcona, and she had done likewise for her younger brother, but if there was any truth to what Zorn insinuated—or if Falcona had any desire for the scientist—it did not matter. She was his guiding light and no one would diminish the glow she generated in the eyes of her younger brother.

A flash of panic shot through the consciousness of Dr. Zorn but being a young man himself, he possessed the strength to overcome his attacker. In one sudden burst, he roughly pushed Estevan away from him, breaking the hold he had upon his neck before it could completely cut off the flow of air to his lungs.

They stood in the darkness, facing one another. It was a stalemate.

Zorn glowered at Estevan. "I'll ask you the same question you asked of me. "Where is Falcona?"

"Go to hell, you bastard," Estevan shot back. "We know everything," the dark-haired man revealed rashly. "We know what you're doing down there in your lab. If you touch me again or threaten my sister in any way, the authorities will hear of your experiments. We'll let them decide whether they are legitimate science or crimes that will put a noose around your neck."

Estevan realized too late that his outburst had just doomed him and his sister to dismissal from Zorn's service but it did not matter. They could effortlessly track the location of the traveling carnival that once employed them and the band of entertainers would surely welcome the siblings' return to their circle with open arms.

Estevan's admission sent a chill through the doctor. The Spaniard was right. If the result of his research was revealed to his peers in the halls of academia, it would be more readily accepted and he stood a decreased chance that his methods would be questioned. But if presented to a Bürgermeister and the uneducated, God-fearing throng that supported him, Zorn would be branded a heretic. Worse, should the lowly Leuthar and Hugo resurface and offer their insight into his work, he would soon dangle from the end of a hangman's noose in the Kleinburg town square. But most upsetting to the doctor was that somehow, despite the abundant protection of his secrecy, the truth had come out. After all that he had done for his house staff, they had betrayed his trust. That was unforgivable.

"How is it that you know what you think you know?" Zorn hissed. "Which of you is the trespasser, you or your sister, or both of you?" he demanded.

Estevan was silent. He had already said too much. It was then that the scientist spied the open door upon the landing of the staircase that traversed the south and east walls of the castle, brightly illuminated by moonbeams that poured through the tall cathedral windows of the second floor of the grand entry hall. Estevan, too, noticed the open door but before he could react, Zorn furiously bolted for the stone stairway. Up the steps he bounded, followed closely by Estevan. The younger man did not know to what lengths Zorn would go to protect his secrets and he feared for the safety of his sister who was surely the author of the door's opening. Esteban had to work fast. Upon the landing, his hands caught one of Zorn's arms before he could pass through the doorway and onto the spiral staircase hidden within the cobweb-enshrouded blackness of the turret.

"Leave her alone!" Estevan shouted, pulling Zorn away from the door, but in a surge of adrenalin, the scientist wildly flung his fist, catching the Spaniard across the jaw.

The blow momentarily stunned Falcona's brother. Zorn took advantage of Estevan's unbalance and struck out with both hands against the chest of his antagonist. The young man fell awkwardly against the precipitous stone stairway and struck his head numerous times on the unyielding granite steps as he tumbled hideously to their bottom.

He did not rise, nor did he move.

Estevan breathed no more.

Zorn looked down upon the corpse of the young Spaniard and then descended into the blackened pit that lie at the base of the southeastern tower.

Curling tendrils of smoke rose from the snuffed wicks of several candles in the gloom of Madame Sabina's inner sanctum. Rested upon the table was the result of an oracle card reading but the woman who had dealt the card had either hurriedly departed or melted into the dark and disappeared. Considering Madame Sabina's reputation with the local villagers, they would all agree that the second option was not outside the realm of possibilities.

The reading she left behind was disturbing and must have been the provocation for her hasty departure. The cryptic message related by the Oracle was "agonizing finale." Most unsettling was the image that adorned the top card. It depicted the face of a haunting apparition, draped in white, with deep black wells of despair in place of eyes.

Into the ebon forest and down the wooded lane that led to Castle Zorn, the cartomancer gingerly trekked on foot, her deep green cloak swallowed by the night's dark maw.

CHAPTER SEVENTEEN
REVELATIONS

A shroud of foreboding gloom lay heavily upon the two women in the dark confines of the laboratory. Dr. Zorn possessed the only key to the door of the underground chamber but the iron gate that led to the southeast turret and freedom for both of them was unlocked.

There was much to which Zorn must answer, but Falcona's inner voice insistently urged her to first consider flight; she could confront Zorn at a later date after she and Estevan had secured a safe harbor with the traveling Romani carnival. At the moment, Falcona wanted nothing more than to take the hand of the red-tressed woman and lead her away from the castle and into the night but a perplexing question still lingered unanswered. She watched as the creation let drop the nightgown over her breasts until the garment's bottom hem brushed the top of her bare feet.

"I must know," the dark-haired young woman uttered delicately as she and the creation sat on the mattress. "It's clear that you left the castle earlier. I traced your footprints from the front door to the tower, then down here. I don't know what you did while you were away. That is none of my business. But why did you come back?"

The creation thought for a moment, clearly wrestling with the conundrum. As she collected her thoughts, she plumbed the depths of her psyche, trying desperately to pull together the stings of ephemeral emotions that could be woven into an explanation for her strange actions. The creation's head swayed gently from side to side as she subconsciously followed one dead-end path after another; she desperately hoped that one of those trains of thought would lead to enlightenment, but a logical justification for her actions eluded her.

Why *did* she return?

She could not reach a reasonable conclusion to her self-examination and admitted the unsatisfying revelation to her raven-haired companion, whose gaze fell upon the now-clean hands of the creation.

One slender hand came to rest upon the knee of Falcona. "I hear voices inside my mind," the creation explained, knowing that as much as Falcona sought to comprehend her bizarre state of being, she could not possibly relate. Falcona was one of the living but the creation continued regardless. "There is not just one voice inside my mind, but many. They are pure and sweet, and I hear their whispers. But when I focus on a singular voice, I can feel a burning rage behind it. There is anger and frustration, and they all urge me to open myself to them, but I keep the voices buried," she paused regretfully, "out of fear."

"I see. Have you spoken of this to Dr. Zorn?" Falcona asked hesitantly.

"I have not," the creation responded.

Falcona was relieved. She had only spent a short time with the creation, but already she had come to feel protective of her and did not want Zorn to know any more about her than he already did.

"They, the voices, they warn me not to tell him," the creation continued, "but they have allowed me to tell you, Falcona. Either they trust you, or they distrust him," she reasoned suspiciously. "But there's more. Tonight, I allowed one of the voices to be heard fully and I gave her a platform on which to express herself. Her tale was hideous and I came to understand her anger and sadness in an instant."

Falcona was bewildered. "I confess, I'm a bit confused. Someone in your mind was talking to you?"

"You asked if I believe in ghosts," the creation noted. "I do, Falcona. The voices within me…They are ghosts," she revealed, to the shock of her companion. "I do not know how it is possible, but this body—built from the dead flesh of untold women—is alive with their voices and their thoughts and their celestial essences. I hear them all," she said solemnly, "And they are not happy."

"How dare you!" the enraged Aldo Zorn screamed from the darkness, his voice entrapping the two women after rebounding from the chill, stone walls of the laboratory. Only Falcona flinched at the utterance, but both women turned to face the barechested blonde scientist as he stalked from the shadows, fists clenched and knuckles white. "After all I have done for you, you would betray my trust?" he shrieked. "Get to your room, now!" he commanded of Falcona, his eyes ablaze with a fury that spoke of crushing disappointment, personal insult, and the slow roil of insanity, bubbling just beneath the surface of his composure. On bare feet, he stalked toward the mattress at the chamber's epicenter as the women stood to meet his advance.

Zorn had not reckoned with Falcona's inner fire. She would not be intimidated by words, particularly not when the safety of the sorrowful red-haired creation was in question. She stood her ground as he approached and defiantly stared into his eyes. "I will do as I please, you arrogant prick," she hissed.

"You've forgotten who is your master?" Zorn spat venomously, now within arms reach of Falcona. "I'll not have my creation soiled by association with a common whore," his voice stabbed as his open palm flew toward the face of the Spaniard.

After a short lifetime of fending for herself and her younger brother in one strange town after the next, Falcona had learned much and was always prepared for the worst in any confrontational situation. She deftly bent back and avoided the hand that was propelled by the entirety of Zorn's unbridled anger. Before he realized that his slap had missed her smooth face, her right hand shot out in a graceful swing that snapped his head to one side and ripped through his flesh, leaving behind three deep scratches across his cheek and nose.

Never in his life had Aldo Zorn been struck in such a way and the shock of the assault stunned him into silence. His utter embarrassment was significantly compounded by the fact that he had been made to look ineffectual in full view of the woman he had surgically constructed from corpses, the woman whom he had designed to worship him as his feet and in his bed. The haze of rage blurred the periphery of his sight, but he knew that the creation must be staring at him, analyzing his behavior, and making a judgment on his character as a man. The commoner who he had rescued one year ago from a life of depravity and lawlessness was unraveling all that had taken him decades to achieve.

The red wave of bloodlust surged through him, but no, to kill Falcona, to throttle her until her face turned blue in front of the creation would leave scars upon the creature's psyche that could never be undone. A different tactic was necessary to regain his dominance of the women in the room. He must take control and shame his house servant before the creation. He must reveal how, in the very chamber in which they stood, she had begged him to fuck her only weeks prior. Not only would the revelation dissolve the strength of Falcona's assertiveness, but he hoped it would elevate his desirability in the eyes of his creation.

To Zorn's dismay, the mind of Falcona worked at an astounding pace and quickly parried before he could even draw his verbal sword. "I know what you did, Aldo Zorn," Falcona seethed. "We both do," she said, tilting her head toward the patchwork woman at her side.

"Shut your mouth, you syphilitic trollop. You're mad, your mind filled with delusional fantasies. Get to your room, I said!" he commanded.

Falcona stood her ground, stepping to one side between Zorn and his creation. "She knows what she is, you know. And we both know what you are," she blurted. "You, Aldo Zorn, are a murderer!"

"A pitiful lie! I've harmed no one, you ignorant bitch. I have never…"

"When you were a child, Dr. Zorn?" Falcona interrupted. "Is it not true that when you were studying to become a doctor, you visited this castle with your father? And I assume by your father's instruction, did you not bring with you a green bottle containing hemlock?"

The face of the young doctor froze into a mask of absolute guilt and terror. "No!" he screamed. "I did no such thing!"

"And did you not somehow poison the owner of this estate, resulting in her excruciating death only days later?" Falcona leveled.

"No!" Zorn screamed shrilly.

"You murdered her, Aldo Zorn!" the young woman shouted. "You murdered Isadora Luca!"

At the utterance of the name, a low moan filled the chamber and grew in volume and intensity until it fully manifested in an ear-piercing shriek that vibrated the very bones of Zorn, Falcona, and the creation. It came from nowhere, yet was everywhere, a cacophonous din that overwhelmed the senses of all in the laboratory. It was a scream of pain and release, as the voicing of her name in the presence of her foul murderer freed the specter of Isadora Luca from the otherworldly shackles that few on this Earth could comprehend. Now she could speak more than just the cryptic phrase that for years she was cursed to ineffectually repeat only to the living. Now the voice of Isadora Luca was no longer cruelly restrained, should she choose to exercise it.

With an extremely odd dismissal of what had just occurred, Aldo Zorn turned and drifted toward his work table. It was as if the scream of an unearthly specter from beyond the grave was nothing more than the innocuous chirping of a cellar cricket. Falcona was livid, every nerve in her body aflame, every muscle tensed, her mind racing with possible scenarios and appropriate— and defensive—actions.

Falcona had lived under the same roof as the doctor for just over a year, yet never had she seen him in such a state of detachment. Perhaps that facet of his personality had always been present but never revealed to her, or he could be suffering from a sudden imbalance of mind, but whatever the explanation, his demeanor spoke of a man on the brink of madness. Or perhaps a man who had already plunged into the dark chasm of insanity.

Zorn's hand ran directionless over the plethora of medical and scientific instruments before him, as if admiring the collection of tools he had used to create the astonishing creature that stood behind him in the dark laboratory.

"You have no idea what all of this means, do you?" he asked dismissively, his question directed at the young Spaniard. "Each singular piece contributes to the whole. Individual notes build upon one another to create the concerto. What I have created is beyond the comprehension of man—perhaps even God—but how I have accomplished what I have does not matter. All that matters is that it *is* done. I have succeeded. I have won." His words recalled Madame Sabina's educational lecture he had received during his visit to her cartomancy shop weeks before, but now the old woman's message had been warped in his mind to satisfy the abhorrent rationale behind his deeds.

With her eyes cautiously fixed on the scientist, Falcona's hand found that of the creation beside her, and as their fingers entwined a light tingling sensation entered her palm. She at first attributed the barely perceptible tickle to her senses being inflamed by fear and rage but as her eyes moved to the face of her red-haired companion, she realized that whatever it was that she was feeling was being generated by the being who stood with her. Beneath the crimson curls, the gaze of the living dead woman focused not on the substance of the room but rather on the beyond, and to Falcona's shock, those emerald irises seemed to pulsate with some inexplicable form of inner light.

The faux sweetness of Zorn's voice broke through her bewilderment. "Oh, I forgot to mention," the doctor hissed with a sneer, "you might want to attend to your brother. He seems to have taken a nasty tumble down the stairs."

A searing jolt of panic shot through Falcona and she immediately pulled upon the hand of the creation. "Come with me!" Falcona cried in desperation, only to be met by a peculiar resistance.

"You go to him," the creation insisted. "My place is here. Please, go," she imparted solemnly.

With that, Falcona rushed to the wrought iron gate, flew through the short tunnel, and bounded up the rusted spiral staircase, her mind registering neither footfalls nor cobwebs as she burst through the silken strands in her haste to reach her brother. It was evident that her employer was not the man for whom she had danced one year ago or the man who she had seduced just weeks prior. She now cursed herself for that sexual act and everything she said and did on that sordid night. The thought that she had shared such intimacy with a monster like Zorn now turned her stomach, but in hindsight, she should have known. She did know. The signs were always there and she had always suspected that he was not what he seemed. Yet, until moments ago, she had always harbored the secret desire that the strapping young doctor would reveal himself to be a man of the strongest moral fiber and perhaps show romantic interest in her.

Now, whether he was lying or not, he had made a direct assault upon her through his implication of evil-doing against her brother. It was probably just another of Zorn's lies. Falcona was well-acquainted with his kind, those whose every waking moment seemed dedicated to the control of those around them and crushing the will of those they considered with as much regard as the dirt upon the soles of their boots.

Falcona's heart beat wildly as she burst through the door at the top of the stone stairs leading down from the entryway to the southeastern tower. *Zorn was lying. He had to be.*

They were alone, Aldo Zorn and the woman he had created, but not a word was exchanged between them. The inflated ego of the scientific genius had been stroked by the admission of the creation that her place was with him. He feared, however, that although she had not fled with Falcona, the sum of the damage done to her budding personality by the words of his Spanish servant could not be calculated.

203

Zorn had screamed his denial of Falcona's damning accusation, but his disavowal of wrongdoing was a façade; Falcona had indeed dredged forth the dread secret that had lain buried within him for two decades.

On that dreary day long ago that seemed to stretch on indefinitely, young Aldo had tried in vain to preoccupy himself with the lavish accouterment of the drawing room in the castle of Isadora Luca. In the next room, his father employed his silver tongue to persuade the widow to allow him to draft a will designating him as the heir to the estate and all of her belongings.

Before disembarking from Hannover on their trip to Kleinburg, Wilhelm Zorn had given very explicit instructions to his young son, who filled a green, glass bottle with a liquid composed of finely ground seed heads carefully plucked from the poison hemlock plant and held in suspension with distilled water. The bottle was carefully stoppered, and the cork was not removed until, by his father's instruction, Aldo poured a scant amount of the fluid into the teacup of Isadora Luca while his father diverted her attention with the copious minutia of the legal document he was drafting upon her desk.

The young boy was aware of what he was doing that evening and understood the implications of his actions, but it did not matter. He was eager to please the father who had, at last, shown interest in him and young Aldo displayed no misgivings about complying with Wilhelm's dastardly request. He was assured by his father that no one would ever know what had occurred on that night. He and Aldo were far too clever for their deed to be discovered, his father told him with a pat on his back. After all, they were Zorns.

The creation watched the doctor drift before the length of the worktable, its wooden surface cluttered with beakers and bottles, hand-scrawled notes, and the paraphernalia of his studies. Zorn's thoughts plumbed the depths of his reason as he weighed his options and to his reticence, no matter how he rebalanced the facts, his conclusions led to only one path forward. It would be a drastic measure and the undoing of years of work, but it must be done. He gathered himself, the reflective object in his grip concealed behind his back, then turned to face the woman he had created with his own two hands.

With a start, he now noticed the haunting iridescent glow of the creation's irises, now greener than the first budding leaves of spring. He knew not what it meant and he didn't care. He knew what he must do next.

As he faced her, the odd nature of the creation's posture gave him pause. She stood tall and statuesque as always but there was a distance to her stare that was both perplexing and disturbing. It was as if she was looking to the beyond, as if gazing into an infinite realm beyond human comprehension, either one never before seen by humankind or one concocted by the imbalanced nature of her psyche. She neither moved nor spoke as the unnatural light in her eyes throbbed, then dulled in intensity, then throbbed again, nearly in unison with the adrenalized beating of Zorn's own heart.

But within that beautiful mind resided an astounding secret, the nature of which the being's architect could never have guessed.

As clearly as one hears the call of the loon as it travels across the surface of a still pond shrouded with fog, so did the voice call out to her within her mind. The words were intangible at first but germinated in both volume and clarity as if some mental apparition had crept forth from her subconscious and was drawing ever nearer, begging to be heard. It was a woman's voice, but not her own, or at least it was not the voice that came from the vocal cords the doctor had implanted in her silken throat. It was someone else, an invisible presence that could not be seen but permeated every fiber of her being.

The presence welled within her, a warm and most intimate sensation. Although the mental invasion was startling, the creation held no fear of malice. The voice was gentle and celestial, but the message it conveyed was one of dark destruction.

"My name is Josephine Engel," the voice resounded throughout the entirety of her mind and body, "and I must be avenged."

CHAPTER EIGHTEEN
DESCENT INTO DARKNESS

Never in her life had Falcona cried with such wretched anguish. She sat on the cold marble floor of the foyer, cradling Estevan's head in her lap, his blood staining her hands. She shook uncontrollably and her tears flowed in torrents as she rocked him in her arms, just as she had when he was only an infant. Every moment of their lives together flashed through her mind; every kind word, every laugh, every argument. Her brother, her best friend, her confidant; he was everything in the world that mattered to her and now he lay cold and lifeless in Falcona's embrace, the pale light of the moon falling upon them through the open doorway of Castle Zorn.

After each spell of shaking and sobbing that erupted from the core of her being, she looked down upon his face hoping to detect some glimmer of life. Perhaps his eyes would open. Perhaps he would laugh the way he did on that summer day long ago when she screamed after the butterfly landed on her nose. Since that day, every time they would see a fluttering insect Estevan would laughingly taunt her, "Look out, Falcona! Here comes a butterfly!" Every time. And she would punch him in the arm and they would laugh together. Maybe his eyelids would flutter now and he would warn her that a butterfly was on her shoulder. He would chuckle and everything would be right again.

But each time she beheld his cold, bloodless countenance her heart was crushed once again, over and over. *He's dead, he's dead, he's dead.* Like a butterfly, his soul now fluttered toward the great Elysian Fields of forever.

In her bottomless despair, Falcona did not notice as the shadows beyond the door seemed to coalesce and move of their own accord, creeping toward her. An ebon shape glided slowly across the floor on cat paws and the glowing eyes of the jet-black feline surveyed her cautiously before slinking past Falcona and the body of her brother. After it disappeared into the deep shadows of the mansion, a second obsidian cat silently crossed the threshold, stalking purposefully, followed by two others. The last of the silent grimalkins made itself known to her, padding softly to her side. Falcona watched mutely as the animal's arched back brushed against her hip, then its muzzle prodded her elbow before it bounded off and melted into the blackness of the room, beyond the dark blood that had pooled on the tile floor.

"I am sorry, my child," came a soft voice from the doorway. Silhouetted by moonbeams, the stooped form of Madame Sabina stood before Falcona, her ancient face nearly concealed by her hooded cloak.

Through her tears, Falcona looked upon the cartomancer with numb detachment. "My brother is dead, Madame Sabina," she wept softly. "He's dead."

The old woman floated across the floor toward the heart-wrenching tableau and gently ran a weathered hand over Falcona's raven hair. "I understand that it is of little comfort to your broken heart, but know that Estevan is happy, and will greet you with open arms when you answer the call of the beyond, a long, long time from now." But Falcona's mind was already racing, and instantly recalled the unfathomable spectacle she had witnessed when Madame Sabina had last visited the mansion.

"Madame," Falcona urged with wide eyes, "you can bring him back, can't you? I saw you do it with the woman in the Doctor's laboratory! Please," she pleaded, "please bring Estevan back!"

The elderly cartomancer sank to the floor at the side of the despondent young Spanish woman and placed a hand against the chest of her deceased brother.

"Falcona, I cannot," she lamented. "It just doesn't work that way. What you saw, the ritual you witnessed, was not what you think it was and not what Dr. Zorn understood it to be."

"But the woman, his creation... she's alive," Falcona insisted, "I've *spoken* to her. She *is* alive!"

"No," the old woman replied sensitively. She sighed, a sound infused with both remorse and pity. "Let me explain," she rasped. Falcona's eyes were filled with desperation and although what Madame Sabina had to say would crush what remained of the young woman's hope, it had to be spoken.

"When someone dies," she began, "their energy—their soul if you will—departs this plane of existence, their destination... Well, even I do not know that. But once our energy leaves us, it cannot be retrieved. Understand, Falcona, that the turmoil we endure in this life is stripped away and left behind as we move on. There appears to be no need for negativity in the next realm. Fear, grief, self-pity, remorse...All are peeled away like the skin of an apple. Those emotions are discarded and without the connection to our energy—our soul—they are without power, and thus become nothingness. They are simply thoughts, intangible and fleeting. The dead have no use for such things. But one emotion can live independently of our corporeal forms. It is strong. It has its own power. And it endures. That emotion is anger."

Madame Sabina stood and surveyed the darkness about her, gesturing toward the castle walls. "Anger can sustain itself. Its essence can become embedded within stone, or wood, or even flesh. In its most pure form, anger that lives in the shadow of those who have departed may dissipate over time. But anger that is fueled by vengeance is something altogether different. Unless it is satisfied, that form of anger is eternal."

Falcona listened patiently and anticipating the resolution of Madame Sabina's explanation, she gave voice to the solution to the mystery of the creation in the castle's basement. Now it all made sense.

"The woman in the laboratory," Falcona slowly spoke aloud, "she was constructed from multiple murdered women. You did not return her soul to her because you could not. But you reunited her body with all of the vengeful anger that still exists, the anger—the energy—of all the women from whom she is composed."

"Exactly," Madame Sabina mouthed dourly. "And they shall have their revenge."

Falcona again began to weep softly, knowing that Estevan was truly gone forever. "Zorn did this. I know he did. I'll..."

Madame Sabina interrupted her declaration of murderous intent. "You might have to wait in line, young lady," the venerable Romani woman quipped cryptically.

With that, she instructed Falcona to treat Estevan's body with the respect he deserved and remove him to someplace comfortable, while she would descend to the basement laboratory and deal with the demented scientist in her own unique way. Falcona agreed and after giving the old woman directions, Madame Sabina made her way across the darkened great room. As she drifted away from Falcona, four small shadow-like creatures flowed like quicksilver from out of the shadows and followed the mystic into the moonlit corridor.

It was ironic, the cartomancer contemplated, that in an ancient edifice whose walls ensconced the vilest of secrets, the passageway through which she traversed was adorned with gaily framed artistic works of beauty and tranquility. It would seem that although Zorn declared ownership of the property and all it contained, he possessed not a shred of gentleness nor whimsical imagination required of a tasteful decorative sense. No, he simply absorbed that which he did not own and claimed it like a birthright. He took whatever he wanted from whoever he wanted and called it his own without a whit of decency or self-consciousness.

She made her way down the hall with a gait that belied her age. Madame Sabina stopped suddenly as she approached the threshold of the spiral granite stairwell which led down to the basement hallway. It was the mouth of the castle's veritable Hell

Curiously, she spoke aloud. "I am here to help you," she said. The dark eyes of Madame Sabina were fixed upon the blackness beyond the arched doorway, but only silence greeted the echo of her voice, reflected down upon her from the vaulted ceiling. But she was not alone.

In the blackness, something moved. It was not smoke, fog, nor the blur of human vision now experiencing natural age deterioration. No. What Madame Sabina observed was an astounding, billowing shape composed of some indescribable matter, materializing directly before her. It floated above the floor and appeared to be attempting to coalesce into a solid form and as Madame Sabina waited patiently and unvexed, folds of ectoplasmic matter resembling diaphanous white material continued to emerge from the nothingness until the personage of a woman completely draped in a death shroud shimmered before her in the moonlight.

The hooded cartomancer reverently straightened her posture as she faced the ghost that haunted the halls of what was now called Castle Zorn.

"Forgive me for being present without an official invitation, revered madame," she said apologetically. "May I ask in whose home I am now a most fortunate guest?"

Although there was no movement of the stale air in the passageway, the ghostly figure undulated gracefully as it hovered before the courteous intruder.

"I am Isadora Luca," the specter announced with pride, her voice thin and distant as if heard from across the expanse of a wide ravine. "And how might you help me, Madame Sabina? Oh, yes, I do know who you are," the ghost imparted with a laugh.

Anyone else would have been chilled to the bone if confronted by a supernatural entity, even more so if it called them by name, but Madame Sabina was undisturbed by the familiarity of the phantasmic being. "My reputation precedes me, it would seem," she replied, before taking a more earnest tone. "If you are here, then you have unfinished business in this world. Let me assist you in getting your affairs in order," Madame Sabina concluded with a devious smirk, and with that, the two women passed from the moonlight to the darkness of the stairwell leading to the laboratory of Dr. Zorn.

The dreamlike whispers of Josephine Engel were only audible in the mind of the creation and were accompanied by a cascade of shimmering lights that overcame her senses. They were nothing that could be seen, as the flashes of brightness were akin to hallucinatory manifestations, but the waves of pure emotion that radiated from the bursts of brilliance before her mind's eye was overwhelming. The creation felt a similar sensation earlier in the night when the burning anger of the woman Gina took hold of her conscious mind and recounted its tale of woe and death, but this…This was something remarkably different. Rather than witnessing a flood of extrinsic memories flashing in rapid succession, Zorn's creation instead experienced complete incapacitation of all of her physical abilities; she could not move, nor could she speak. Neither did she see the recollections of the woman who called herself Josephine Engel. There was something else there, an intangible force whose presence seemed at odds with the voice of Josephine that cried out for vengeance.

Then, like a single flute cutting through the din of an orchestra, the disruptor of her mental harmony was revealed.

It was a second voice.

"My name is Magdaline Zorn," it growled, "and I will have my revenge."

With that, a surge of psychic force pushed forth, seeking control of the mind it inhabited, and though its intent was honorable, the results were disastrous for the scarlet-haired creation. Two intelligent yet completely foreign mental essences collided head-on with her own, each wrestling for control of the body they co-inhabited. It was as if three mighty timbers floating downstream arrived at a river's narrowest passage at precisely the same instant. None of the three could progress because of the interference of the others, and the flow of the river—or in this case the flow of consciousness—ceased with startling abruptness.

Zorn watched dumbfounded as the body of his scientific achievement stiffened and fell to the floor like a marionette whose controlling strings had been cruelly severed.

The doctor flew to her side and examined her, but there was no response. Although the eyes remained open, the odd glow they had earlier radiated had now been snuffed. By all appearances, the composite human he had built in his lab, the abominable creation who was a walking dead woman, the being who had cruelly spurned his sexual overtures now failed to exhibit any of the functions that had previously replicated those of a living being. Further, her skin once again exhibited the surgical handiwork of the scientist, every scar and every suture once again visible across the entirety of her lovely form. The startling illusion of perfection was an unexplained phenomenon, but now it was as if there was no mind to conjure the visual subterfuge.

There could be no doubt.

For reasons unknown, she was now truly dead.

The doctor stood forlorn over the pale body. The physical frame was salvageable. Doing away with the body of the corpse-like Venus would be unthinkable. He had spent far too many years acquiring the perfect specimens of every aspect of her physical being and much like the old dowager from who his father had inherited the castle, he could not bear to part with his belongings, regardless of their viability.

But no, the issue was not the flesh; it was the brain that was malfunctioning. That organ must be expunged from her skull casing and burned in the furnace, just as he had done with all of the other unusable human remains that did not meet his stringent standard of perfection.

Now quite resolute, Dr. Aldo Zorn produced the long knife he had kept concealed behind his back, the one with which he had considered using to slit the throat of Falcona had she chosen not to flee the laboratory. He would now begin with the immediate surgical removal of the offending gray matter within the skull of the creation.

The wheels of the surgical table creaked as he pushed it to the center of the laboratory, now lit by several lanterns hung about the room to provide adequate lighting for the medical procedure he was about to perform. He lifted the body and dumped it unceremoniously upon the table and ripped the nightgown from it. Even in its lifeless state, the exquisite beauty of his creation gave him pause. There was no reason to saw open the braincase that very night, as he had no donor from which he could procure a replacement for the offending organ, but the bitter sense of betrayal her failure generated within him must be quelled. His actions were those of a spoiled, impatient child, who would smash the puzzle he could not solve rather than employ logic to arrive at the solution. It was a mental state that was at complete odds with the meticulousness by which he had worked for years.

The red haze of violent anger that had settled over his intelligent composure now drove him to acts that could only be described as madness. It was not even a surgical scalpal that he held, but a long, crude carving knife. It didn't matter. He must act now and cut open the head of the one who had denied him his due glory.

But before the blade could slice into the porcelain-smooth flesh of the creation's forehead, a rapping fell upon the heavily-reinforced laboratory door. There were three knocks in quick succession, followed by a pause, then a single knock.

Zorn's focus was shaken and he snapped his head toward the offending noise. Not only had he been disturbed, but the sound was familiar, a haunting half-memory that lie tantalizingly out of the reach of his full recognition.

Again, the sound repeated with the same rhythm. Three knocks, a pause, then a single knock. He wished to scream, to hurl the full fury of his anger and frustration toward the offender behind the door, but the knock...He *knew* that knock. His mind raced, leafing through a lifetime of experiences cataloged for later study and review.

Three knocks. A pause. Then one knock. Where had he heard that before?

The hand that gripped the knife fell limply to his side as realization and cold sweat washed over him.

Years ago, days stretched into long nights as he toiled in the lab at his Hannover estate. There, he had pored over the complex equations that would provide the backbone of the scientific principle that would fuel the creation of a regulation chamber. Within months, the chamber had been successfully constructed and his focus shifted to the development of the fluid by which the cellular activity of dead tissue could be successfully resuscitated.

Throughout that frame of time, his seclusion and concentration would occasionally be shattered by a cordial rapping upon his laboratory door. Three knocks, a pause, then a single knock. The same sound that he now heard at the door of Castle Zorn's basement chamber. His pulse throbbed in the sides of his neck as his heart leaped to his throat.

"Magdaline?" he called out. His voice teetering on the precipice of hesitation, perhaps even panic. The knock he heard was the same as the one his now-deceased wife would use in her attempts to draw his attention away from his work.

"Please let me in, Aldo. I'm worried about you."

Zorn flew to the door and pressed himself against the wooden portal, his eyes darting as he strained to hear through the heavy planks. "Magdaline…I'm very busy," he sputtered.

He knew she was dead. It was he who wrapped his fingers around her neck and squeezed the life from her. It was he who carved the flesh from her still-warm corpse and preserved her face in the chilled confines of his regulation chamber. And it was he who dismembered and incinerated her body and orchestrated the interment of an empty casket in the Zorn family plot. Dear, sweet Magdaline could not possibly have been on the other side of the door but that assumption could only have been reached by a logical mind. Zorn was beyond that now and his imbalance made it possible for him to ignore reason. Instead, he embraced the dark maw of madness that held him firmly in its icy grip.

"Aldo, my dear," the voice implored, "I forgive you. Please let me in."

With that, Aldo Zorn unlocked the door and opened it wide.

CHAPTER NINETEEN
POINT OF NO RETURN

———————•————————•—————

Zorn refocused his eyes as he peered into the darkness of the access hall outside the warmly lit laboratory. Standing calmly before him was a figure, draped in a long dark green cloak that concealed the head and face of the unexpected visitor. But upon his closer inspection, the disturbed scientist found that the woman was not Magdaline at all, but rather Madame Sabina, a wry smile on her cracked lips.

"We have much to discuss, Dr. Zorn," the old woman croaked.

Reality, as best as he could comprehend it at that moment, was swirling about him, and though he was utterly shaken by the cruel ruse that had just been played out, Zorn was resilient. "We do have much to discuss, you deceitful old bitch," he spat. "There! In there lies the damage you have wrought upon my work and my dreams…And my life! My creation is dead and all of this is your fault!" With that final declaration, it occurred to him that the knife was still in his grip.

"I've done nothing but what is right, Dr. Zorn," Madame Sabina hissed. "Not what is right for you, mind you, but what is right for all those poor unfortunates who gave their lives simply to feed the disgusting sexual urges of a frail little man."

Zorn knew not how to react. What had occurred over the past two weeks between him and his creation, how he had attempted to touch her and was spurned, how he had pleasured himself on multiple occasions while lasciviously ogling her dead flesh…No one could know that. No one *must* know that. It was a revelation that brought a flush of heat to his face as utter, crushing embarrassment flooded through him. "That's not true!" he screamed. "You have no proof of these lies!"

Madame Sabina glowered at the flustered man of science. "No proof? That depends on what you consider proof," she taunted. "I only have the word of Isadora Luca, whose ghost has been watching every perverted movement you have made since you invaded the sanctity of her home."

Aldo Zorn thrust out one hand and plunged the knife deep into the chest of Madame Sabina, who crumpled to the floor of the dark passageway.

The predicament in which Zorn now found himself was a quagmire that could quickly engulf him if he did not act with haste. Although the focus of his every waking minute over the past few years had been the achievement of his ambitions, now the fear that his crimes would be uncovered overrode all other concerns. The woman on the silver table could be explained away easily enough as a body on which he practiced his surgical skills but should the corpses of Estevan and Madame Sabina be discovered, he would have no believable explanation that would exonerate him from wrongdoing. It was likely that no one knew that the old cartomancer had come to his estate that night, but still, the disposal of her body needed to be achieved immediately if she had been followed. Incineration would take much too long, he concluded, but there was another simpler option to rid himself of her withered cadaver.

There had been no sound from the upstairs rooms, but it was a foregone conclusion that by then Falcona must have discovered her brother lying at the base of the staircase. What she was doing at the moment mattered not to Zorn; once Madame Sabina was gone, he would silence his Spanish servant. He would then conceal the bodies of her and her brother in the same manner in which he planned to dispose of the elderly Romani woman who was the author of what he hoped would be a short-lived scientific failure. Soon enough, the brain of the creation would be destroyed and he would begin anew, and perhaps this time the perfect woman he had constructed would retain the vital spark known as the human soul.

But first, the bodies.

Barefoot and wearing nothing but his thin sleep pants, the young doctor carried the remains of Madame Sabina into the night. Above him, the curled fingers of ebon tree limbs evoked within his mind the grasping hands of the law that would surely drag him to the gallows should his crimes be discovered. Onward he tread, following the overgrown path that led to the abandoned mill where he had disposed of the carriage of Josephine Engel several weeks prior.

Zorn stood upon the precipice of the sinkhole beside the crumbling mill, cradling the body of the dead woman, and into the black abyss he peered. At the bottom of the pit, the body would decompose and be devoured by the rats that dwelt within the cavern. No one would ever find her. The full moon watched the horrifying tableau without judgment.

As he began to heft the body to hold it out over the mouth of the pit, he looked down upon her one last time. He did so not with any sense of respect or honor, but rather, with disgust.

But to Zorn's horror, the body that he carried in his arms was not that of Madame Sabina. Instead, cradled in his arms lay the white-shrouded ghost of Isadora Luca, whose soulless black eyes stared into his with a condemnation that instigated a shriek of abject terror from the doctor.

Again he screamed as he fell away from the pit. The immaterial shape he had carried from the castle hovered above the death chasm. From beneath the undulating white cloth that enrobed it, a bone-white hand reached out to him, an accusatory finger pointed directly at his fear-struck face as he lay upon his back.

"You will pay, Aldo Zorn," the unearthly specter wailed. "It was you who murdered me and I will haunt you for the rest of your days!"

Zorn's next recollection was of pain radiating from the soles of his feet, which had carried him across the sharpness of fallen branches and briars in an unconscious flight from the vengeful spirit that sought his death. Both of his feet bled profusely as entire chunks of flesh had been ripped from his soles as he fled in terror and the deep red glistening tracks delineated his frenzied path across the stone entryway of Castle Zorn. Although he had departed the mansion through the side entrance of the castle's southeastern face, the front door provided the quickest entry into the sanctity of his home.

His flight carried him through the great room of the castle, but the body of Estevan was nowhere to be seen. As he ran, he noted the track of blood smeared across the floor, which revealed that Falcona had dragged the body of her brother to some other location within the estate. To where, he did not know, but he could not be concerned with that now. He must return to the only place where he might enjoy refuge: his laboratory.

Zorn bolted the length of the art-lined hallway and vaulted down the spiral stone stairwell. His heartbeat pounded in his ears, but his initial panic began to subside as his logical mind offered the supposition that perhaps what he had seen was simply a delusion. Whether the specter was real or a product of a mind overwrought by exhaustion could be examined at length once he reached his laboratory.

Within seconds, the doctor had traversed the pitch-black hallway and swung closed the iron-reinforced laboratory door as quickly as possible. But as speedily as he had sealed himself within his inner sanctum, he had not closed the door fast enough. Unseen in his frenzy, four ebon shadows flowed like roiling smoke across the floor and shot into the lab past his feet just as the portal slammed shut.

Zorn bolted the door securely and breathed a sigh of relief, but before he could even turn, a silken voice reached out from behind him to take hold of his frayed nerves.

"How was your walk, Aldo? Anything exciting happen?" the voice purred sarcastically. He turned sharply to behold a woman who sashayed into the lamplight in the center of the laboratory. The dark-haired visitor was unknown to him.

She was young, perhaps only in her early thirties, and even with her head covered by her cloak hood, her striking beauty immediately enraptured the doctor. She had large dark eyes, their lids painted by deep earthen hues, and she fluttered her thick black lashes in mock appreciation of his attention. High cheekbones and a strong nose were complemented by plump, wide lips. Contemplation of her olive-hued skin was not necessary for Zorn to identify her Romani heritage.

She stopped in the center of the room and looked upon the patchwork woman who lay unmoving on the surgical table. "Don't touch her!" Zorn shouted. They were the only words that would come to his lips, so hypnotized was he by the presence of the strange visitor. She looked his way and giggled dismissively, then removed the hood and cloak that she wore over her dress and let it drop to the floor.

It was the same dark green cloak that the ancient cartomancer Madame Sabina had worn each time the doctor had met with her.

"Who are you and how did you get in here?" Zorn demanded of his unwelcomed guest as he paced cautiously toward her. *What did she know? What had she seen?* He could not be certain but after furtively glancing to the floor, he snatched up the knife he discarded after thinking he had killed the old witch Madame Sabina. "You will tell me who you are!" Zorn commanded, the knife held firmly in his grip.

The mysterious young woman stared into Zorn's eyes, then looked at the knife clenched in his fist. "What do you think you're going to do with that? Stab me? Again?"

How had the night come to this? Too much was happening in rapid succession for the doctor to make sense of it all. All he knew was that everything around him and every aspect of his life was spiraling out of control. There must be answers and there must be order, but his thoughts were adrift in a sea of uncertainty. He felt as if he was slowly drowning.

But what did she just say?

"Stab you again?" Zorn repeated. "I've never seen you in my life!" Games, a conspiracy by a shadowy enclave of enemies, all of it was an effort to drive him mad. Who was responsible? His mind raced to recall the names and faces of every one of his scientific colleagues who had ever disparaged him or his theories. It was them, he was sure of it. They were all out to stop him in a destructive campaign driven by jealousy. The words of the dark woman shook him from his paranoid vision.

"You know me, Aldo Zorn. I am Madame Sabina," she said with a smile.

"What is this rubbish?" he screamed in response. "What are you trying to do? Get out, do you hear? Get out of my house!"

The shapely visitor was unmoved and completely dismissed his demand as if he had not even spoken.

"The Madame Sabina who you so viciously tried to kill with that knife? She was an illusion, as you must have figured out by now," the woman explained. "Isadora Luca was right. Mimicking the voice of your dead, deceased wife sure did get under your skin. You know, Madame Isadora wants nothing more than for you to suffer eternal torment, and to be honest, you deserve it." In complete disregard for her safety, the young woman strolled about in a directionless manner as if unconcerned that she was locked inside a room with a homicidal maniac.

Dr. Zorn's composure was completely off-balance, but he was sure of one thing: This younger Romani woman was working in concert with the old charlatan Madame Sabina. Somehow he had been drugged and all of the horrors that he had witnessed that night were nothing more than hallucinations.

"I'll no longer be a party to this idiotic charade," he blurted. "You will explain to me exactly what this is all about, or God help me, I'll use this on you," he threatened chillingly, holding up the polished blade. "You've done something to me, you old bitch. You've poisoned me. What I'm seeing is not real. I see a young woman, but I know that standing before me is a withered old charlatan with one foot in the grave." The young woman giggled dismissively.

"The Madame Sabina who you've met, who visited this very laboratory?" she said, but as the words left her lips, Zorn's vision began to blur.

He focused again upon the woman but as his vision cleared, he found before him not the young beauty, but the ancient crone. "This is the woman who you met," she said, touching her chest. "But here's the funny thing," she continued, "the *young woman* is not the illusion. The *old* woman, what you see now, *this* is the illusion."

Zorn strained to maintain the focus of his vision as the ancient cartomancer who stood before him again shifted and warped, the wrinkles of her face filling as did the curves beneath her cloak. Once more, the younger personage of Madame Sabina was revealed. "I can't very well stroll through decades looking like this without the self-righteous religious simpletons of the world proclaiming me a witch, can I? 'The ancient old lady' is a pretty effective disguise, wouldn't you agree, Dr. Zorn?"

Inwardly, the young doctor was dumbstruck by the sights he had just witnessed. None of it made logical, scientific sense, but neither did the animation of a composite of dead human tissue grown in a vat of chemicals. What he saw before him was not magic, it was not supernatural, it was an as-yet unexplained scientific principle and nothing more. He thought for a moment, and with crystal clarity, the path forward revealed itself. A curtain of tranquility fell over his demeanor and an unnerving smile crossed the lips of the scientist.

For the entirety of his life, Aldo Zorn had heard local legends and whispered stories of fearsome witches who fornicated with Satan and wielded hideously evil powers. The tales permeated every aspect of European society, from filth-encrusted alleyways to the opulent ballrooms of Hannover. Most intelligent people dismissed them as fairy tales designed to frighten children, while others believed in the absolute veracity of the accounts of women with powers whose roots extended to Hell itself.

Without question, Zorn was certain that his scientific genius could unravel the mystery of the witch, which could be easily accomplished through the dissection and analysis of such a being. Only he could excavate the foundation of what the common man called "magic" to reveal the scientific principles from which it was constructed. Only he could learn the secrets of the dark ones and once mastered, he would weave the science behind that magic into his creationist endeavors.

Standing before him was the embodiment of the perfect experimental subject. His fingers tightened around the handle of the knife.

"Haven't you figured out that you're dabbling in a world you could never comprehend? For a man of science you show remarkable ignorance," she cooed. "This woman on the table. You've deluded yourself into thinking that you created her. You did not create her. She is the product of the union of multiple women and men. You've not created," the youthful Madame taunted, "you've stolen."

Zorn looked cooly upon the raven-haired Romani, who stood just four paces from him. "Enough, Madame Sabina, or whoever you are. It's late and it has been a long night. What you're doing now is stalling for time. You know what is to come, don't you?" He raised the knife and wiped the blade against his palm as if to polish its surface in preparation for use. He took one step forward, but the young woman was unmoved. "What happens next is that you contribute to the furtherment of scientific knowledge through your brave sacrifice." He held up a hand as if to silence her, but she had no intention of speaking. "No, no, don't speak. You can keep your final outlandish insults to yourself. That's all you have left, isn't it? Insults."

"And what is your intention, exactly?" she quipped unflinchingly.

"What do you think? I have the knife, and you are alone," the doctor imparted flippantly.

A devious smile played on the lips of Madame Sabina. "Oh, that's where you're wrong," she uttered melodically. "You see, I'm *not* alone."

As Zorn processed the meaning of her threat, he failed to notice the shadow. It flowed across the floor near the far wall of the laboratory, undulated and twisted like blood in water, then by some unseen force the obsidian ball of ectoplasmic matter catapulted through the air at near the velocity of a bolt of lightning. His eyes widened but the attack was so sudden that Zorn could do nothing but bear the brunt of whatever it was that had flung itself at him.

It hit him in his upper chest with much lesser impact than he expected, but it clung to him and in his panic, he tried to brush away the ebon fog with his free hand. To his dismay, his defensive maneuver was futile, as his hand passed through the phantasm. He watched in utter disbelief as the mist-like thing began to congeal into something solid, its claws digging into his chest.

It was a cat, black as pitch, and its eyes glowed a fiery yellow, like blazing embers floating into the night sky. The hellish creature continued to embed its claws into him, but in a burst of sheer panic and self-preservation, Zorn managed to grip it around its slender neck. He furiously bared his own teeth as he squeezed, intending to crush the life from the nightmarish creature before it could inflict further physical harm to him.

But as he held the tiny beast at arm's length, the savage feline burst into flames. The doctor watched in disbelief as the fire enwrapped his hand and forearm with a life of its own, clinging to him as it seared through his limb's outer layer of skin. He waved his arm frantically as he fell about the room and at last the sentient flame dimmed and dispersed into the black mist from whence it had originated, swirled in the air like a corkscrew, then shot back into the shadows behind Madame Sabina.

Zorn examined his blistered and blackened arm in shock, a strain of mocking laughter echoing in his ears. "Now. Tell me again what you intend to do to me?" the dark Romani cooed.

Enraged beyond all reason, Zorn hurled his full fury at the young woman and charged toward her with the knife held high. This time, she would die.

But the blade would not fall upon her. Zorn was again hit by a streaking ball of black energy. The ebon force smashed him in the chest with the force of a rock-hard fist, staggering him. It shot away just as a second phantom attacker stuck his knife hand, sending the killing instrument clattering across the stone floor. The ghostly force solidified into yet another black feline, driving its curved talons into the flesh of his arm. His attempt to rip it free with his blistered and charred hand was in vain; the blue-eyed antagonist melted upon his touch, its entire body becoming transparent and shattering into a shower of water before he could grasp it.

The doctor tried desperately to gather his wits, but he was mesmerized by what was occurring. Inexplicably, the individual droplets of liquid that had covered him and splashed to the floor rose into the air of their own volition and hovered before him. The ghostly liquid congealed into a swirling black orb that shot away and dissolved into the shadows of the laboratory as quickly as it had appeared.

So vexed was Zorn by the successive attacks that he failed to notice Madame Sabina leaning over the body of the creation, her lips close to the dead woman's ear. "Listen to me," she whispered. "Don't repress the voices inside you. Embrace them and allow them control. Just step aside and let their anger bring you life. But, ladies," she warned. "One at a time, please."

Zorn was panting furiously and although the soles of his feet were torn and his left arm was covered by weeping burns, it was the scratches across his face left by Falcona's slap that generated the most pain. If only she was present. Unlike the beasts that had attacked him, she was composed of flesh and blood, and her body would easily succumb to the frenzied pounding of his fists against her porcelain features. She could feel pain. She *will* feel pain. He must find her, for upon her he could unleash his unbridled wrath.

The thought was barely completed when he was struck again by another of the black demons, this one hitting with such force that it lifted him off his feet and flung him against the damp stone wall. The force would not relent, however, and it felt to Zorn as if he was being battered by hurricane winds that kept him helplessly pinned. His feet kicked ineffectively as they could not reach the floor. The black orb had disappeared and it was the force of the wind itself that pinned him just below the ceiling of the laboratory.

He could not move, nor could he speak, and slow, creeping panic spread across his face as he realized that the very air within his lungs was being sucked out by the invisible attacker. Pinpricks of light began to dance before his eyes and he could feel his heartbeat slow as his body was increasingly deprived of oxygen. He was about to die.

But not yet.

"Not yet!"

As abruptly as it had ensnared the doctor, the wind ceased and retreated to the shadows when the voice of Madame Sabina cut through the chamber. Zorn dropped to the floor and gasped for air, his mind reeling from the ordeal he had just endured. But Madame Sabina's command—along with the sinister undertone of her voice—ensured him that his torment was not yet ended.

Zorn had never been that close to death and the chilling realization that his mortality was not without bounds was sobering. The indignant nature of his madness was not similarly affected, however. He stood, straightened his pants, and theatrically brushed his hands together. Zorn arrogantly ran his fingers through his thick blonde hair as if making himself presentable before a gathering of elites and smiled smugly at the young cartomancer standing at the center of the room. "This will end now," he hissed.

Behind Madame Sabina, a finely sculpted leg dropped from the surface of the surgical table. One dainty foot, embellished by scars and sutures, made contact with the floor, then the other, and the creation stood stately at the side of Madame Sabina. Once again, her emerald eyes burned with an inner fire. She glared menacingly in the direction of the man responsible for her creation.

At the feet of the women, four black housecats purred and rubbed affectionately against both of them. The eyes of the creatures glowed in the dim light; green, gray, yellow, and blue.

227

Earth, wind, fire, and water.

"Elemental forces," Zorn sputtered in realization. "Those animals...they're..."

"Physical manifestations of my power. I could conjure them in any form; bats, wolves, whatever. But it just so happens that I like cats."

Zorn thought for a moment, then recalled, "The candle in the shop."

Madame Sabina smiled politely. "Yes, that was a small warning of what you were dealing with, but not surprisingly, you did not heed it." With aloof indifference, the young woman strolled away casually, leaving the red-haired creation alone in the center of the chamber. Like a classic statue chiseled from marble, the pale figure stood silently.

Zorn sharply pointed a finger at the cartomancer. "You are the one responsible for her condition. You and Falcona. Both of you. I was a fool to trust the advice of that whore. Had I continued my research undisturbed, I would have found the anomaly and corrected it. And I will still achieve that goal, believe me. Look at her. She stands, so all is not lost. No matter what you did to try to sabotage my work, it failed. You have failed," he screamed with finality.

"Have I? Why don't we ask her opinion," Sabina chirped, tipping her chin in the direction of the creation. "Tell him who you are, my lovely."

An unnerving smile pulled at one corner of the lips of the creation as she narrowed her glowing eyes. "My name is Josephine Engel."

A bolt of sheer terror ran the length of Zorn's spine and jabbed into the base of his skull. He stood mutely, unable to comprehend how any of this was possible. Through the means of some unknown flourish of sorcery, the undead woman had identified the name of one of the donors used in her construction. The creation told him she had no recollections of past lives, but it was not Josephine's brain he had implanted within the carcass; he only made use of her blood and the scalp from which erupted a cascade of red hair. There could be no retention of memory in sanguine fluid nor flesh, and thus, the revelation must be all part of Madame Sabina's plan to torment him. The cartomancer must have had some connection to Josephine Engel or perhaps even her husband and Madame Sabina simply suspected Zorn's involvement in her disappearance and was now using that suspicion to taunt him by secretly feeding Josephine's name to the creation. That had to be the answer.

He tested his theory. "What is your name again? Josephine Engel? Tell me about yourself, won't you?

The creation glowered at the scientist from beneath the overhead lanterns. "What would you like to know?" she asked politely. "Would you like to know of my likes and my loves? Of my upbringing and family life? Perhaps you would like me to tell you of my happiest recollections, of the things that warmed my heart." She paused, then continued in a very deliberate fashion, emphasizing each word and syllable of her question. "Or maybe you would prefer to know what was going through my mind when you and I stood in this very room, just before you took the scissors and thrust them just here," she pointed to the underside of her lower jaw, "and drove them upward into my skull?"

It was a recollection that no one else on the Earth could possess, save him and the woman who he had murdered in cold blood. Zorn's lower jaw was slack, his mouth agape, but no words came forth. His dread was palpable and a swirling maelstrom of horror churned by his incrimination buffeted what remained of his crumbling composure.

Madame Sabina relished his pain. "Oh. I believe there is someone else who would like to speak to you, Dr. Zorn." The young mystic looked coyly to the creation, whose eyes burned with green fury.

"Aldo, I have something to say as well," the creation intoned slowly.

No more! Say no more, his brain screamed and his tongue, at last, found words. "Who are you!" he demanded. "What do you want from me?"

"All I wanted was for you to spend time with me, Aldo. Was that too much to ask?"

"What…?" he sputtered.

"I would have been happy with your recognition of my devotion, or an occasional kind word, even telling me that you liked my dress. But you couldn't. It was beneath you. I was nothing more than a trinket to play with when you felt like fucking. That's all I was good for. But I was determined that I could change you and make you see. Because I loved you." The creation—or rather, the voice that spoke—paused to plumb the depths of her anguish one last time. "All you had to do was tell me, 'Magdaline, I love you.'"

Zorn had to remind himself to breathe.

"Instead, you unlocked the door of your laboratory in our home in Hannover. I was barefoot, in my nightgown. You ushered me in and showed me your experiments. You showed me this," she said, holding up her right hand, "floating in a tank of green liquid." She clenched the hand into a fist and continued. "That was just before you put your hands around my throat and crushed it until my neck snapped."

The eyes of Madame Sabina shot from the creation to Aldo Zorn. He was sweating profusely and the only spark in his eyes was that of madness and fear. "Well?" Madame Sabina asked. "Anything to say?"

"Just this," Zorn growled venomously. "I will not be judged nor condemned by the words of women. You have no proof of any of the lies spewed by this…this manikin. She is simply repeating whatever bullshit you've fed to her, but it is irrelevant. She is not a real person, is she? She does not breathe, her heart does not beat. She is nothing but a mere ragdoll, to be tossed about and mended when she needs repair, to be played with or ignored, depending on my whim. She is not truly human, which makes her words or what passes for thoughts irrelevant."

The longer he stewed in his toxic anger, the more color infused his face, neck, and bare chest. "You cannot possibly comprehend the miracle that has been achieved through my intellect. I have done this," he shouted, shaking both hands in the direction of the silent creation. "I made this. This is my miracle and you will not take that achievement from me. Why are you even here? What purpose does your presence serve? None. Other than to try to inflict pain upon someone who can feel no pain, because the innocent man does not bear a noose around his neck, does he? I have done no wrong, can't you see that?"

He glared at the creation and pointed an accusing finger at her face. "And you, you should be groveling at my feet for making you everything that you are! For giving you life! You will learn to bow to your master, for I am your everything, don't you understand that? Without me, you would be nothing but chunks of putrifying flesh strewn about alleyways or bloated and bobbing against dock pilings. You would be infested by worms devouring you from within or rotting beneath cedar planks in the cellars of maniacs. I saved you from death and you will show me the proper respect, just as one would respect God."

"You pompous, arrogant idiot," Madame Sabina laughed. "There is no God." She sighed, adding with frustration, "There's no hope for this one."

With that, she curtsied to the creation in a manner befitting one in the presence of a queen and moved to the farthest wall of the chamber. The creation did not respond, keeping her eyes fixed upon the doctor.

Madame Sabina looked to Zorn, then down to the ebon felines who lovingly nudged her legs. "I gave this beautiful woman before us the gift of remembrance," she said. "It is a terrible burden but it was the least that I could do to help her understand who she is and to assist her in making sense of the bright, shining stars who dwell within her. But you should know, too," Sabina chirped deviously, "I gave her a little something else, too. An extra 'gift,' you could say."

The young cartomancer and the crimson-haired creation exchanged a glance. Zorn noticed and watched in bewilderment as Madame Sabina slinked with her back against the wall as if to create more distance between her and the creation. Something was about to happen, but he knew not what.

With a slow stride that spoke of both complete confidence and regality, the creation took several steps in Zorn's direction. He nervously shrank from her approach, his bloody feet leaving smeared tracks on the stone floor. His retreat was an instinctive reaction in self-defense and he immediately regretted it. He must show the creation that he would not be bent, nor would he be broken. He tilted his chin upward to meet her advance but his supposition that she would strike him dissolved as she came to a stop just beyond his reach, both of her feet planted firmly together.

Whatever incomprehensible power roiled within her, whatever cruel intent she held in the forefront of her mind, he could not guess. The only visible indication of her state of mind was the burning blaze behind her emerald eyes, a cold fire that remarkably drifted upward from her face and twisted like smoke in the air above her head.

A shiver as if someone had just stepped on his grave shot through the entirety of his being when Zorn looked into those eyes, for the only thing he could read in them was death. With the grace of a ballerina, she wove her hands through the air like feathers upon a fickle wind, rising then falling, then rising again. The motions were mesmerizing, the beauty of their dance shattered by the eruption of white-hot bolts of lightning that shot forth from her fingers and into the chest of the startled scientist. They hit with the force of a sledgehammer and knocked him from his feet, his back smashing against his work table, breaking beakers and shattering the delicate glassware that had been utilized in her creation.

Zorn slumped to the floor amid various splattered liquids and shards of glass and looked at his aching chest. In its center was a large circle of blackened flesh and through the shredded cheesecloth that was his skin, pink ribbons of pectoral muscles were revoltingly exposed.

"That was from Josephine Engel," the creation hissed, mockingly.

The doctor screamed in equal part fear and pain as the scent of his charred flesh wafted into his nostrils when he frantically gulped for air. Again her hands wove with hypnotic fluidity before another attack was unleashed. This time, the blue-white bolts danced across the floor around his legs as he kicked in a desperate attempt to avoid harm. Not fast enough, it was as if time had ceased to be as Zorn watched the flickers bolts converge into one, striking him between his legs. The doctor's scream was like one ripped from the depths of Hell as within his sleep pants his testicles swelled and burst, ripping his scrotum to shreds and splattering blood across the crotch of his clothing.

She looked upon the wretched man of science as his entire body trembled uncontrollably. She smiled. "That was from Magdaline."

"What did I do? What did I do?" The words were malformed, his lips shaking to such an extent that he could barely coordinate the use of his mouth.

The creation paused and composed herself once again, muscles relaxing and hands to her sides. As Zorn writhed in abject pain on the floor, there was no pity to be found in her eyes.

"What did you do?" she repeated. "Aside from your punishable crimes of the murder of Josephine Engel and Magdaline Zorn, you attempted to create a human being without ever understanding what it is to be one. I might not live but I'm more human than you, you piece of shit."

The entire frame of Dr. Aldo Zorn was rocked by the relentless electrical death that shot forth from the hands of the creation. Like a web of lightning, it enveloped his body and gripped him in its savage embrace. It was as if a thousand needles were being pounded into his body and the beat of his heart accelerated to an unbearable rate. He tried to scream, but no sound issued forth from his mouth as a thick, white tendril boiled every drop of saliva from his throat and snaked down his esophagus, leaving behind a blistered and shriveled tongue.

What took only seconds to transpire felt like an eternity and Aldo Zorn was acutely aware of every devastating effect the murderous attack had upon his body. He was being ripped apart from the inside and could do nothing to stop it, a mute witness of his own excruciating execution.

No emotion played upon the face of the creation as every cosmic particle of her fury poured forth from her hands, but at last, a smile crossed her lips when the eyes of Aldo Zorn grew blood red, then black, then exploded from their sockets in a miasma of crimson gore.

With one final burst of rage, the cleansing bolts of death converged upon his head and lifted his twitching body from the floor to float suspended in the air before her. "This, Aldo Zorn," she said with furious intent, "this is from me."

The brain of the scientist boiled within his skull and as death spasms rocked his quivering frame, the skin of his face and head ripped open as bone and gray matter exploded outward, leaving nothing but ragged shreds of flesh and muscle draped upon his shoulders. As abruptly as it began, the attack ceased and the smoking, devastated corpse of Dr. Aldo Zorn crashed to the floor like a ragdoll.

A deathly silence settled across the lantern-lit chamber as the patchwork woman considered the smoldering carcass of the man responsible for her creation. She tossed her crimson hair as she turned toward Madame Sabina, who walked to the creation's side, followed by the four prancing ebon elementals. Sabina looked at the corpse and wrinkled her nose. The stench of burnt flesh was nauseating.

"I didn't get a chance to tell him what that other gift was that I gave to you, but I guess he knows now," Sabina said, then spat upon the headless corpse. "It's a shame there's no Hell because if anyone deserves to burn for all eternity, it's him."

An immediate concern entered the cartomancer's mind, and she took both hands of the creation into her own. "How do you feel? Are you alright?"

The red-haired woman thought for a moment, then replied. "I feel…lighter in some way. And sad."

"Why is that?" Sabina queried with mild concern.

"Because they're gone. Josephine Engel and Magdaline Zorn. I let them in, as you directed, and in that instant, I came to know them on the most intimate of levels. I became both of them, and they became me. Our voices were like a choir, singing in harmony inside of me. There was no division; we were one. But now, there's only silence." Her chin dropped and she turned away. The admission was painful.

Sabina gently lifted the chin of the creation so that the tangles of her hair no longer concealed her pretty face, then looked directly into the emerald eyes, no longer glowing with eldritch fire. "It's alright to be sad. You've lost two friends. But the negative energy that bound them to this world has been dispersed, along with the painful aspect of them that was left abandoned when they crossed from this plane of existence: their anger. They have been avenged and now they fly free. You have righted two hideous wrongs and if it was possible, I'm sure Josephine and Magdaline would tell you they love you for giving them the greatest gift they could ever have received."

Behind them, the hinges of the iron gate leading to the secret passage hidden in the southeast tower whined as Falcona pushed against it. The blood of Estevan was still on her hands, a large kitchen knife gripped tightly in one of them. She had seen it all and after suffering through the death of her brother and witnessing the horrifying showdown that had just occurred, Falcona was quite pale. She padded silently to the other two women and did not flinch at the sight of the true form of the creation. The patchwork woman felt no need to summon the

235

illusory veil of perfection; she stood before Falcona as she truly was, for she had nothing to hide from the young Spaniard.

Falcona tipped her head to the cartomancer. "You are Madame Sabina?" she asked, to verify that all she had absorbed in the past few minutes was the truth.

"I am," Sabina assured her, then looked to the knife in Falcona's hand. "That was for Zorn?"

A tear rolled down Falcona's smooth cheek. "My brother is dead," she mewed.

Sabina placed a warm hand against Falcona's arm. "You've never taken the life of another and I'd like to see it stay that way. I understand your heartbreak. Believe me, I've been around long enough to see far too many I cared for grow old and die around me. But Aldo Zorn got what was coming to him and your conscience will remain unburdened by guilt."

Falcona nodded in acceptance. "Thank you, both," she said, then threw her arms around the creation and crushed herself against her. After several moments of cleansing embrace, Falcona looked to the darkness of the laboratory rafters, encased in cobwebs. "What about Isadora Luca?" she asked.

Madame Sabina tilted her head, then listened for a moment. "She's gone. Her chains have been broken, too," she said with a smile. "We have much to discuss, the three of us. Let's get out of this hellhole, go upstairs, have a drink, and figure out the best course of action. Agreed?"

Falcona and the creation nodded. Sabina retrieved from the floor the cloak she had earlier discarded and handed it to the creation. "You're really quite spectacular, but that body is a bit distracting," she chided. The creation draped the dark green cloak over her nakedness and the three women ventured into the black hallway, leaving behind the sickening stench of the still-smoldering remains of what had once been Dr. Aldo Zorn.

CHAPTER TWENTY
DENOUEMENT

The dark pallor that hung over the estate was not a physical manifestation, but an emotional impression generated within the minds of those who viewed Castle Zorn from pastoral Kleinburg. On the pages of the stately dwelling's narrative could be found the details of the mysterious death of the reclusive widow Isadora Luca, the questionable bequeathment of the property to Wilhelm Zorn, the subsequent degradation of the grounds, and the hermit-like nature of its most recent master, Dr. Aldo Zorn.

The synthesis of those peculiar events created an air of unease within those who contemplated the secrets that lie behind the castle's cold stone walls. Had the villagers known the depths of depravity to which Aldo Zorn's scientific experiments plumbed, they would have emphatically expunged their hamlet of the castle's dark influence by promptly burning it to the ground. But on this morning, the rays of the rising sun illuminating the face of the mansion seemed to cleanse it of its darkness, or so it was in the mind's eyes of Falcona and Madame Sabina.

It had been a long night and the evil in the heart of Castle Zorn had been vanquished. The victors had not escaped unscathed, however, as Falcona suffered heart-wrenching despair due to the tragic loss of her brother. There was talking and there was crying; there were reassuring embraces and a plot hatched that would conceal the truth of what transpired at the heart of the castle the previous night. But there was no sleeping for Madame Sabina and Falcona. There was too much work to be done.

Birds sang joyously in the trees that flanked the rear of the estate as Falcona's hands lovingly smoothed the earth over the grave of Estevan. The shadows of the aromatic pines were retreating, drawing with them the chirps of nocturnal crickets that blanched at the coming of the dawn.

Madame Sabina sympathetically squeezed the hand of Falcona, standing silently beside her. There were no words to be shared, nothing left to be said. The young Spaniard blew a kiss to the plot of ground nestled within the embrace of the forest and the two young women turned and walked slowly to the castle. Above them, black smoke wafted from one of the residence's weathered brick chimneys and dissipated into the crisp spring air.

While Falcona and Madame Sabina attended to the interring Estevan's body, the creation saw to the elimination of the corpse of Aldo Zorn and all written evidence of his work. In the darkness of the laboratory, the crimson-tressed woman stoked the flaming coals within the great black furnace that hungrily consumed the body of the scientist, along with every scrap of paper on which he had detailed the accounts of her creation. The flickering of the fire danced in her eyes as she watched the destruction of a lifetime's worth of work. She could not help but smile knowing that never would another be subjected to the spiritual and moral torture that had been thrust upon her pale shoulders.

In that fleeting instant, she felt true peace.

Until she heard the voice.

It was weak and thin and welled from some dark corner of her mind. It was woven of fear and anguish, but most of all, it spoke of a thirst for vengeance. The creation focused her thoughts upon that singular echo, and at last, the voice became clear.

"My name is Ivonette," it intoned, "and I must be avenged."

For over two hours, Falcona and Madame Sabina searched the castle, but to their dismay, they could find no trace of the creation. Every room and every corner of the estate was scoured but there was nothing to indicate that the object of their quest had ever been there at all. At length, the two women sadly conceded that their expedition was futile.

The sun's golden rays warmed them as they sat together on the long couch before the vast picture window on the eastern face of the castle. "She had to find her own way in this world," Madame

Sabina rationalized. "We should not mourn her departure. We should be happy for her."

"I know," Falcona responded sadly. "I just wish I could be there for her if she ever needs a friend. Or if I need a friend." With that, the exhausted Falcona melted against the breast of Sabina and succumbed to the call of Morpheus.

"Don't you worry, Falcona," Madame Sabina whispered. "You'll always have me."

To the joy of the woodland crickets, night had fallen. But the nocturnal chorus of the insects grew silent as a shadow fell upon the door of the country estate of Erwin Engel. The shadow of a woman.

It had taken several weeks before anyone in Kleinburg noticed the absence of Josephine Engel. Questions about her whereabouts had begun to surface, but Erwin had no idea what had become of his wife. It was concerning to him, but his fears had nothing to do with the well-being of his spouse. Erwin's anxiety was initiated by his presumption that an investigation into Josephine's disappearance might lead the local authorities to delve into his personal life, which, in turn, could uncover his affair with—and murder of—Ivonette. Engel assumed Josephine had finally had enough of his philandering and had fled the village of her birth to create as much distance between them as possible. *Good riddance*, he thought.

After having returned home that night from the Kleinburg rathskeller, he quickly fell asleep in a drunken stupor, still clothed, his new engraved pipe clutched in his hand. But the knock on the front door roused him after only a few moments of rest and greatly angered him.

"Who the hell is knocking on my door at this hour?" he blurted. He stood, stormed to the door, and flung it open. "What the fuck do you want?" he screamed at the unknown visitor.

Though she was enrobed by the night, the alabaster quality of the woman's face fairly glowed. Engel was taken aback by the beauty of the mysterious stranger who stood beyond the entry-way. She was clothed from head to toe in a dark green hooded cape that was tightly tied closed across her front, but in his usual lascivious manner, he crudely surveyed her body, his gaze leveling on the fullness of her bosom. He cared not if she noticed his infatuation; in fact, he hoped that she would. In his drunken state, the questions of who she was or from where she had come did not even cross his mind. She would be just another conquest that he did not even have to leave his home to pursue.

"I'm sorry to disturb you at such a late hour," she said apologetically. "I'm traveling alone, and I'm afraid I've become a bit lost. I know Kleinburg is somewhere in that direction," she motioned toward the distance, "but I don't want to drive my carriage any farther if I'm going the wrong way." When she raised her arm to point toward the forest, the gesture caused her cape to part slightly and afforded Erwin a quick glimpse of the side of one of her breasts.

Beneath the cloak, she was completely naked, he shouted to himself in his mind.

Engel's heart skipped a beat and he involuntarily gulped in a breath due to the unexpected sight. His reaction did not go unnoticed. Beneath the copious curls of red hair that framed her face, her eyes rolled seductively back to him and a smile crossed her lips.

"So. Can you give me what I need, or shall I apologize for disturbing you?" she playfully asked. He attempted to feign indifference but the haste at which he ushered her into his home and locked the door behind her was all too telling.

"Brandy?" he offered, filling his glass from the crystal decanter on a silver serving cart in his study.

Her posture was perfect as she sat, legs crossed, upon the red up-holstered lounge. "Oh, I won't need it. I'm hot enough as it is," she purred. Only one oil lamp lit the room, but even with its wick set at the smallest flame exposure, the yellow light was enough for him to drink in every aspect of her beauty.

Engel greedily gulped down the contents of his glass, then placed his unlit pipe back in his mouth, anxiously biting on the mouthpiece as he ran it back and forth between his lips. The blur of alcohol dimmed him somewhat, but it was readily apparent that the woman was there for one thing: she wanted his hard cock inside of her and she wanted it now. What else could he assume from her dress, her words, and her teasing demeanor?

There was something about her that gave him pause and gnawed at his subconscious. Had he met her before? He was sure he had not, yet there was something remarkably familiar about her that he could not quite put his finger on. He blurted out what was nagging at him.

"Forgive my faulty memory, but have we been previously acquainted?" he asked.

"If we had, don't you think you'd remember me?" she tossed back at him, one hand seductively rubbing across the material of her cloak just above the small protrusion on the face of her breast that indicated the erectness of her nipple.

He was enraptured by sexual fantasies of taking her then and there and could think of fairly little else. "What you're doing is teasing me, aren't you?" he slurred with unfiltered directness.

"I am."

"Because you want me?" he assumed.

"No. Because I want to see you squirm."

There were two ways that Engel could interpret the statement. He hoped that his first, more base assessment was true, rather than the latter. Before he could think more about her words and what they might portend, she breezily changed the subject.

"That's a beautiful pipe," she remarked, bringing to his attention how ardently he had been mouthing the smoking instrument. He withdrew it from his mouth and admired it, the initials E.E. engraved on its polished silver bowl. "Was it a recent purchase?" The peculiar nature of her question failed to register concern in his mind.

"It was," he said proudly. "Quite expensive."

The visitor was unimpressed. "What happened to your old one? Did you lose it?"

It took a moment for the weight of her statement to sink in, but within a few seconds, his unease was written all over his face. "What did you...What do you mean?" he asked nervously.

"Did you lose your last pipe and that's why you bought a new one?" she said, taking the smoking instrument gently from his hands as only the closest of friends might do. It was quite forward of her, but something in him allowed her to take the pipe from him, even though he wished to resist her.

Playfully, she continued. "Do you know where I think your old pipe is? I think it dropped from your coat pocket when you were in the apartment of a young lady named Ivonette. You remember her, don't you Erwin Engel?"

Now he knew. Now he understood the reason why the woman was there. It was blackmail, pure and simple. Somehow she had uncovered his crime and was now about to threaten him with exposure unless he paid her handsomely. Upon the realization, the drunken fury of Erwin Engel erupted.

"What is it you want, you whore?" he screamed.

"'Whore?' That's funny," she growled. "That's what you called Ivonette the night you strangled her."

Erwin Engel thought he understood the intent of the midnight visit with crystal clarity but his assessment of why the woman had come to his home was completely wrong. It wasn't money she wanted. No. She wanted something else.

"How do you know these things?" he demanded. He was a fly entrapped in a web of his own weaving.

"I know more than you could possibly imagine, Erwin Engel." She twisted the knife by repeating his entire name a second time.

"How? Tell me, you witch, or I swear I'll..."

"I'm no witch," the mysterious visitor interjected. "I am Ivonette."

"What are you talking about?" Engel sneered, and to his dismay, a startling transformation began to take place before his eyes. It was as if her skin itself blurred and became liquid-like, then resettled into focus. That skin, once smooth as silk, now bore a network of hideous scars and sutures across the entirety of its surface.

In horror, he backed away from her but there was nowhere to go.

"The blood of Ivonette flows through my veins," she shared, "mingled with the blood of Josephine, your wife. She is also within me."

"Josephine is dead? How? Why do you say that?" he gasped. "She simply deserted me, that's all."

"No. She is dead. She is now a part of me, along with many others. Their names would mean nothing to you," the creation explained, "but they are everything to me. They are who I am. I am one woman, and I am every woman. I am every vile and perverse sin ever committed against the original owners of this flesh. I am that pain. I am every victim hidden in the nightmares of so many murderers, screaming out for vengeance against those who would avoid justice." She paused, her stare boring into the eyes of the visibly shaken owner of the estate. "Those like you, Erwin Engel. The women inside of me...One by one, they will be avenged."

Engel's mind reeled from the words of the woman and what he had seen. It was a nightmare, perhaps a hallucination brought about by the night's drink. Or was she real? He could not be certain of anything.

To make sense of it all, to get to the bottom of just what this woman knew and what secrets she possessed, he must pry from her whatever he could, beginning with her identity. "What is your name!" he demanded.

"What is my name?" She pondered the question thoughtfully. "If name and nature can be one, then my name is Ragdoll," she growled.

With that, a terrifying supernatural fire erupted behind her green eyes, causing them to glow like those of an English Jack-o'-lantern.

Before he could draw a breath, the crimson-haired visitor thrust upward with the stem of the pipe. The swift motion caused the pipe stem to puncture the underside of his lower jaw and impale his tongue.

Erwin Engel spasmed furiously as blood sprayed from the sides of his mouth. He reached for his throat to remove the object, but the woman had already retracted it. Crimson gore poured profusely onto his shirt from the gaping black hole under his chin. Instinctively, he swung wildly with one fist while trying to stop the flow of blood with his other hand, but in his drunken imbalance his punch missed his intended target and he fell awkwardly against the serving cart.

The entire world was spinning for Erwin. When he fell, all had gone black for a split second and when he regained his faculties he realized that he was lying on the floor in a pool of bourbon and broken drinking glasses, his back against the overturned silver cart. His eyes darted around the room seeking focus and the attacker, but the blinding pain that shot from his ruined tongue into his jaw and ear canals brought flashes of light that obscured his vision. Even if he had seen her, there was nothing he could have done to prevent her next vicious assault.

With one hand, the woman tore open his bloody shirt, sending silver buttons clattering across the floor. With her other, she stabbed downward with the broken rim of a whiskey glass and slashed across his stomach, through flesh and fatty tissue. She reversed the course of her hand and cut backward, now slicing completely through his abdominal muscles.

Erwin Engel tried to scream but could only make a sickly hissing sound that sprayed bright red blood into the air as he tried to buck the woman who straddled him, but there was such a copious amount of his vital fluid on the floor that his desperate attempts to get traction were fruitless.

Even if he could have stood, it would not have made a difference. It was too late.

With cold detachment, the murderous visitor thrust her hand through the bloody folds of skin, fat, and muscle and twisted her fist within his gut. As he watched in abject horror, she ripped from him his small intestine and held it up for him to see. Deftly, she wrapped the warm internal organ twice around his neck and attempted to strangle him with it but her strength was too great. The fragile tissue of the intestine ruptured and shredded, causing her slender hand to rip away from his neck. The motion sprayed deep red blood and feces against the wood-paneled walls of Erwin's study.

As the length of the gory assault ticked away in seconds, so too did the life of Erwin Engel tick away. Though he retained consciousness, his body was in the throes of shock and he twitched uncontrollably. The woman who had savaged his flesh looked at the rope of intestine in her hand that had ripped free from the rest of the impromptu noose. She threw it across the room dismissively.

"Fuck it," she said, as she brought both of her fists down upon his face, smashing it with such force that his facial bones shattered and his entire head collapsed in a spray of brains and blood that shot across the floor in a revolting crimson halo.

In one night, Gina had been avenged, Josephine Engel had been avenged, and Isadora Luca had been avenged. The voice of Ivonette had grown silent in the mind of the creation, for the spirit of the dead woman now joyously winged into the nothingness of eternity, away from that intimate inner chamber, the psyche of the woman who called herself Ragdoll.

Justice had been served.

Pale moonlight illuminated her as she quietly closed the door behind her and stood upon the stately entryway of the Engel estate. Her porcelain fingers ran over the raised scars and stitches of her arm and trailed through the gore that stretched to her elbows. Each segment of her body, each section of dead flesh, all of the muscles beneath her skin, the entirety of her physical being, all had been stolen from the sacred remains of untold victims. But how many women they were, she did not know. She looked to the black forest at the end of the drive and bare feet gracefully trod across the gravel as she disappeared into the night.

For that moment at least, her consciousness was a placid pool devoid of the haunting voices of spectral forces thirsting for vengeance.

However, she knew that soon enough those voices would return and her journey had only just begun.

I would like to heap gratitude upon the following people who helped make this novel a reality, thanks to their support of the Kickstarter campaign to fund its production:

A. Hooper
Adolfo Ramos
Adrian M.
Adrian Ropp
Aexoyir
Alan McAnelly
Algie Lane III
Andrew Sharp
BMM
Bob Meracle
Bookkitten Silvia P.
Bryan L. Crow
C.C. Reid
Chris Vaughn
Christopher Bardell
Christopher Paul Carey
Craig Hackl
Curtis Schultz
Dan Charleston
David Bitterbaum/The Newest Rant
David Blake
Destroyer of Worlds
DJP
Elise
Eugene Alejandro
Everette Hartsoe
Frank Kowalczyk
Gary Phillips
Greg Bary
H. Yanoska
Heather R.
Holly G!
Ian Bannon
James and Heather LePore
Jason Hutchens
Jay Allam IV
Jeffrey Behrend
Jeramy Lee Perez
Jim and Rhonda Lancaster
Joe McCulloch
Joseph Holesovsky
Joshua Yarborough

Julie Pizor
Just Cruising By
Kailie Bill
Karl Robinson
Keith Howell
Khadija Hussain
Magnus Emilsson
Mark S. Neira
Martial M.
Melvin D. Emerson
Michael "Necro Monkey" Schultz
Mike Beck
Mister Steve
Morgaine Hughes
Nathan R Plunkett
Nicholas Ahlhelm
Nick B.
Owen John Ryan
Pablo A. Eekman
Phillip T.
Princesse-dokidoki
Quilliam FP.
Ray U.
Richard E. Paulk
Richard Novak
Richard Parker
Robert Verderber
Roderick "Ranma711" Cardwell
Rogulynx
Ron
Ryan Doan
Scott Hart
Seth Alexander
Shayna Kohan
Spikeh
Susan O'Fearna
Thomas Richardson
Thor
Tony Anjo
Victoria Swanwick
Win Scott Eckert

ABOUT THE AUTHOR
MIKE WOLFER

In a professional career that has spanned over thirty years, writer and artist Mike Wolfer has been a prolific voice in the world of independent comic books, with much of his work dedicated to tales of horror. Although he has written various comics titles ranging from *Night of the Living Dead* and *Friday the 13th* to *Zorro* and even *Casper, the Friendly Ghost*, Wolfer is currently best known for his work in the Edgar Rice Burroughs Universe on such titles as *The Land That Time Forgot, Pellucidar, The Monster Men, The Moon Maid, Jane Porter, Victory Harben,* and others. But Wolfer's long-time fans first associate his name with his self-published erotic horror offerings, *Widow* and *Daughters of the Dark Oracle*.

Daughters of the Dark Oracle: Doll of the Dead is Wolfer's first published novel. He lives in Wyoming, Delaware with his creative partner Natalie Jane, and a whole bunch of cats.

OTHER TITLES AVAILABLE FROM
MIKE WOLFER ENTERTAINMENT:

   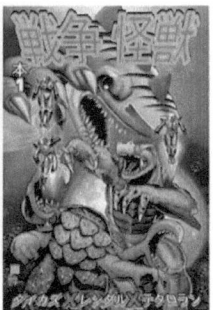

Daughters of the Dark Oracle Volume 1:
The Curse of Ragdoll graphic novel

Daughters of the Dark Oracle
Oracle Card Hornbook

Widow Archives Volume 1: Flesh and Blood graphic novel
Widow Archives Volume 2: Kill Me Again graphic novel
Widow Archives Volume 3: Metal Gypsies graphic novel
Widow Archives Volume 4: Bound by Blood graphic novel
Widow Archives Volume 5: The Origin graphic novel
Fangs of the Widow Annual

War Monsters Volume 1 graphic novel
War Monsters Volume 2 graphic novel
War Monsters Volume 3 graphic novel
...and many more!

For a full list of available titles and pricing, email
mweorders@gmail.com
or visit
facebook.com/mikewolferentertainment